# THE MIRRORS

*Nicole Cushing*

# Nicole Cushing

# THE
# MIRRORS

Nicole Cushing

# THE MIRRORS

## Nicole Cushing

PRESS

# THE MIRRORS

Trade Softcover (MSRP $19.95)
*ISBN: 978-0-6924427-8-4*

E-book (MSRP $7.95)
*ISBN: N/A*

SUMMER, 2015
First Edition

Book Design/Layout by JaSunni Productions, LLC
Printed/Bound in the United States of America.
No animals were harmed in the making of these books. Go veg!

Published by

## Cycatrix Press

http://www.JaSunni.com
Email/Contact: JaSunni@jasunni.com

JaSunni Productions, LLC
16420 SE McGillivray Blvd.
Ste 103-1010
Vancouver, WA
98683
USA

Foreword © 2015 by **S. T. Joshi**
Preface © 2015 by **Nicole Cushing**
Cover Art (*The Mirrors*) and Standalone B&W Detail Illustrations
© 2015 by **Zach McCain**
Author Photo © 2015 by **Nicole Cushing**
Book Design © 2015 by **JaSunni Productions, LLC**

\*\*\*\*\*

"**The Truth, as Told by a Bottle of Liquid Morphine**": originally appeared in
*Phantasmagorium* online, June 1-7, 2012, ed. Edward Morris, (Gorgon Press)
and was later reprinted as an exclusive e-book for members of the
DarkFuse book club (DarkFuse, 2012).

"**The Cat in the Cage**": originally appeared in *Eulogies II: Tales from the Cellar*,
ed. Christopher Jones, Nanci Kalanta,and Tony Tremblay (HW Press, 2013).

"**The Orchard of Hanging Trees**": originally appeared as a reading on
episode 277 of the podcast *Pseudopod*,
ed. Shawn Garrett (Escape Artists Inc., 2012),
then appeared in the April 17th, 2014 issue of *DarkFuse* magazine,
ed. Shane Staley (DarkFuse, 2014).

"**The Fourteenth**": originally appeared in *The First Book of Classical Horror Stories*,
ed. D.F. Lewis (Megazanthus Press, 2012).

"**A Catechism for Aspiring Amnesiacs**": originally appeared in
*Lovecraft eZine 12*, ed. Mike Davis, A. J. French, and Bruce L. Priddy
(Lovecraft eZine, 2012); then appeared in *Lovecraft eZine Megapack–2012–
Issues 10 Through 20*, ed. Mike Davis (Lovecraft eZine, 2013);
then appeared in *Lovecraft eZine–Making the Cut–2012:
Tales Selected for Honorable Mention in The Best Horror of the Year Volume 5*,
ed. Mike Davis (Lovecraft eZine, 2014).

"**White Flag**": original to this collection.

"**The Company Town**": originally appeared in *The Grimscribe's Puppets*,
ed. Joseph S. Pulver, Sr. (Miskatonic River Press, 2013).

"**The Choir of Beasts**": originally appeared in *The Choir of Beasts*
(three story limited edition chapbook),
ed. Jordan Krall (Dunhams Manor Press, 2013).

"**All I Really Need to Know I Learned in Piggy Class**": originally appeared in
*Werewolves and Shape Shifters: Encounters with the Beast Within*,
ed. John Skipp (Black Dog & Leventhal, 2010);
then appeared in *Tales to Terrify Volume 1*,
ed. Lawrence Santoro, Harry Markov, and Tony C. Smith (Tony C. Smith, 2012),
then appeared as a reading on episode 60 of the podcast
*Tales to Terrify* (District of Wonders, 2013).

"**The Last Kid Scared by Lugosi**": original to this collection.

"**I Am Moonflower**": originally appeared in *Weird Tales 361*,
ed. Marvin Kaye (Nth Dimension Media, 2013).

**"The Meaning"**: originally appeared in *Polluto 9¾*,
ed. Victoria Hooper, Adam Lowe, and Chris Kelso (Dog Horn Publishing, 2012).

**"The Suffering Clown"**: originally appeared in
*Mighty in Sorrow: A Tribute to David Tibet & Current 93*,
ed. Jordan Krall (Dynatox Ministries, 2014).

**"Eulogy to be Given by Whoever's Still Sober"**: originally appeared in
*TWO: The 2nd Annual Stupefying Stories Horror Special*,
ed. Bruce Bethke (Rampant Loon Press, 2013).

**"Youth to be Proud Of"**: originally appeared in
*Bust Down the Door and Eat All the Chickens, Issue Y'aing'ngah*,
ed. Bradley Sands, Garrett Cook, and Andersen Prunty (2010).

**"Subcontractors"**: originally appeared in *Strange Aeons 15*,
ed. Laurence Amiotte, Rick Tillman, K. L. Young, and T. E. Grau (Eryx Press, 2014).

**"The Peculiar Salesgirl"**: originally appeared in *Polluto 10*,
ed. Victoria Hooper, Adam Lowe, and Chris Kelso (Dog Horn Publishing, 2013);
then appeared in *Postscripts to Darkness*,
ed. Sean Moreland, Aalya Ahmad, and Ranylt Richildis (Ex Hubris Imprints, 2014)

**"Non Evidens"**: originally appeared in *Women Writing the Weird II:
Dreadful Daughters*, ed. Deb Hoag (Dog Horn Publishing, 2014).

**"The Squatters"**: originally appeared in
*A Darke Phantastique: Encounters with the Uncanny and Other Magical Things...*,
ed. Jason V Brock (Cycatrix Press, 2014).

**"The Mirrors"**: originally appeared in *Nameless Digest V2, No.1*,
ed. Jason V Brock & S. T. Joshi (Cycatrix Press, 2014).

*****

*****

# Dedication

To the memory of my grandparents.

# TABLE OF CONTENTS

**Foreword**
*by S. T. Joshi*
11

**Preface**
15

## BROKEN MIRRORS

The Truth, as Told by a Bottle of
Liquid Morphine
19

The Cat in the Cage
27

The Orchard of Hanging Trees
33

The Fourteenth
45

A Catechism for Aspiring Amnesiacs
54

White Flag
61

The Company Town
71

The Choir of Beasts
76

All I Really Need to Know
I Learned in Piggy Class
93

The Last Kid Scared by Lugosi
101

I Am Moonflower
106

The Meaning
108

The Suffering Clown
111

# FUNHOUSE MIRRORS

Eulogy to be Given by Whoever's Still Sober
125

Youth to Be Proud Of
139

Subcontractors
146

# BOUDOIR MIRRORS

The Peculiar Salesgirl
159

Non Evidens
167

The Squatters
190

# CODA

The Mirrors
201

Story Notes
209

About the Author
220

# FOREWORD

## By S. T. Joshi

Nicole Cushing's stories grab you by the throat—and don't let go until they have slapped you around a bit. I know of few writers of contemporary weird fiction whose stories pack the raw emotional power that hers do—and, as her preface to this book suggests, many of their elements are drawn from the experiences of her own life. But that would mean little unless she had the literary skill to transmute those experiences into powerful tales that speak poignantly of pain, loss, tragedy, heartbreak—and terror.

A surprising number of Cushing's tales are of a provocative "what if" sort and might almost be classified as science fiction; but there is more than enough fear, gruesomeness, and supernatural horror to place them well within the confines of the weird tale. What if (as "White Flag" suggests) homeless people of the future have had their life expectancy vastly increased through advances in medicine—but still remain destitute? What if ("The Company Town" proposes) a company can arrange for the suicide of individuals and whole families trapped in an unending welter of depression? What if (as in "Subcontractors") a plague is so widespread that it causes private individuals to become amateur morticians? What if (as one of the most innovative and carefully worked out stories in this book, "Non Evidens," extrapolates) some babies are born invisible?

It can be seen from the above synopses that a good number of Cushing's stories deal intimately and unflinchingly with the psychological traumas of their characters while at the same time broaching broader sociopolitical concerns. An extra dimension of complexity and poignancy is added by Cushing's occasional experiments in narration. The two stories that open this collection are told from the standpoint of, respectively, a morphine bottle as it dispenses its transitory aid to cancer patients and a cat that acts as a bland witness to a depression-plagued suicide victim. A cloud of melancholy hangs heavy over this book—a point made not in criticism (even though this bleak atmosphere, reminiscent of nineteenth-century Russian literature, is generally at odds with the resolute cheerfulness that dominates the self-image of most Americans) but in praise of the simultaneous power and delicacy of Cushing's psychological analyses of her characters. In some cases, her telling portrayals of depression can create terror on their own: "The Fourteenth" is nothing more than an account of a woman who seeks solace in music following the death of her husband—but fails to find it.

One might suspect a Ligottian influence in all this: certainly, Ligotti's *The Conspiracy against the Human Race* is about the last word on "anti-natalism" (the belief that human beings would have been better off having never been born). Ligotti's work clearly underlies such tales as "A Catechism for Aspiring Amnesiacs," a vibrant second-person narrative featuring a rumination on oblivion as a balm for the ills of life, and "The Choir of Beasts," where a plague has caused the collapse of civilisation and a reversion to barbarism. But Cushing wouldn't have responded to Ligotti's pessimism and misanthropy if she had not felt it deeply herself.

The sociological or cultural dimensions of Cushing's work comes to the fore in such a tale as "Eulogy to Be Given by Whoever's Still Sober," where a horror writer plans to culminate a wild party with his own death. This sardonic indictment of the excesses of our celebrity culture mingles terror and grim satire in equal doses. In "The Peculiar Salesgirl," a shop sells new skin to women: a more pungent condemnation of the objectification of women (not to mention the race prejudice—based solely on such a superficial factor as one's skin colour—that continues to bedevil our society) would be difficult to find.

Let it not be thought, however, that Cushing's tales are dour exercises in heavy-handed moralising. We find a vibrant and distinctive imagination in both the conception and the execution of such tales as *"Non Evidens"* and "The Mirrors" (which somewhat similarly deals with the anomalous plight of certain people who fail to have their images reflected in mirrors). These and other narratives—such as "The Last Kid Scared by Lugosi," where Béla Lugosi is resurrected on the one hundredth anniversary of the film *Dracula,* and "The Suffering Clown," where the clown in question is endowed with terrifyingly cosmic powers—show that Cushing is well aware of the need for weird tales to be truly *weird.* This genre is different from standard social realism precisely because it allows the author's imagination free rein to envision a world very different from what we see around us; but those imaginative flights must be directed by an aesthetic sensibility that uses fantasy, horror, and supernaturalism to tell profound truths about human beings as they function in our complex and bewildering society. Cushing's tales do exactly that.

This is Nicole Cushing's first full-length collection, and its variety, profundity, and underlying unity of thought and conception are enough to make any young author proud. I hope that the final impression most readers will derive when they finish this book is a thirst for as much more work by this gifted writer as they can find. I know mine was.

—S. T. Joshi
*Seattle, Washington*

# THE MIRRORS

# PREFACE

"There is no nobler chore in the universe than holding up the mirror of reality and turning it slightly, so we have a new and different perception of the commonplace, the everyday, the 'normal', the obvious. People are reflected in the glass. The fantasy situation into which you thrust them is the mirror itself. And what we are shown should illuminate and alter our perception of the world around us. Failing that, you have failed totally."

—Harlan Ellison

Chances are you don't know me, but I'm worried that after reading this book you will. Because a short story collection (maybe even more than a novel) lays bare all the obsessions of an author. It gives the reader a chance to note—in the space of a single volume—recurring patterns: topics the author can't seem to tear herself away from; topics that keep showing up time and time again despite her wishes that they wouldn't; incriminating topics, which reveal her to be something other than normal.

There are twenty stories in this book, and as I assembled it I imagined the manuscripts tacked to a bulletin board in a courtroom. Exhibits A through T in a Kafkaesque daydream.

"Note," the prosecuting attorney says, "how many times she writes about suicide. Poverty. Estrangement from family. Addiction. Note not only *what* she writes about, but also *how strangely* she writes about it. Clearly, this author is deranged. The state asks, your honor, that you immediately remand her to the nearest psychiatric hospital, where she shall be injected with all sorts of medicine to grant her passed-out, chemical bliss. For if one does not love reality, then one must be compelled to leave it."

In response to these charges I offer a complicated plea: simultaneously guilty and not guilty.

The prosecutor cackles. "Ha! Simultaneous, conflicting pleas. See, I told you. Deranged! Deranged!"

"But wait . . . I can explain! I only offered a complicated plea because it's a complicated matter. The stories in this book aren't *purely* autobiographical. And yet—like most fiction, I suppose—there is an *element* of autobiography in each tale. Yes, I'll admit that much. And if that admission leads the readers in the jury to find me guilty . . . deranged . . . so be it. But allow me to discuss all the nuances involved. When I sit down to write a story, a strange phenomenon occurs. I call it dual possession. The character possesses me—occupies my heart as I tell the tale. At the same time, though, *I'm possessing the character*. During the writing of the story, we dwell inside each other."

The prosecutor points at me. "Dual possession? Heh. *That's* your defense for the content of these stories? Deranged! Clearly deranged! Now what have you to say about the *odd manner* in which so many of them are told?"

"They're not *all* weird."

The prosecutor smirks. "'Weird' isn't the word I used, young lady. I used the word 'odd.' Surely you'd have to admit that most are, at the very least, *odd*."

My goose, it seems, is cooked. The prosecutor is hell-bent on finding me deranged and is completely unreasonable. So let me take my appeal, instead, directly to you—the readers. My jury.

All my stories are mirrors, reflecting me and my surroundings—albeit, as Ellison said, turned slightly. Tilted. Warped.

The stories in the first section of this book are filthy, cracked mirrors reflecting my darkest scars. There are scars left where hunger clawed at me for a year or two. There are scars left by family estrangement and sick relationships. Scars left by depression, death, grief, and other troubles. All the injuries themselves are in the past now. I survived, and am grateful I survived. But the scars demand to be addressed. Fiction is one of the several ways in which I've addressed them. I call this section "Broken Mirrors."

If "Broken Mirrors" sounds a little too intense, flip forward to one of the other sections. "Funhouse Mirrors" is a section of more comedic (or, at least, absurd) stories. Now, because *I* wrote them, they're still fairly grim. But at least each wince is offset by a chuckle. That counts for something, right? Or maybe you'll want to check out the "Boudoir Mirrors" section first. That section assembles my stories about identity, gender, and sexuality. The "Coda" is self-explanatory. If you only read one story in this book, read the single story comprising that section: "The Mirrors."

Allow me to conclude this statement in my own defense by instructing you, the jury, to take a good look into these mirrors. Your judgment of my madness or sanity should hang on a single question: is it *only me* you see reflected, or do you not also find *glimpses of yourselves* in them as well? If I'm mad, maybe you are too.

Maybe we all are.

*—Indiana*
*December 2013*

# BROKEN MIRRORS

# The Truth, as Told by a Bottle of Liquid Morphine

**I**n the beginning, there weren't all those shady characters around: it was just me, the rest of the medicine, the woman, the man in the bed, and his cancer.

*Lots and lots* of cancer—metastasized from the lung to the bone, to the liver, to the brain, until the doctors shrugged and, frankly, just gave up looking for all the new places it had spread. That's what the hospice nurses alleged, at least, in whispers when the woman went skulking off to her bedroom. When they thought the patient was asleep and nobody else could hear them.

They might have been furtive, but an objective third party (like myself) didn't need to be an R.N. to see that the patient (identified, per my label, as Jacob J. Amberg, Trailer Lot #52, Pleasant Summer Drive, Wurzburg, Indiana) suffered the burden of multiple malignancies. After all, I wouldn't have even been there if straits weren't dire. Moreover, I could see (through the brown tint of my bottle) the tumor in the patient's jaw that made it look as if he was always working on a gobstopper or wad of chewing tobacco. I could see the way he'd wasted, too, when compared to better-nourished people—the way his belly was a pit, rather than a mound. The way his soft, almost-feminine skin wobbled over bone when he got the tremors ("terminal restlessness," one of the nurses dubbed it).

I perked up a little at the mention of the word "terminal," because I thought that perhaps this meant I might soon find myself useful. Truth be told, I felt lazy. The oxygen machine had been pumping away dutifully—day in, day out—for days now. I envied it, because it was doing its part to keep Jacob J. Amberg alive. I envied the Ativan and Haldol that had already gotten their shot at calming him. I envied all the pills warding off constipation, all the swabs that had their life's purpose fulfilled in the cleaning of his mouth. I envied, if you can believe it, even the adult diapers. At least they were doing their part. I, on the other hand, had to *wait* (rather like the gentleman,

Aroldis Chapman, brought in to pitch the final inning of those Cincinnati Reds games the woman put on the television each night). After seeing enough of those games, I realized I was like the "closer" in a ball game. Not to be called on unless absolutely necessary, after the other pitchers couldn't go on any further.

The nurse told the woman just to use Vicodin at first, and I admit that I felt a swell of pride in knowing that I was considered superior to my peers. So powerful was I, as a pain reliever, that I might have the unfortunate side effect of depressing the work of Jacob J. Amberg's lungs. Better, they said, to avoid using me until the Vicodin stopped working. If I'd had a mouth, like the nurses, I would have smiled (or maybe even gloated) at the implied compliment. As it was, I only managed to force a little bit of extra shine onto my glass when a stray glint of sunlight made it through the dusty mini-blinds.

Such praise was, for a time, the only thing that kept me from going mad from all the waiting. I *wasn't* being lazy, I reminded myself; I was simply being reserved for a more opportune time. To kill the hours (and, as it turned out, days), I tried making telepathic conversation with the other medicines, but they all seemed either too busy or too glum to reciprocate. Jacob J. Amberg himself wasn't talkative either. During long stretches of the day he would sleep. If he did awaken, he might say a word or two. "Chicken," he'd say. "Cloud. Dirt." One might have imagined that he was reciting whatever vocabulary he had left, in alphabetical order. I suspected that those fleshy balls in his brain were gaining weight at the expense of his sanity.

After a day or two, the woman couldn't bear it. She'd spend hours off in her room while Jacob J. Amberg alternated between states of sleep, raspy breathing, and joint-jiggling bouts of *terminal restlessness*. She turned on the television to keep him company, then paced away to her room. But neither *The Price is Right* nor any of the indistinguishable talk shows that followed or preceded it offered the man much in the way of solace. Nothing did. I suppose that's why she walked away. It can be hard just to sit there and see it, unable to do much. I suppose she and I had that in common. She could take her eyes away from it, though—at least for short respites. Not me. I kept the vigil going. I had no other choice.

There came a time when Jacob J. Amberg stopped

speaking entirely. I perked up and thought this meant I would finally have my chance to be of service. While his breath had long been raspy, it now sounded gurgly. The nurses tried to explain to the woman that this was simply a function of the weakness of his esophageal muscles. No longer could they be counted on to swallow his saliva. But the woman shook her head and whimpered. "The death rattle," she whispered, "the death rattle."

The woman was, by now, almost as fatigued-looking as Jacob J. Amberg. I began to feel concerned about her. I never saw her eat much. Sometimes she went off to a cubbyhole furnished with a tiny rust-pocked stove, took a brick of noodles out of a cellophane package, and heated them in a pot of hot water. There weren't many of those bricks in the trailer. On days she didn't eat those, she ate a few hard-boiled eggs. Jacob J. Amberg wasn't eating *anything* anymore (although he might drink from a bottle of Ensure, once a day). I looked back and forth between the two of them to see who was wasting away the quickest. Jacob J. Amberg seemed to be in the lead, but he'd had a head start.

One day, the woman asked a hospice lady if Jacob J. Amberg might be better off in a nursing home. The nurse told the woman that this wasn't the best choice, as it was likely just a matter of days (if not hours) until the man "passed away." Did she *really* want to move him? Could she afford a nursing home? No? Then there would be red tape to consider. Was he already signed up for Medicaid? No? That would take months . . .

The nurse did all the talking that day. The woman didn't say anything. She looked beaten. The man's cancer didn't beat her. *Terminal restlessness* didn't beat her. It took a nurse to do that.

After the nurse left, the woman got a book with thin, pulpy, yellow pages and looked at listings starting with "F." She started to make a call on her cell phone, but it wouldn't work. "I can't be out of minutes," she said to no one (not knowing that I and the other medicines were listening—though in truth I was the only one paying attention). She started sobbing. "I gave them money last week."

I didn't know what she could have meant. If I expected anyone to run out of minutes, it would have been Jacob J. Amberg.

When the nurse visited again the next day, the woman left the trailer altogether, taking a jar of coins with her. She said she was going to buy more minutes, and she could only do this if someone else could stay there. At the time I didn't understand. I thought she was referring to some way of extending Jacob J. Amberg's life by putting her treasure into a machine, perhaps, or offering it unto a god.

The woman was gone for a long time.

The nurse looked frustrated. She glanced at her watch. She took her cell phone out of her purse and began gabbing. I heard her make snide remarks about how "Mrs. Amberg" was so coldhearted that she left the man to go into town. She confided in her colleague that "these types were always the worst." She said she hoped the hospice would speed up its plans to phase out its sliding scale program. She got off the phone when she heard the growl of an engine and crackle of gravel in the driveway.

When the woman came back, the nurse frowned. "You may want to consider starting him on the liquid morphine," she said. "We can't say these things for certain, but he's very close. What I mean is, tonight may be his last night."

"All right," the woman said, eyeing me with some collision of respect and contempt. "I have minutes on my phone now. Is it okay to call you if things get bad?"

The nurse assured her that she could call twenty-four hours a day and someone—not her, of course, but someone on-call—would come out if it was an emergency. The woman feigned thanking the nurse. The nurse feigned sincerity when she told the woman she was welcome, then left to go visit her next patient. I'm a relative newcomer to watching humans interact, but between the man, the woman, the nurses, and television, I'd had a crash course on the subject. The only person who wasn't feigning a thing was Jacob J. Amberg.

Through his gurgling, he seemed to be groaning. Perhaps, I thought, this was my chance to shine.

The woman retrieved the book with the flimsy yellow pages again. She turned to "F" once more. She pushed buttons on her phone, then spoke to someone. She did this many times, tearful throughout the whole ordeal. The conversations must not have been good ones. "I still owe from Daddy? . . . So you won't? . . ."

Finally she had a conversation that proved more promising. "He's dying," she said. "Jake," she explained. "How much will it cost? . . . What's cheapest? . . . I don't want him burnt, Billy, you know that's not what he'd want. He told me he wanted to be buried near his momma. Made me promise not to cremate him. You got to help me."

Then something said to her over the phone unfroze her face from its perpetual grimace. She no longer begged. Now she planned. "You think so? . . . I got some good stuff left . . . uh-huh . . . morphine." She'd said my name. She'd said my name, and hung up almost right afterward.

She made some gestures toward Jacob J. Amberg. She embraced him, stroking his hollowed-out cheeks with the back of her hand. She told him she'd only leave him alone that way for a little while, and that she was only leaving him alone because she *absolutely had to*. Then she grabbed me by the neck and hauled me away.

ℛ

She hadn't lit up a cigarette in the trailer, because of the oxygen. But in her ancient pickup truck, riddled with rust, she was unencumbered by such restrictions. She rested me in one of two cup-holders down by the gear shift. A hot, half-empty beer can sat to my left. I thought (foolishly, I later learned) that this prosaic neighbor of mine proved how fortunate I'd been to come into this world as a medication of no low status.

We arrived at a place called "Tuckwell Home For Funerals." That's what the sign said. Paint chipped away from the building's façade. Grass erupted from cracks in the sidewalk. It didn't look like a pleasant place. She tucked me into her purse (a filthy environ, full of dust and grime and even a pair of whiskey shot-bottles) and only took me out when she sat down in an office.

There was a man sitting across the table from us. He was stocky, short-haired, and smiling. He seemed to have been acquainted with her previously. He made small talk with her about how, since the housing market tanked, he didn't mind leaving real estate for this job. He enjoyed the business of helping people in their time of need, he said.

Then he picked me up, appraising me like the jewelers on the Jared Diamonds TV commercials. "Not bad," he said, "for a down payment."

"Half now," the woman replied, "the other half after he's buried."

He leaned all his girth away from the table, frowning. "Ella Jo," he said, "come on, now, be reasonable. I'm the one taking the risk of getting caught selling it. You know what the sentence for distribution is these days?"

She gritted her teeth and grabbed onto me, squeezing tight. For a tense second I thought she might knock me right across his head. Tears fled from her eyes like survivors from a sinking ship.

"Okay," the man—Billy Tuckwell—said. "Half now, half after he's buried, plus two thousand dollars you'll owe on a payment plan."

The woman—Ella Jo—looked down. "That's the best you can do? After years huntin' and campin' together with Jake? I know he wasn't the most sociable person in the world. He was too shy to make it out to the Elks Club or the Masons or the Kiwanis or whatever it was you had your hands into, but you at least treated him decent. You were the closest thing he had to a friend. And after all that, all those years, this is the best you can do?"

"Now, Ella Jo, don't you get up on your high horse. I offered you the cheapest—and you declined, remember? Said he wouldn't want to be burned."

Ella Jo nodded. Sighed. "Okay, then."

The man fetched a mason jar. "Pour it in now, if this is what you're sure you want to do."

With a trembling hand, she managed to pour just a little less than half of me into the jar. Billy Tuckwell grabbed me out of her hands and shook me, attempting to measure the remaining quantity to ensure Ella Jo had kept her word. He shook his head. "That's less than half you just poured. But I'll let it slide for now."

Then they talked about matters more mundane (to me, at least). What songs should they play over the public address system during the visitation? Would there be a pastor officiating the funeral? Did she have any pictures she wanted posted near the casket? Had she thought through which clothes she'd like him in? How should they trim Jake's beard?

I supposed I could have listened to all that, but I found myself too stunned by the sudden, unexpected absence of just less than half of me. I knew Jake and Ella Jo were each—in their own manner, either from cancer or poverty—wasting away. It just hadn't occurred to me that I would, too.

⌘

"Jake." Jacob J. Amberg was sometimes called "Jake." Just as the woman was sometimes called "Ella Jo." Just like William Tuckwell was sometimes just plain "Billy." It was a lot to learn, but I was getting the hang of it.

When we got back to the driveway outside of Trailer Lot #52, Pleasant Summer Drive, Wurzburg, Indiana, we could hear Jake's moans through the thin walls. When Ella Jo opened the door and rushed over, she plopped me back where I'd been and caressed Jake's hand. "It'll be over soon," she said.

I saw a grimace on Jake's face. I'll never forget it. I felt so impotent. For all my strength, I could only help him if Ella Jo poured me into his mouth. But she wouldn't. I knew that now. She tried to calm him by fetching the two shot bottles of whiskey out of her purse and pouring them down his throat. He coughed. Gurgled. All that did was make him more restless.

The night went on like that. Ella Jo would stay with him until she could no longer stand it, then turn out the lights and leave for a long time. When he quieted down, she'd peek out of her room and walk out, maybe hoping it was over. But it wasn't to be finished for a long, long time. When she realized this, she retreated back down the dark hallway.

As always, she didn't leave Jake completely unattended. There was me, of course, plus the television. First David Letterman. Then Craig Ferguson. Then old movies. The first featured a man with fangs who drank other people's blood. The second showed images of dead people rising en masse from their graves. I wondered just how that could work. I decided that none of the zombies could have died of cancer. The disease had rendered Jake bed-bound. If, after Billy Tuckwell buried him, he were to come alive again, he would, in all likelihood, just lie there in his coffin, groaning. At the most, the soil at his grave might seem to rumble from his writhing in *terminal restlessness*. But he wouldn't be able to so much as knock Morse code on his casket, let alone dig his way out.

Jake's life ended shortly after the last movie and just before dawn. I'm no expert on the afterlife, but based on his grisly expression I suspect the only light he saw in the end was the flicker of his television casting a feeble glow into the trailer's gaping darkness.

I was there at Jake's burial, officially for business reasons (though in my heart—for lack of a better phrase—I really was grieving). Ella Jo and I were the only mourners. She waited by the grave until the bulldozer plopped the last dirt on. Then she drove to visit Mr. William Tuckwell and delivered me into his waiting hands, just as she'd promised.

Billy has seen fit to sell me a little at a time, as that's how he makes the most money from me. It's a slow death, and utterly devoid of the glory I imagined for myself. Instead of saving the day by rescuing seasoned adults from the agony of cancer eating away at them from the inside out, I'm poured down the throats of people barely older than children so they can numb themselves to the dread of all the decades left to live.

In the end, is that enough purpose to expect out of life? Should I content myself with the notion that I'm still at least in some way helpful? No. I don't think so. The only way I think my existence will have been in the least bit worthwhile is if I'm returned to the custody of a certain desperate widow, so that she might consume me in sufficient quantity to finish herself off. If you care to feign interest in *my* interests, that is my final request—to leave this world slaking the death-thirst of a kindred spirit who has learned the truth about this world, just as I have.

# THE CAT IN THE CAGE

The cat batted the thick, orange extension cord with his soft white paws; catching it in his teeth, gnawing, oblivious to the fact that Sheila planned to use it to hang herself.

"Stop it!" Her voice cracked, her face grew hot. Her mind reeled, still catching up with the new reality. Dan did it this time, after years of threats. He really left. Said he couldn't stand the stench of booze on her breath anymore. Since giving up drinking never worked for long, she decided to quit breathing instead.

Suicide (as a daydream, a temptation) first latched onto her in middle school and, like a lapdog, never left for long. The urges came and went over the years, but, unlike the men in her life, didn't wander far. Sometimes accompanied by well-thought-out plans, but often not. Once or twice she'd even started writing the note, but discarded it. This time she decided not to bother. Writing a note slowed her down and invited doubt. She didn't want doubt. Not anymore.

For decades, she'd just wanted to shut off the hurt in her head. She'd just wanted *peace*. The move from the city was supposed to help, but didn't ("geographical cures never do," her A.A. sponsor had lectured). A suicide cure just might, though.

She'd never before worked up the moxie to go *this* far. She didn't need the cat messing around, distracting her. Truth be told, she didn't need the cat *at all*.

But there he was, legally in her care. Well, maybe not "legally." It wasn't like adopting a child or anything. She hated it when the animal shelters called getting an animal "adopting" one. She'd been adopted (not from an animal shelter, but out of a foster home). She didn't like the comparison.

But her sponsor had told her that a cat would help, so she got one. Her sponsor had told her to do a bunch of other shit, too. Shit that came out of the big blue book they read out of at meetings. Pray to a god who wasn't there. Apply the twelve steps to all her affairs. Give up her own will to that of the group.

Nope. Nope. Nope. She couldn't do it. Not any of it.

Get a cat? Yes. She could do *that*. Of all her sponsor's suggestions, taking in a stray made the most sense. It didn't require her to duck her head in the sand like a faithful, unquestioning ostrich. It required no prayer; the only time she'd have to spend on her knees was in front of the litter box. Better than begging for help from an imaginary friend. Better still than praying to the porcelain god while puking up gin and ramen noodles.

And for a while it worked. Sure, he got into everything. Jumped all over the place. Knocked over more lamps than she ever did while tipsy. She hated him. But he was warm and fuzzy when she was cold and clammy. He had this endearing, meek meow that sounded like a bird. The good behavior "calming collar" she'd bought for him at the pet store had a pleasant odor. The package said it gave off mother cat pheromones. She didn't know if that was true or not; to her it just smelled like lavender. Nice to whiff when she cuddled him. She loved him.

She always hurt those she loved. She hurt the cat by drinking.

They weren't all full-fledged benders like this past week; just little slips sometimes. But they never ended well. She'd forget to scoop out the cat poop for a few days, and then the poor thing would resort to shitting in the house. Or she'd forget to feed him, and he'd start to get aggressive. Scratching her. Biting her. Sometimes on the face.

She had scars from the last time. They were the only thing that cut through the blackout to remind her of what happened. She imagined herself a latter-day Hester Prynne, the scarlet bite mark etched on her forehead stigmatizing her to all feline society as a neglectful owner.

So her addled brain constructed a new syllogism. She couldn't stand the guilt after coming to and realizing she'd accidentally starved the cat. If she got drunk, she'd accidentally starve the cat. Therefore, she couldn't get drunk.

It worked better in theory than in practice. Her sobriety had been hanging by a thread, then snapped. She gave in to this last surge of cravings because Dan came home from work in a bad mood and started listing his grievances: her reclusiveness, her distance, her frigidness, her letting herself and her housekeeping go. He didn't care that she was doing the best she could. The place hadn't been uncluttered (let alone cleaned) in months.

And then, when she drank, that was the last straw. He said he had to go "clear his head" up at his brother's house in Muncie. They had no children together (no strings, no one to hurt by separating), so he could do that. After he "cleared his head" for a month, maybe (*maybe*) he'd be back.

She looked up at the ceiling for the heavy hook she'd spied earlier, but got distracted by cobwebs. She almost stopped what she was doing to take a dust mop and clear them away. She didn't like the idea of people coming in and seeing stuff like that. Dirt. Disorganization. Flaws. People would talk if they saw the house in this condition.

But she couldn't keep everyone out forever. Not if things went as planned. She'd have to be willing to let go of her need to control everything. In a month, give or take, Dan (or someone) would find her. Then the A.A. people would stand in church parking lots, smoking cigarettes, and gossip about her death. Some of the meaner ones might even pass on rumors about the coffee stains on the counters and the carpet gone too long without vacuuming. So what? She could tolerate being gossip-fodder if it meant an end to the misery.

The cat rubbed against her leg, forcing her glance downward. He looked up at her with big, yellow-green eyes and let out a timid squeak. He knew her moods. He had to know she wasn't wanting to cuddle, but tried to suggest snuggle-time anyway.

She bent at the waist and scowled. "Am I going to have to put you in your cage?" It wasn't an idle threat. There was, in fact, a cage (big enough for the cat to jump up on plastic ledges and play with catnip-laced toys; big enough for his bowls and his litter box). But, facing facts, it was still a cage.

Dan didn't like calling it a cage. He called it the "kitty condo." He was always sugarcoating shit ("just a month away to clear my head").

The cat flinched and went back to playing with the extension cord.

She let him do that, for now. It would keep him busy while she got the ladder. It didn't weigh much, but its bulk made it hard to maneuver while she was still hungover and clumsy. It lurched too far to the right, knocking over a heap of mail that had accumulated on the coffee table. She didn't bother cleaning it up. It didn't matter anymore.

Nothing would matter, soon.

She spread the ladder's legs and tightened the hinges to keep it in place. Then she turned to get the cord.

The cat looked over his shoulder, caught in the act as he bit and clawed at the cord for all he was worth. She sighed and lurched toward him.

He ran, taking the cord with him down the hallway, into the kitchen, dragging it against the linoleum.

"Get back here!"

He scattered four paws on the floor in quick bursts of energy, slipping and sliding. But the heavy cord weighed him down. He could drag it away, but only so far. She caught up with him, grabbed him, but he twisted in her grasp. She didn't *mean* to shake him, but in her haste that's just what she did. He swiped his paw against her cheek. Another scratch.

"That's it. I'm done."

She picked him up. More scratches and bites as she trucked him to the unused dining room—the room he had all but taken over. Stray litter and crumbs of cat food were scattered over the hardwood. She winced and threw him in the cage. Home incarceration in the kitty condo. She closed the latch, locking him in for good measure, and retrieved the cord.

She went back to work, trying to remember what the website said about making the noose. In the end, she did the best she could. Improvising, as she always had. Throwing something together and hoping it worked. She climbed the ladder and placed the noose on the hook where the planter had hung before she'd killed the fern. She experimented with it to see if it might bear her weight. It seemed sturdy.

It took some doing to get the knot tied so that it would actually *stay* tied. The noose wasn't perfect, but it didn't need to be. It just needed to do the job. She placed it around her neck and, for some reason she wasn't sure of, started sobbing.

The cat let out a squeaking, brittle meow. She looked down from her perch and saw him in the next room, his eyes and voice coordinated in a campaign for release. *Let me out and I will love you,* he seemed to be promising.

But no one had kept their promises. Her mom hadn't when she chose crack over groceries. Dan hadn't when he left.

The cat hadn't when he scratched.

She inhaled, took one last look at the mess her house had become (the mess her life had become), and kicked the ladder out from under her, falling a short distance before catching. The drywall cracked, sprinkling dust into her eyes, but the ceiling held. The noose tightened, crushing the breath out of her, swelling her throat.

But she didn't die. Not right away.

Her heart raced and she'd wished she'd gotten drunk before she'd tried this, but she knew she would have fucked up even more if she'd been totally trashed. The cord burnt and her lungs wanted to breathe even if she didn't and her chest felt as if it would burst from the blossoming ache, but it didn't. Not yet. She felt herself flush and she just wanted it over. And it would be, soon but not soon enough.

The cat spied her swaying and made shadow-boxing motions, as though she was just a big toy teasing him into pouncing. Only he couldn't, not after she'd locked him up.

Then (*only* then) as she swung from the noose did she look down into the cage with bulging, teary eyes, and see his empty bowl.

# The Orchard of Hanging Trees

I t's another cool April morning in Hell, and the hanging trees (just saplings, really) are starting to sprout fleshy, strangled buds that look and sound like choking fetuses caught up in tiny umbilical nooses.

Their embryonic faces haven't yet developed features, but I know that as the days get longer their lips will grow into a grimace; their eyes will ooze agony. I have already been warned that their first cries (when they can utter them) will be those of breathless suffering. Their first words, pleas for help. The curses will follow shortly thereafter.

But right now, as fetus-flowers, they only emit shrill, eerie mews. Even this meager vocalization makes me shudder. I lower my glance from the entire orchard, feeling disgust for the day ahead. I whistle a tune to distract myself from the noise of thousands of semi-sentients who exist in a state of more or less continuous suffocation. Those to whom full sentience will bring only misery.

I am not, after all, a monster—even if I am in the employ of Hell. Even if (as my fellow laborers predict) some of the fruit will grow up to call me "demon," this is an absurd epithet. I do not *want* to be in this position. But *my* cares, *my* wants, *my* sense of being an individual with free will—these are things of the past. Shams more easily harbored during a lifetime marinated in a sweet sauce of ignorance.

"Stop the whistling. I'm onto you!" the foreman shouts. "You have to listen to them. The ones that aren't yet whining are the ones that need watering." He looks a little like me, only older. Some of my fellow laborers call the foreman an "arch-demon," but I say that is as absurd as the fruit calling us "demons."

Still, he knows too much about this place. I suspect some force (perhaps a spell cast by the Devil himself) skews perception here. Maybe the Devil *wove skewed perception into* the fabric of Hell's reality. I conjecture that the foreman may be a member of some species far older than humanity, one that knows more about this place than humanity ever will. He certainly seems to know more about me than he should, if he was (as he pretends to be) just a strange human soul that I'd never met before coming here.

"You ignored the suffering of your fellow men easily enough in life. That's why the Devil recruited you for this position. It takes a strong stomach. It's not for lightweights."

How can I argue with that? He's right. Perhaps he even means it as a backhanded compliment, but I suspect he means it only in a way that's intended to increase my suffering. Those of us who watched people hurt in life and did nothing to lessen that hurt are doomed to do the same after death. We are doomed to labor in the orchard of hanging trees.

I spoke earlier of the delusion of free will. Sham enough, to be sure. But the chief delusion afflicting humanity is this: the conceit that death is content to remain a dot on the horizon. That it *won't come soon* or that it happens to *someone else*. The delusion that death is *not here* and *not now*. Anyone with a shred of wisdom will tell you that the hand that holds the reaper rules the world. But wisdom is a commodity in short supply on Earth. Ignorance is far more adaptive; ignorance of suffering (the ability to completely look the other way) the most adaptive variety of ignorance around. Bliss beyond bliss; the sort of ignorance that I hope to possess someday.

I can't remember how I died any more than I can remember how I lived. The foreman gives me insights into the latter, if only to justify why I must do what I must do.

I can *half* remember my entrance into Hell. I recall waking up in the middle of the orchard, as if from a fitful sleep. An onyx slab towered over me, on which was written The Great Commandment. At least, that's what the foreman told me it said when he found me there and translated it. He said it was engraved with an inscription, but all I saw were claw marks.

"Your job is to tend to the trees and their fruit," the foreman said, gesturing toward the monolith, reading off of it. "You are not to pick the fruit. You are not to release the fruit from their nooses to end their torments. If you try, you will be cast out of Hell and into The Dark." He then pointed a knotty, crooked finger at a gaping black blur suspended just above the ground, outside the orchard's gate.

"What's that?"

"A door to where space, time, matter, and energy do not exist. Here in Hell, you may suffer vicariously by seeing others suffer, but at least you will *be*. You will have consciousness. The 'real you'—for lack of a better phrase—lives on. There, however, you die. I mean, *really* die. All that is *you* will cease to exist. Here, you can get by the way that you did in life, by doing your job and looking the other way. But the moment you enter The Dark, you die. And you can never come back."

It's a warm May morning in Hell. Sunrise; and the hanging fruit are children now—*actual* fruit, not just flowers—with thin rope around their necks. They dangle from branches in a coughing chorus. The trees themselves have grown to nearly one hundred feet tall. Some of the fruit (a minority, those who appear to have a glimmer of intelligence in their eyes) have made the connection between the rope around their necks and the suffocation they suffer. These ones struggle against the noose, trying to pry a space, however small, between it and their neck with soft, doughy fingers that are not up to the job. A few of them succeed, if only for a few seconds. Just enough time to get out a few sobs. Or, rarer still, a few words. "Save us. Save us!"

Today I'm assigned to prune branches. "Let the sun shine in," the foreman says. "Some of these fruit are awfully small. The Devil doesn't want duds." He gives me a hand pruning saw, a rare privilege here. A tool that looks as if it could easily cut the rope that strangles the fruit. This must mean that he trusts me. Or perhaps he is *testing* me. Or maybe he just really wants to *torment* me further by *giving* me the means to end the fruit's suffering, after giving me The Great Commandment forbidding me from doing so.

I can only speculate, and speculation only increases my discomfort. So I stop speculating and just do what I'm told. It's easier that way; and one should accept any ease offered in Hell.

I tell a co-worker to help me carry the ladder toward the trunk of one of the trees. He looks into my hands, sees the saw, and defers to the newfound authority it confers on me. I like seeing him obey my command with alacrity.

He helps get the ladder into place. I instruct him to wait at the bottom and secure it with his own weight. I climb until I reach a sturdy branch upon which to make an excursion. I pass hanging fruit on my way.

It makes no sense that they know the saw can save them. They've spent their whole life being strangled. They can't know anything different. But somehow they have an awareness of their torture, and I hear them whimper and see them fling themselves around like fish fallen on land. As if they're begging for help. I bite my lip for a moment, then grit my teeth. Yes, I can help them. But that is not my job. I have been entrusted by the foreman with an important duty, one that I will not shirk out of a personal whim to assist fruit be something other than fruit.

Hell is bigger than any one soul's whims. Just as my co-worker had to bend to my will, I must bend to the foreman's. The foreman must bend to the Devil. And the Devil must bend to God, if there is one. That's the only way to remain sane here. One must go along with the chain of command, to get along. If you think about it too much, if you question it, you lose one of the few things you have left. You lose *yourself*. You end up being cast out into The Dark.

I do not want to be cast out into The Dark.

So I ignore the cries of the hanging children and take my saw to stray branches. I apply the teeth of the saw to the trunk, and in a matter of moments the stray branch—a branch that has yet to find its use—falls to the ground. Say what you will, I at least have purpose. My actions matter.

I begin to take the saw to yet another branch. A dark one, emerging from a lush flurry of leaves, but itself leafless. Bare and bearing no fruit. I put the saw's teeth to it, about to start in, when it twists around and bares *its* teeth.

"You damned soul!" he hisses. "How dare you take so crude an implement to the hide of—"

I shudder at the sight of the snake. I lose balance. The creature coils its tail around the entire trunk of the hanging tree and lurches its thick, muscled body forward to break my fall.

"Y-you! The serpent! I *know* you."

I hear my fellow laborer shout from the ground. I can't

understand what he's saying. But he sounds concerned. I don't yell back. Not yet, at least.

As I regain my balance, the serpent rears its head up to look at me once again. It places its nose close up to mine and flicks its tongue, getting the scent of me. "*I* do not know *you*, in particular. Just your kind," the serpent says. "I am long acquainted with the tribe of men, but have not—to the best of my recollection—come across *you* before. And I have a very good memory. I can not see how *you* could have come to know *me*."

I strain my memory. This serpent appears to belong, in some way, to the world I knew before Hell. But I cannot imagine how, unless a character from some old story matched his description. But this memory seems even older than that. This serpent seems older, somehow, than stories themselves.

"I don't know how," I say. I feel foolish.

"I suspect I am correct and you are not. In any event, you have come at an opportune time. I am about to feed on the fruit of a hanging tree. The leaves and branches whisper to me that it is a grand spectacle!"

I brandish my pruning saw. "You will do no such thing! The fruit of this orchard are under my protection!"

The snake laughs a deep, dry, guttural laugh. More like the laugh one would imagine coming out of a dragon. He looks at one of the naked, hanging children. A boy, blue and gasping for breath. "Is this what Hell calls 'protection,' demon?"

I want to object to his name-calling. I am not a demon. But besides that, he does seem to have a point. I blush and extend my hand toward little boy blue and his kin. "All this isn't my fault. The foreman says that if I cut even one of them down to ease their suffering, I will be cast out of Hell and into The Dark!"

The snake smiles. "The Dark, eh? I see no Dark. I only see sun and leaves and hanging children."

Exasperated, I sigh and part the branches so that he can see the black void off in the distance, open like the maw of a beast. "If I'm cast out into The Dark, I will cease to exist!"

The snake laughs louder and longer than before. So long and loud his body spasms, shaking the tree. Almost shaking me out of it. When he is through he looks at me. "Is *that* what they tell you?"

My stomach drops. I don't like being laughed at. I don't like the uncertainty he introduces. I don't like how he insinuates that my foreman is a liar. But even though I am a minion of Hell, some residue of self-will can't help finding the possibility of escape appealing.

But another part of me—some part of my *humanity* lurking deep, deep in the marrow of my bones—tells me the serpent lies. Still, I'm intrigued. I tell myself that it's better to know my enemy than to be ignorant of him. I tell myself that if I listen to the lie the snake tells me, then I know the snake a little better.

"What is The Dark, then, if not a void?"

"My home. The hole in which I burrow each night. I am the serpent of beginnings and ends. The ancients of your race called me many names. Tiamat, Ouroboros, just to name two."

"You go into The Dark and do not cease to exist?"

"What is existence?" the snake says.

"I don't understand that question."

"Your kind never will. Allow me to elucidate. I cannot guarantee what would happen if you were to venture into my den. There might be a whole other world awaiting you there, where you never suffer and stay forever young. Or perhaps my hole would be the snuffer that would extinguish the flame of your consciousness. Or it could be that I would just *eat* you once you got in there, and the 'you' would cease to exist and become a *part of me*. A part of *eternity*. Who knows? For all my importance, I am just a snake—a player in this play just like you. I did not write the script."

I *know* the snake has to be lying. It knows what happens when men and women enter The Dark. Surely, it knows whether or not it will *eat* me. It knows, but answers in riddles.

"Just stay away from me," I tell him. "And stay away from the whole orchard, while you're at it!"

"I will do nothing of the sort. I will eat one hanging child each day, and one each night." With that he rears up, widening his jaws to the point of dislocation, and begins devouring the blue boy, feet first. The lad makes whimpering sounds, like a cornered rabbit. I look away. I start to descend the ladder. When I reach the bottom, I tell my fellow laborer that I am finished with that tree and we should move on.

"Are you sure you're up to it, sir?" he says. "You look as

though you've seen the Devil himself."

The foreman looks in my direction as though he, too, suspects I am shaken. I just look down at the ground.

It's a scorching June afternoon in Hell. The sun hovers right overhead, so that the hanging trees offer only stingy shade. I linger by the trunk to stay cool. I look up and appreciate how my careful pruning and watering have led to the bounty I see dangling above me.

The fruit have already ripened into young bucks and maidens. They try to loosen their nooses to no real avail. Just as they have grown, so has the rope — thick as an actual hangman's noose now, and just as tight on their necks as in earlier months.

Occasionally, some of them *briefly* succeed in clearing a tiny space between the noose and their neck, and manage to vent their rage against me. They call me "fool" when they aren't calling me "demon." There's a blonde up there, just dangling by her noose, who is screaming herself hoarse. She is attractive, having grown tan up there, naked and baked each day by Hell's sun. Her breasts sway as she rocks back and forth on the creaking branch. She screams in her ragged voice that I must save her to save myself.

I am a practical man who knows there is no salvation. The onyx slab says so. The foreman says so. My fellow laborers say so. They say it, I believe it; that settles it. The serpent plays dumb, but I suspect even he knows we are right.

I do not believe saving her will save me. But I do suspect she can be provide me some benefit. As I consider that, I feel an almost-foreign stirring below my belt. I can't remember how long it has been since I've had a release. It seems as if it has been ages since I've even *wanted* release. But now I do. For the first time in Hell that I can recall, I yearn for it and have a plan for getting it.

And, for once, all this work seems worth it. Let her call me "demon," as long as she says it on her back, with her legs spread.

Perhaps noticing my distraction, the foreman approaches me. "I hear noises up there day and night," he says. "I think we have a pest damaging our harvest. How are the fruit?"

I tell him all is well, but that I'll be glad to check it out. I say this, perhaps for the first time, semi-sincerely. I will be glad to examine the fruit. Or at least the lovely.

He seems satisfied by the answer, and that makes me relax. But I am worried by the possibility that he, like the serpent, knows more than he's saying. Maybe he knows about the serpent and expects me to tell him about it, as some test of my honesty and devotion. It has been up there for a month now. It has eaten some fruit. One by day, one by night, each day, each night—just as he said he would. But there are thousands of hanging fruits in the orchard. With that rate of success, he's more worm than dragon, ruining relatively few trees here and there. A *pest* (as the foreman said), no more. Even with him here, Hell's work goes on unimpeded.

I grab my pruning saw, have my assistant help me with the ladder, and decide to climb up to the lovely. She and I need to have a chat.

Although she hangs lower than most fruit, her branch is still higher than my reach at the top of the ladder. Undaunted, I climb the tree itself until I arrive at her place on it. I smile, holding out the saw.

I look her over. The perspiration pours off her brow and onto her breasts. It drips off her nipples, down her belly, and drenches her sex. I know it's just sweat, but I like to imagine that she's aroused. Ready to use. Wanting me as much as I want her. I am able to ignore, for the moment, the noose. Able to ignore her choking.

Maybe she detects my lust. She takes her dainty hands up to her noose and pulls it away for just a moment. "Demon," she hisses, "save me and save yourself. You are dam—"

I ignore her, the way I always ignore fruit. I run my hands through her light, soft hair. I let my fingers—now calloused from all the orchard work—graze her neck. I cup her breasts. Jiggle them. She takes her hands away from the noose and tries smacking and clawing me away. I just move down to her crotch and, when she smacks my hands away from there, her ass.

She makes loud, choking whimpers.

"Shhh," I tell her. "I'll save you all right. Save you for later!" I grin.

On the way down a jury of fruit—bystanders to my flirtation with the blonde—cast judgments on me. "Demon!

Rapist!"

I know in my heart that I'm neither. I didn't even have the opportunity.

It's night and the orchard is cool. It takes me twice as long to haul the ladder out from the shed alone than it would with my assistant, but no one can know what I'll do tonight. I don't *think* what I'm doing is against the rules. Yes, I plan to cut her down, but I'll find a way to hang her back up when I'm done. I'm just not sure if the foreman would approve, and I don't want to take any chances.

The hanging fruit flail in summertime. All their kicking and gasping makes the leaves rustle. A good thing, too. My movement in the tree might be overheard if they weren't moving all the time.

The full moon glows red, as it always does in Hell. Even up in the branches, it isn't hard to find her. After spending time with her earlier in the day, I think I can smell her. She sees me and starts bucking her body backward, then lets herself go forward as though to make herself into a hanging projectile.

She misses, and on the backswing I grab her. My heart pounds in my chest, and for a moment I am unsure if I am truly dead and damned or, rather, alive. It sure feels like the latter.

I hold her tight and kiss her swollen lips. "Look, I'm going to cut you down off of here. The least you can do is grant me one favor."

She stops fighting.

I cut her noose. Damn, I did it. It sways on the branch in the aftermath of our tussle. It's strange seeing the noose without a choking fruit in it.

She coughs and clears her throat. Her voice sounds raspy, brittle, and about to break. "You don't understand, you fool. You *demon*. You don't understand this is all . . . all just a test! Let me go to The Dark. Follow me there. It will be . . ." More coughing. "It will be your salvation."

I stop. I look at her. I now remember the story. The old story. The serpent convinced the woman. Then the woman convinced the man. And then they were, both of them, exiled from Eden. I will not be led by this wily tart into non-existence.

I exist. Not only exist—thrive! I will continue to exist, her wiles notwithstanding. "You've been deceived, woman. Come, let me plow some truth into you."

She screams and screams again and jumps off the tree. "You cruel bastard. You deserve it!" She lands, I hear bones crack. I see her figure twisted in unnatural angles.

I see a shadow-projectile dart through the rose-tinted night. I see fangs glint in the moonlight. I see its jaws widen around her feet. I see a tail sweep back and hit my ladder, almost knocking it to the ground. I gasp and begin to race down. I cannot be left up here. I would be mocked. I can't let myself be mocked. Not a man in my position.

"Let the serpent take you!" the woman screams. "Let him take you back to The Dark, or just run there yourself. It's almost too late."

Lights come on in the quarters. There is a clamor. The snake has devoured her up to her hips now. Now up to her neck. Now she's in, and her cries stop. Now he slithers off toward The Dark.

Now the foreman comes out of his quarters. "Tell me, son, what's the meaning of all this."

"The woman in the tree . . . the serpent told her to go to The Dark. And she told me to go to The Dark. But I didn't."

He looks toward the escaping snake. Looks toward me.

"Well done, my true and faithful servant."

"But what about the serpent? We should go after it. We should kill it."

"The serpent has been around for a long time. It will be around for a long time. There is always a second chance."

I smile and return to my bunk. Despite my unsated libido, I drift off to the deepest, most restful sleep I have had here yet. Perhaps I am finding my niche.

I wake up trying to cough, but can't. Trying to breathe, but can't. Trying to flail, but can't. I feel the burn of something tight and hard cutting into my throat as it yanks me upward.

I try to pull it off, but I have no hands. I try to look around, but I only see murky, dark shapes. I feel only the whipping wind of an early spring morning, so strong against my body that I sway back and forth on the tree.

I don't understand.

*Your kind never will.* I can't hear, but the words are burned into my brain by something antediluvian. Something I've heard before.

*Even with the help of the young lady, who tried to warn you, you do not understand.*

I explain to the serpent, in my thoughts, that I am confused. In the old story he deceived the woman, and the woman deceived the man, and the man suffered because of it.

*Each new story is carved out of pieces of the old, reassembled. You should not have relied so much on old stories. You should have relied on your heart. That is the soil from which all new stories grow. But what do I know? I am just a player, not the playwright.*

I try to attend to the serpent's telepathic message, but I panic. My heart beats much faster than I am used to. I squirm. I mew. I want out.

*You had a second chance. Your sin on earth was ignoring the suffering of others.*

I tell the serpent that I never hurt anyone.

*Nor did you help them.*

I explain that I just minded my own business.

*You fool! The other men and women in your family, your town, and the world were your business. You could have helped them, but you looked the other way. Minded your own business while sick people suffered from want of medicine, and hungered for lack of food. That is what led to your damnation in the first place. Your second damnation only came when you failed to learn from the first. You could have freed the fruit. Or, at the very least, you could have joined me in The Dark. It is not so terrible a place, compared to the orchard. It is the only place that offers escape from suffering. But instead you did your job, and nothing else.*

I ask the serpent if he might eat me now. I tell him I think I am ready.

*You have lessons yet to learn, son. I am sorry. I can only eat one fruit each day, and one each night. You are not yet ready for me. You are just a fetus-flower. You are not even a fruit yet, let alone ripe. It may take several growing seasons before we meet once more.*

I try to pay attention to any other lessons he has to share, but his thoughts recede from my consciousness, and in their wake I feel only the burning. The hanging. The airless, limbless,

suffering.
    I did it again.
    I did it *again*.

It is another cool April morning in Hell, and I am just one of a thousand fetus-flowers sprouting on a branch. A fleshy, strangled bud. A choking fetus on a tiny, umbilical noose.

My embryonic face hasn't yet developed features, but I know as the days get longer my lips will grow into a grimace. My eyes will ooze agony. My first cries, when I can utter them, will be those of breathless suffering. My first words, pleas for help. The curses will follow shortly thereafter.

"Fools!" I'll say. "Demons!"

# THE FOURTEENTH

Shostakovich's Fourteenth Symphony drifted toward you from the hallway. You were in the kitchen peeling potatoes because you wanted to make dinner for a change, instead of going out. This all happened on the fourteenth of August, the day Hank died.

You only knew which symphony it was because Hank had taken the time to instruct you in such matters. In the first years of your marriage, you'd taught him about books and he'd taught you about music. You didn't care much for the modern Russian classical stuff (especially the work from the Soviet era). You felt it was too bombastic. You told yourself that the Russians stopped making good symphonies when they started making AK-47s. Then he had you listen to an old Melodiya recording of the Fourteenth, and you ate crow. Those opening strings, meek but beckoning. What power they had! That little, pale, bespectacled Dmitri snared you in a net made from those strings.

You sat on a stool, hunched over the kitchen sink, and tried to determine if it was the first movement or the tenth. (They sounded alike at the beginning.) The music was muffled, as though it came from three houses away. But the sound didn't come from the window, from the outside. Moreover, you knew that the neighbors three houses down were not the sort to hire an orchestra to perform Shostakovich. The Flanagans couldn't even find the classical station on the radio if their lives depended on it.

You abandoned a half-peeled potato, rinsed your hands free of the skins, and padded across the rug and down the hallway. A Russian soprano's voice called out to you like a morbid siren: "Po'et byl mertv. Lico ego, khranja / vse tu zhe blednost', chto-to otvergalo . . ."

You were good, but not great at translating Russian (you took three years of it at Wellesley). You caught enough of the meaning to know this was the tenth movement. The one that quoted a Rilke poem about a poet's death.

The Flanagans didn't know who Rilke was, but just to make certain you weren't selling them short you walked back toward your kitchen and out the French doors to the deck. You heard nothing but the purr of lawnmowers pushed by hired landscapers, the splashing of water in below-ground pools, and the shrill giggles and shrieks of well-fed children. The symphony of the late-summer subdivision. That was the problem with this neighborhood: people didn't teach their kids to keep the noise down.

When you were raising Tommy and Jennifer, you taught them that screaming was uncouth. And it worked. They learned how to control themselves without such outbursts. That's why they went to Brown and Swarthmore while their contemporaries landed at State U. But nowadays, random poolside screaming was de rigueur.

By the time you walked back in, the music had stopped. *Of course it stopped,* you told yourself. The tenth movement was near the end. The symphony must have finished while you were outside. You went back to the potatoes. In between swipes with the peeler, you paused, hoping to hear a fresh round of strings. In its absence, you started humming.

Everything was done by six-thirty. But Hank called right around that time to let you know that there were still some loose ends to resolve before making the deal. The senior partners were breathing down his neck to make things happen, to pull more magic out of his sleeve. Just another day (two, at the most) and he'd be home. You wrapped both plates in foil and went to bed early. Turned out you weren't that hungry.

The crash woke you just a little before midnight. It came from the hallway. Then there was music. The Fourteenth, this time the eleventh movement. The ending. The soprano again. Singing louder than she had at supper time. "Vsevlastna smert' / Ona na strazhe . . ." —"Death is great. We belong to her."

Your nightgown swished through the air-conditioned dark as you walked into the hallway. Something had torn asunder a huge section of wall—a full meter in width and half that in height. Dust and shattered drywall littered the carpet. You would have fumed and cursed, had you not come to realize that the music was being played on the other side of the hole. That must have been where it had been coming from earlier, as well. Music wasn't the only thing that gushed out of the gaping wound in the wall, either. Moonlight did too.

Your cell phone chirped and chimed on your nightstand, and you winced at the cacophony it imposed on the Shostakovich piece. You considered letting it go to voicemail, but then you thought it might be Hank. You walked away from the moonlight, the music, and the hole and went to pick up the phone. It wasn't Hank. It was a woman you'd never heard before. She spoke too quickly to understand.

"Mrs. Abernathy?"

"Beg pardon?"

"Mrs. Abernathy? Is this the wife of Henry Abernathy? This is Katrina from Houston Emergency Medical Services. Ma'am, I'm sorry. You might want to sit down before I tell you this. Earlier tonight. He collapsed. Your husband, I mean."

The Fourteenth grew louder. The soprano shrieked. The paramedic-woman kept talking on the other end of the phone, but you could no longer piece together what she was saying. Wood blocks from the orchestra's percussion section pounded against one another, making sounds like slowing heart-beats. Then the strings whirring, whirring, like a child's top slowing down; devolving from a tight spin to a clumsy wobble.

The woman on the phone raised her voice, apparently frustrated with having not been heard but trying to rein in that frustration for the sake of politeness. "There's a hole in the hallway," she wailed.

You almost said, "I know, and there's moonlight and music pouring out of it." Then you realized she was talking about a different hole in a different hallway. Far away.

"That's where he fell. We think he was on his way back to his room when he collapsed. He fell so hard he made a hole there. It was a stroke, ma'am. The ambulance couldn't do anything. He's, he's died, ma'am. Pronounced dead, that is." A pause. "Ma'am?"

You pulled the cell phone away from your ear. In the hole—the hole in *your* hallway—music still blared. The symphony should have come to an end, but instead the strings remained in a holding pattern, whirring. The top still wobbled, long after it should have stopped. It was as though the symphony was being played on a skipping record.

Your out-of-shape knees ached as you knelt on the floor. You stuck your head into the hole and saw a vast landscape of sand dunes on the other side, illuminated by the full moon. An orchestra and singers occupied one of the dunes. The string players' bows worked diligently, playing the same notes over and over. The soprano's eyes caught yours. She grinned and beckoned you to come watch the last moments of their performance. In the hollow under the dune, a well-dressed audience listened. Dapper gents in tuxedos and ladies in silk gowns.

"Ve are vaiting for you," the soprano hollered in Russian-accented English. "Come now, the orchestra can not feenish unteel you arrive."

You set the cell phone down on the hallway floor and crawled into the hole. Into the desert night.

You found yourself adorned in a red strapless gown of the sort you hadn't worn in twenty years. Heels, too. Awkward for marching through the desert. You decided to take them off until you reached your seat. You felt hard, sharp fragments of shells or rocks in the sand. Some tortured the soles of your feet. Some crunched under your step. Wind whipped through the night, tossing dust into your eyes and throat. You coughed, but persevered until you arrived at the appointed dune.

The moment you took your seat the string section performed new notes—as though a record had just become unskipped. You'd never heard the Fourteenth performed live before. You felt yourself grow dizzy with each jab of the violin bows, as though *you* were the top whirring and wobbling—the world around you spinning but slowing. When the symphony ended, you struggled to rise to your feet for the standing ovation. Members of the audience flung bouquets of white lilies toward the soprano. The conductor, a thin gentleman with longish, Oscar Wilde–like hair and a pencil mustache, swept them up and presented them to his prima donna. More applause.

He approached the bulbous, antique microphone at the front of the stage and spoke to the audience. He, too, had a thick Russian accent. "Teenk you lahdeez end geentlemun.

Now, for yew-ur enjoyment, zee cournival." Applause, this time accompanied by cheers and laughter. The previously prim and proper crowd shed evening jackets and scarves and took on a deportment more fitting a fraternity party than a reception.

The sky lightened from black to dark blue, and on the horizon you spotted the first hint of daylight. You followed the line of concertgoers to a dune in back of the stage, where a crude collection of amusements had been assembled in a semicircle. A rust-pocked Ferris wheel. A carousel, bereft of horses to ride and furnished instead with an array of grotesque, saddled chimeras. A concession stand selling black cotton candy. In the middle of it all, a man (Indian? Pakistani?) took a hoe to a pile of hot embers. Smells of burning things lingered unpleasantly in your nostrils.

The soprano approached you and smiled. "Behuld," she said. "Zee firevalker."

The firewalker nodded, acknowledging the soprano's introduction, and began his demonstration. With each step, there were crackling sounds from the coals. The crowd gasped and oooed and ahhhed and laughed and applauded.

A voice drifted toward you from behind, from the place where you'd entered this desert. A woman's voice, filtered through the mechanism of a cell phone. "Ma'am? Are you all right, ma'am? I'm so sorry to have to make this call, believe me. Are you there?" Then, to someone else, frantically, voice cracking, "She's not responding."

You began to turn away from the firewalker. You weren't interested in carnivals, and Hank . . . Oh yes, you remembered now. Hank had just died. You strode purposefully away but felt a cold hand on your bare shoulder. "Not yit," the soprano said. "Ve all tek turns. Now, chu valk on zee coals."

"But my husband, he . . ."

The voice on the cell phone again: "Ma'am?" Then, to a coworker: "What do we do now?"

The soprano took you by the hand as though you were a child. "Chu moost be brev. I inseest." Then she walked you through the sharp sand. When you arrived at the pile of coals, the crowd inhaled a collective "ahhhhh," then started the chant: "Wid-ow, Wid-ow, Wid-ow."

The landscape brightened another shade, moving past twilight into full dawn. The soprano giggled and shoved you onto the hot coals before joining into the chant, herself. "Vid-ow, Vid-ow . . ."

As the desert sun began to bulge, huge and warty over the horizon, you saw that a glowing, superheated femur splintered under your feet. On the ground a few feet ahead of you, you saw a smoldering skull—a collage of white bone, gray ash, black smoke, and orange heat.

You were treading on cremains, not coals.

You wailed as flames began licking your legs. You started to run off of the pyre, but soon found there was nowhere to go. The orchestra members, singers, and carnies blocked your exit. You turned toward the soprano, shrieking as you began to smell the scorching of your own skin. "Help me!"

The firewalker started a new chant, and the rest of those gathered joined in. "Sut-tee, sut-tee, sut-tee . . ." Suttee—the act of a Hindu widow tossing herself atop her husband's funeral pyre. Now largely abandoned, illegal, but still reverberating throughout history and legend. A sign of true wifely devotion.

Then full daybreak. A howling sirocco gusted over the scene, whipping up the flames in a frenzy around you. The last sight you saw before being wholly consumed was the way the wind cut through all the faces surrounding you. The way ball gowns and tuxedos went limp as the flesh that had inhabited them was revealed to be nothing but ash. The way the desert wasn't a desert at all, but rather a wasteland of cremains—dune after dune of human ash littered with tiny chunks and splinters of bone that had survived the ovens.

You awoke to find the paramedics—locals, not their Houston counterparts—hovering over you. A young man with a buzz cut. "Stay with us, ma'am. Stay awake."

All you could say is, "My husband . . ."

The paramedic looked you in the eye. "Your children are on their way. Think about your children. Stay awake. You took a nasty spill right into the wall. Broke all the way through the drywall. This cut on your head is gonna need stitches."

So you got stitches. They kept you there until Tommy and Jennifer arrived to take you home. Then came the blur. Hank's body flown back on an airline he'd always hated. A sit-down with the funeral director (something you didn't remember in the days afterward, even though the children insisted you were there). Hank's family driving in from Connecticut. A brief viewing (for close family only) before his cremation. He looked gray and sad. Then days in your pajamas and housecoat. Days without showering.

The memorial service. A polished brass box, no bigger than an old record turntable, embossed with his name. It bore all that was left of him, burnt and pulverized into thousands of tiny, dead pieces. Kind words from one of the senior partners about the void that he'd leave in the firm with his passing. Even the Flanagans came.

You insisted the funeral home play Shostakovich. You wanted them to play the Fourteenth in its entirety, but compromised with the mortician and your kids, who said this was impractical and might upset people. You decided to use only the last movement. You translated the libretto for the occasion and inserted it into the service leaflet. "Death is great / We belong to her, we whose mouths laugh. / When we believe ourselves to be within life's care / she dares to cry within us."

His family came over to you and offered platitudes that he was in a better place. "Don't cry," his mother (an ancient, hyper-religious shrew) said. "The Lord needed another angel." You didn't have the energy to object. One by one, the mourners paid their respects to you. How oddly similar it all seemed to the receiving line at your wedding.

The funeral director patted your shoulder. "You should come to the reception now, ma'am."

"In a moment. You go on ahead." You needed some time by yourself before moving on to cake and punch and mints. Besides, couldn't the funeral director see that one mourner remained in line to pay his respects? A little, pale man wearing thick glasses.

"They vunted deez service to be comforteenk," Shostakovich said, "to say dat death eez oonly zee begineenk. But eets not a begineenk, eetz zee real end. There vill be noothink aftervards. Noothink."

You got up and embraced little Dmitri. "Thank you," you croaked as tears slalomed down your cheeks. "Thank you for telling the truth."

He nervously pushed away from you and lit a cigarette.

Took a little bow. Then shuffled toward the door. He ran his fingers through his hair and coughed. You'd embarrassed him.

March fourteenth, seven months later. You were in the kitchen microwaving a potato because you wanted to make dinner for a change, instead of going out.

The kids weren't due home for spring break for another week or two. They'd bounced back after the memorial service. They'd only stayed with you a few days afterward, because, well, they'd had a lot of material to read to start off the semester. They'd told you they'd been offered extensions on their assignments but didn't want to use them because extensions only *delayed* the stress and didn't *eliminate* it. Their professors were breathing down their necks already, they'd said.

Tommy had seen to it that the hole in the hallway was repaired. You told him there was no rush. (Actually, you didn't want it repaired at all. You wanted to keep a portal open between this world and the Desert of Ashes. But, of course, you couldn't tell Tommy that.)

Shostakovich's Fourteenth Symphony drifted toward you from the hallway, and you let out a wistful sigh. It was the first time you'd heard it since the day Hank died. The fourth movement this time. The one about a suicide moldering in a cemetery, buried without the benefit of the holy sacraments. (The libretto, from Apollinaire: "Three large lilies, three large lilies on my crossless grave. / Quite alone, quite alone and accursed as I, methinks.")

You needed to find your way back to the concert. To the carnival. You had friends there (or at least, companions). You'd given Hank's old toolbox to Tommy so he could use it to assemble Ikea furniture for his dorm room, and he hadn't brought it back. So you had no hammer with which to bust up the wall. The music got louder and you became more desperate. You even considered, for a moment, heaving Hank's brass urn against the wall, but ultimately that felt too disrespectful.

In the end, you created a new pyre. You used faded wedding photos and baby book pages as kindling. You stacked them against the wall where the hole had been the first time. You hoped that a fire could burn its way through, reopening the portal. Then you struck a match, set it all ablaze, and bent down to the ground with tired joints. Softly, you whispered the chant: "Sut-tee. Sut-tee . . ."

The soprano grew louder with each rising flame. You smiled for the first time in years.

# A Catechism for Aspiring Amnesiacs

Only the most desperate among us feel a tug toward the Time Altar. Fewer still embark on the journey to find it. The outcome is too uncertain. You could end up with exactly what you want, or you could end up with the opposite. Only the Beast, Oblivion, decides what you get. All you can do is figure out what It's hungry for, and try to be that.

To render yourself acceptable for sacrifice, follow these suggested steps.

First, you must either shun or be shunned by your family for a period of no less than five years. Relationships are like clouds that obscure, roil, and churn, suggesting picture after picture to our pattern-seeking heads. To be touched by Oblivion, you must trust no one. You must be immune to seeing things in the clouds that aren't there.

Next, follow Interstate 65 to the Rust Belt town of Verderben, Indiana. Take in the local color. You'll see one of the region's many abandoned factories just off of Spring Street. It's now put to use as a Halloween spook house, open only a few weeks in October. The garishly painted hearse lingers in the parking lot year-round, though.

You'll smell raw sewage from the treatment plant. You'll drive on crumbling roads, over rusty railroad tracks. You'll dodge a handful of bleary-eyed addicts trudging across the four-lane highway in no particular hurry. You'll fear that they might even throw themselves underneath your car. Don't. This particular gaggle of humanity hungers for nothing but the next fix. They're merely meandering from their residence on one side of 10th Street to that of their dealer on the other.

Keep driving straight. Observe the payday loan establishments, churches, and whorehouse motels by the roadside. All three of these temptations cater to your needs in the crassest, most incompetent manner. Signs outside these establishments suffer from misspellings, superfluous quotation marks, and misplaced apostrophes. The relief they offer is ephemeral. Just like pictures in the clouds. Commit that to memory: *just like pictures in the clouds.*

You'll continue to drive north until you pass another abandoned industrial site on your right. Unlike the haunted house downtown, this one goes on for hundreds of acres. It's an abandoned power plant. Rows of tall, blighted buildings infect the otherwise-empty landscape. All the paint has peeled off, revealing bare cinderblock. Windows have broken. Cement has cracked. A half-dozen smokestacks poke out of the ground like the fingers of a dead, deformed giant rising from a shallow grave.

Continue on the road for seven miles. You'll pass Fluvia. This hamlet's largest business is the methadone clinic. Rumor has it the proprietors aren't as strict as those who run a similar venture across the Ohio River in Louisville, Kentucky. During the work week the parking lot exceeds capacity and junkies pull up onto the side of the road, just past the clinic. There's a farm there. They grow feed corn. Sometimes in the autumn, the edges of withered stalks graze the junkies' cars.

To find the Time Altar, you must look for it during the work week. This means that you must neglect your job. Employment is just another social tie that must be broken for Oblivion to find you acceptable. Employment may be even more insidious than family, as a bond that promotes a pro-Something point of view. It's a bait and switch. You think you're signing up to provide labor in exchange for money, so you can eat and drink and wear clothes. They don't tell you that in the process, you're asked to at least grudgingly go through the motions of agreeing with a mission statement (no matter how ill-conceived—and they're *all* ill-conceived). They don't tell you that when you take a job, you become a part of a vast, interconnected matrix of meaning that insists first-quarter goals are real (just as the child insists there really is a face in the clouds).

To find the Time Altar you must drive further north, to Fluvia State Park. You must go there during the off-season. Preferably a day in late November when the sky is gray—when the clouds huddle together in one dark, inescapable mass so solid and unceasing that the imagination can't conjure pictures out of it. Around this time of year, the grass turns a straw-like shade of brown. The brown ground and the gray sky are like the jaws of a vise and each day is like the whirring of a lever bringing them closer together.

You'll find the booth at the entrance of the park abandoned in the off-season. Admission is free, so you'll drive on through. It takes longer than you think to get to Trail 3, and by this time in your trip your anticipation will be great. Many pilgrims have experienced tachycardia once they realized they were so close.

You'll find few cars, if any, in the parking lot. You'll find the trail inordinately steep. First descending, then ascending, in a zigzag through leafless trees. If you're over thirty-five (as, let's face it, almost all pilgrims are) your knees will hurt. No pain, no gain.

You'll arrive at a clearing. You'll see a bridge. Walk across it.

On the other end, you'll see a small historical marker telling you you've crossed over to a place called Rose Island. Note that there are no roses in the immediate vicinity. Read the marker. Note the photographs printed onto it. Note the black-and-white photos of tourists in a swimming pool—the men in early twentieth-century leotard-like bathing suits. Note how the ladder used to go in and out of the pool was constructed with what looks like thick plumbing pipes, curved outward at the end. Note the steamboats chugging up to the hotel. Note a map indicating that there once was a carousel, a café, a picnic ground where churches held feasts away from the summer heat of Louisville. Note how few photos remain. Note how even those extant are blurry with the motion of giddy toddlers who are now broken-hipped old ladies (or corpses). Note that there's a certain out-of-focus quality to the photos that makes all the subjects appear misshapen.

Read how the Great Flood of '37 wiped it all away; how all the mares of the merry-go-round were submerged under the weight of the Ohio and all the muck and branches that came with it. Consider how all the rugs and walls and food must have become sopping wet and ruined.

Walk onto Rose Island. Take off your clothes. Clothes are like families, like jobs. There is the pretension of Somethingness to them which would be sacrilege at the Time Altar. Feel the sting of the wind on your bare flesh. Walk, wincing as the rocks and sticks all over the brown ground jut themselves upward to torture your feet.

Take the path and you'll begin to see the ruins of the amusement park. Crumbled foundations, now covered with moss. Fractured fragments of wood, painted yellow, stick out of the ground like rotten teeth. They're what's left of booths that sold ice cream and lollipops.

Follow the path to the left. Keep walking and you'll find what remains of the swimming pool. Note the filthy water, crusted over with scum. When the wind blows over the surface, it looks like a flexing muscle covered in green-black skin. Note how the ladder down into the pool is constructed of thick, rounded pipes—just like in the photo at the entrance.

Farther down the path, you'll see a slab of limestone, some one hundred feet high, erupting out of the forest floor. Locals call it the Devil's Backbone, but its actual name is the Time Altar. The park hasn't carved a path up to this formation. You must leave the trail to access it. It slopes groundward on one side, and that's where I recommend you make your ascent. The going is still steep. You may tumble and break your neck right there (and never even have the chance to meet Oblivion). Then the joke, as they say, would be on you.

Note the denser-than-expected vegetation at the top. In days of old when the Altar was venerated as such, this wouldn't have been the case. There would have been ritual space—a stone circle atop the stone Altar, which would have foretold the days and the times Oblivion rose out of Its sinkhole to feast. We, the pilgrims of the present day, have no such advantage.

We must walk atop the Altar until we find a clearing. (The vegetation doesn't stop until one approaches the edge of the formation.) If you fear heights, I suggest you cast your glance at the limestone at your feet (and not over the cliff, at the resort ruins). In any case, really, you should bow your head in submission to Oblivion. You should prostrate yourself before the Eater of Time.

Everything written so far is more or less commonly accepted by the coterie of pilgrims. This is what all of us who feel called to Oblivion agree on.

From here on out, though, there is room for debate. Some of us feel that it's helpful to ruminate on the stretch of time in our lives we want Oblivion to consume. There's a theory that It feeds only on passages of time that were particularly eventful, upsetting, or uplifting. There's a theory that thinking about these times, with great focus, tells Oblivion that we are worthy, that our past is peppered with enough trauma to render it tasty enough to feast on.

Most of us who want our time-aspect consumed do it to escape a particularly bruising past. We are those who were molested and didn't dare tell; those who lost wives to cancer, sisters to prison, brothers to fundamentalism, jobs to China. Allowing such memories free rein amounts to masochism, but what are we to do? We need to let Oblivion experience what our past was like—at least from our own limited human perspective—if It is to deign to feed on us.

The goal, you see, for many of us (including, as you may have guessed, yours truly) is to achieve a degree of amnesia so severe that one can never snap out of it. Many of the addicts on 10th Street employ drugs to reach a similar effect. That approach works for some, but runs into the inevitable limitation of expense. Plus, there are the risks of violence attendant to the advanced junkie's pursuit of forgetting. There's the fact that over time, you'll always need more to get the same effect. The methadone clinic is for those who seek to wean themselves off heroin or Oxycodone. A.A. is for those nabbed too many times for DUI. The Time Altar is for those of us who have been there, done that, and can't bear it any longer.

It's a symbiotic relationship—we need to lose our pasts and Oblivion needs to eat time.

There are stories from the 1950s—long after the flood waters receded—of passing boaters spotting feral, naked men roaming Rose Island. Successful pilgrims, these old wives tales say—traumatized vets of Normandy and Bataan who had so much of their past consumed that they lost their capacity for language. Ultimate ignorance, ultimate bliss.

It is rumored that Oblivion sometimes decides to eat aspects of time besides the past. "What if you go there wanting to forget the past," a gadfly might say, "and the Old Beast decides It wants your future instead, leaving you with nothing *but* the past and the present, condemning you to *relive* past problems over and over? Then what?" It is rumored that Oblivion can create demigods by removing a sacrifice's time-aspect altogether. Some say time is just a cocoon we're wrapped up in while our species is still young and Oblivion is only there to free us from its confines, so that we might actually experience dimensions previously undreamed of.

Much conjecture, no proof. There are scoffers who have heard of our little sect through the Internet who say that we of the Cult of Amnesia are victims of a mass delusion, swept along the wave of a communal bad acid trip. "How do you even know Oblivion exists?" they say. "Have you seen It? Has *anyone* seen It?"

When I prostrate myself on the Altar, I dare not look over my shoulder at the sinkhole Oblivion is said to call home. None of us are worthy of such a sight. Once, though, after several hours of resting with my cheek against the limestone, I felt something expansive and undulating place Itself between me and the weak November sun. I dared not lift my head. *Of course,* I dared not lift my head. There's no reason to believe the specks of crude, mammalian jelly in my orbs would be up to the task of glimpsing the Time-Eater, Itself. But I couldn't help but dart my vision over the limestone, spying what fragments I could of Its writhing, tesseract-like silhouettes. Shapes bubbled through the air behind me like boiling water, substantial—broken—reconstituted—twisted; casting shadows engulfed in themselves. Some might say these were multiple phenomena, but my pattern-seeking head knows they were merely parts of a greater, extra-dimensional whole (of which there was vastly more than I could see).

That's how I would sum it up: there is *more,* vastly more of It than there ever will be of us; greater Somethingness in Oblivion than in sunlight and sin, than in mission statements, heroin, factories, and farms—than in all the sublime trash of our world piled together.

As is obvious from the fact that I'm writing this catechism, the Time-Eater didn't feed on me that day. It instead lingered uncomfortably long, then let out a noise like a whinnying toad. I know it is blasphemous to anthropomorphize Oblivion, but I'll confess to you this: I think It was laughing.

If it really did feast on the pasts of World War II vets in the '50s, then my own past will never measure up. While the troubles of my life are enough to plague my sleep with nightmares, they may be too mundane to prove appetizing. If that's the case, the passage of time's my only hope. Maybe It will grow hungry enough in future years to lower Its standards. Or perhaps more interesting traumas await me; and these will render me more palatable.

In any case, I will never stop trying. I will go to the Time Altar Monday through Friday, in autumn and winter. If you come to offer yourself, be forewarned I'll have gotten there first. I'll have already prostrated myself on the choicest spot of limestone. I am, I believe, the most desperate of all desperate men. Too broken to be made whole, too timid for suicide. I will wait for It to show. I will tolerate Its contempt. I will pray for the passing of my past.

"Amnesia may well be the highest sacrament in the great gray ritual of existence."

—Thomas Ligotti
*In a Foreign Town, In a Foreign Land*

# WHITE FLAG

ene stood under the boiling sun and suffocating sky, in line for a place on the floor at the shelter. It was a white flag day at Westside Christian Mission. The shelter had hoisted a frayed, once-ivory-now-dingy banner right underneath Old Glory as a signal to homeless folks that no matter how foul their odor or how empty their stare, no matter how often they screamed for the invisible bugs to get off of them or how many fights they'd been known to start in the past, Westside wouldn't turn them away. A white flag flying over the shelter meant that they'd throw aside all the usual restrictions and squeeze in anyone and everyone wherever they could. Gene had heard through the grapevine that the mayor made Westside Mission do this whenever the thermometer surged to three digits or plummeted to the freezing point. No one in Louisville wanted a dead derelict on their conscience.

As Gene finished his last cigarette a weaselly little guy joined the line right behind him. He wore a stained, ragged black tank top, gray bellbottom slacks, flip-flops, and a thin brown mustache. His skin had been bronzed from weeks or months in the sun. The way he folded his skinny arms over his chest reminded Gene of a dead body in a coffin.

"In the homeless shelter of the future," the little guy said, "there will be no lines."

Even on a good day, Gene wasn't the sort of man who took kindly to smart alecks or psychos trying to make conversation. There were a lot of them in the shelters, but most had already gotten word that he preferred to keep to himself. Most took a gander at his size and decided not to risk pissing him off. Gene was tough, one of the toughest on the streets—both in his body and in his mind. Tough, like a living, breathing callus.

He listened to what the little guy had to say, spat on the sidewalk (half expecting it to sizzle), turned back around to face the shelter, and let out a non-committal "Uh-huh."

"You see, in the year 2078 all social workers had their jobs changed to microchippers."

"Uh-huh." *Geez*, he wished he'd saved himself a Marlboro for the wait.

"Instead of signing people up for food stamps or tracking down places they might be able to stay for the night, their only job became to catch vagrants and inject them with a microchip that could be used to track them down. You see, by then drones had become inexpensive enough that cities could buy hundreds of them to patrol the streets. Any time their temperature sensors indicated it was one hundred degrees or above, they'd swoop down from the sky, remotely activate the positioning signal from the microchips, shoot out a big net, and snare some unsuspecting guy who was napping behind a dumpster. That way, they could take him to a shelter whether he wanted to go or not. They'd drop him right in front of the building at some predesignated time. No waiting. Worked pretty well, too—as long as the drones' temperature sensors were in proper operating condition."

Gene turned back around to look the little guy in the eyes. "Hey buddy . . . it's hot out, yanno?" He waved his gnarled hand at the sky, as if to add: "Too hot for gabbin'."

"I just thought you'd be interested," the little guy said. "About what's waiting down the road, in the future."

Gene looked up and down the line, at the other street people. Missing teeth. Missing limbs. Missing sanity. He let out a hoarse, ugly chuckle. "I don't think anyone in this crowd is gonna live that long. So shaddup."

"But that's another thing that changes, over time. In the homeless shelter of the future, alcoholism, tooth decay, eczema, tuberculosis, and STDs have been eradicated. By 2342, the life expectancy of the average homeless man rose to eighty-seven. That of the average homeless woman made it all the way up to one hundred and eleven. Of course, to be fair, the average life span for a *housed* individual skyrocketed to one hundred and thirty. So the disparities were still there. But still, I think you'd have to agree that eighty-seven isn't so bad, eh? Of course, I found it *less* encouraging that the leading cause of death among the homeless of that era was good old-fashioned suicide. Throwing themselves out of flying buses was the preferred method, for whatever reason. Melancholia . . . still no cure for that."

Gene scowled. "I wish *you'd* thrown *yourself* out of a flyin' bus!" Then a pause. "Melan-what?"

"How silly of me . . ." the little guy said. "That's what they called it back in the eighteen-hundreds. By the way, did you know that the first homeless shelter in your nation-state was the New York City Rescue Mission, founded in 1872? I went to visit there a few trips before this one. I don't recommend it. They didn't treat people respectfully *at all* back then. But I digress. Melancholia . . . in your time you call it something else . . . starts with a 'd' . . . on the tip of my tongue . . ."

The line moved forward half a step.

"When we get in there," Gene said, "don't even *think* of takin' a space next to mine, ya hear? This is the white flag line for a shelter. This ain't the express lane at the grocery store. We *ain't* makin' small talk, and I *ain't* your friend."

"Oh . . ." the little guy said. His eyes twinkled as he put two and two together, finally catching on. "I'm sorry . . . forgive me. Etiquette changes so much over the years. I just came back from 2779. Now, the way it works in *their* homeless shelters is that it's considered stuck-up not to say a word to anyone."

Gene sighed. "This is what I get for stayin' in Louisville for a whole year. End up out here in all this heat next to a fuckin' nut-job who won't stifle himself. Should've gone up to Chicago. Cooler up north. They're nicer to you up there, too. Buffalo, now that was a really sweet deal. Except in winter."

"So you came down here to get out of the cold?"

"Brilliant guess, Einstein."

"So you drift from *place* to *place,* just trying to find a town that's a smidgen better than the last? That's sad . . . not to mention unimaginative. Limiting."

Gene grabbed the little guy by one strap of his tank top and whispered into his ear. "I'm warnin' you, nutsy, shut up or I'll break those twiggy arms of yours! Just be quiet for another half-hour or so, and we'll be in and I can forget I ever met you." Then a pause. "Hey, and another thing . . . where do you get off callin' me 'sad'?"

The line moved up another half-step.

"I used to be a scholar," the little guy said.

"Yeah," Gene said. "I went to school once, too. So?"

"I was a historian. You see, in 2835, when I turned

thirty-six and finally became a real adult, out on my own year-round—the year I matriculated into grad school . . ."

"Oh Christ, more wacko nonsense!" Gene turned his back to the little guy.

The little guy tapped Gene on the shoulder.

"Look," he said, "I have an idea that can get us out of this line and into another shelter. And we wouldn't have to stick out our thumb or walk a thousand miles to get there. That's what I've been trying to tell you all this time. But you won't listen."

"I've been in this lousy city a *full year*, mister. This here's the only place that has room to let everyone in when it's hot."

"Just hear me out. You see, in 2835, time travel became reliable enough to allow historical excursions, regulated by the Bureau of Chronicler Affairs."

"Nutsy," Gene interrupted. "The staff in the shelter are gonna *love* you."

"Do you mind if I continue? Without interruption? I'm just trying to help us both get to the homeless shelter of the future—a place without lines. I'm giving you an *opportunity*. Just give me a chance to tell you about it. If, after hearing what I have to say, you decide you're *really* not interested, I promise I'll be quiet afterward."

Gene cracked his knuckles.

The little guy frantically fumbled for something in his slacks pocket. A pack of cigarettes. Some brand Gene never heard of. Chesterfields.

"Okay, okay," the little guy said. "I can see you need something more than just the assurance that my motives are pure and the promise that I'll eventually shut up. So how about *this* . . . If you just give me a chance to finish what I have to say, I'll let you have this pack of cigarettes."

Gene grinned. The little guy didn't realize what a lopsided trade he was offering—a whole *pack*. He'd kept his distance from little psychos for such a long time that he'd forgotten how easy they were to con. It was like he'd suddenly gone from losing the lottery to winning it. "Oh, hell," Gene said. "Sure. Gimme your spiel. We got nothin' but time and, besides, it's too hot to whup your ass."

The little guy's shoulders drooped and something like a smile scribbled itself across his face as he relaxed. "Great!" He took a deep breath and tried (unsuccessfully) to wipe the sweat off his brow with his equally sweaty forearm. "Here goes. Because I'd always dreamed of being a chrononaut, I applied to grad school and became a research assistant for a time travel historical expedition. But I didn't get accepted to any schools that were doing the really high-profile work, unfortunately. No trips to the times of the pharaohs, the French Revolution, or the Niger Delta Wars for me. The best I could do is to get assigned to a project to assemble an extensive survey of homeless shelters throughout the ages."

"What's this have to do with not havin' to stand in line?"

"Like I said when we first met, in the homeless shelter of the future—by which I mean, the future from *your* point of view; the present and past from *mine*—there are no lines. Now let me finish. I thought you said you weren't going to interrupt me."

"Ain't no interruption, just a question. Here's another: If it's so much better in the future, why ain't you there?"

"It's not as easy as just *wishing* to time travel. We have to find another scholar who's traveled back to this time and stowaway in his timeship."

Gene smiled. He had the little guy right smack dab in his crosshairs. "See? That's where your story don't add up. If you're from the future, how come *you* don't have a timeship?"

The little man shook his head. Rolled his eyes. "That's like me asking you how come you don't have a car."

"What's *that* supposed to mean?"

"Well, let's put it this way. Once, sometime in your past . . . did you *used* to have a car?"

"What kinda flunky do you think I am? Of course I had a car once. I'll have one *again* someday, too, once I get back on my feet."

"Let me ask you this: Did you ever have to *live* out of your car?"

"Well, sure . . . when things started to go downhill."

"Well, for awhile I had to live in my timeship."

"*Your* timeship?"

"Okay," the little guy fessed up. "The *university's* timeship. It's just that when my mom came down with a bad case of the cerebellum blur, I had to divert some of my student loan money to her medical care."

"The Sarah-what?"

"Don't ask. That's the one part of the future you definitely *don't* want to know. Anyway . . . that left me short of money for room and board at the university, so I tried to just live on the timeship in between excursions. No one really seemed to mind. Then I started taking it away for unscheduled excursions, just so nobody else would use it. I told everyone I was just trying to get extra credit. Like you, I had to be a drifter. Only instead of going from place to place, I went from *time* to *time*, saving up a little money . . . looking for items from one time I thought might become valuable antiques in another. Visiting the homeless shelters, too. Sometimes I told myself that I was there to do real research. And I even halfheartedly tried to make notes and discreetly record images so that I'd have something to show for my efforts, but—if I was really honest with myself—I was mostly using them to get a hot meal."

"So you're expectin' me to believe that you went from bein' a college kid to livin' in shelters?"

"Well, things got really bad off when my timeship got stolen."

"Stolen?"

"Well, when I sold it to a pawn store. Which, you know, is *practically* like being stolen. I had a buddy in another department at the university who promised to come back and get me. I thought I could sell the ship, take the earnings, and buy some gold, platinum, I don't know, *something* that would hold its value until 2835. The plan was that he would then come pick me up, and I would sell the precious metals when I arrived back in 2835 and help pay for Mom's treatment."

Gene nodded his head, appreciatively. "Not a bad plan, really. You'd just have to explain to the college how you lost the ship."

"Yeah," the little guy agreed. "And, in my plan, I'd tell the university that it was stolen. Because, you know, *practically* it was."

"Damn straight," Gene said. He wiped his sweating forehead with the hem of his T-shirt, revealing the jungle of hair where his belly should have been. "I mean, not that I'm sayin' I actually *believe* you. Just that, if I *was gonna* believe you, that story would make sense."

They took another half-step forward.

"So all I gotta do to is find a timeship and stowaway."

"I think you're gonna be out of luck, kid. Like I said, I've been around here a year. And I ain't ever seen no timeships."

"Of course you've never seen them," the little guy said. "The historians couldn't get very reliable records if everyone knew they were being studied. Timeships . . . they're always camouflaged."

"Camouflaged?"

"Yeah. Cloaking technology. All the timeships for the early twenty-first century, for example, are cloaked to look like ice cream trucks."

For the first time in months, Gene smiled. The idea of time-traveling ice cream trucks struck him as pleasant, even fitting, as ice cream trucks always seemed to him not quite right. Like something that had seen its heyday about forty years ago but still lingered, in an almost-creepy kind of way, into the present. "You gotta be shittin' me. Listen . . . let's say, just for a second, that I *did* believe you. Why bother tellin' me all this? I mean, if you're worried about people knowin' they're bein' studied, then you just blew it, big time."

"Because I'm not much of a scholar anymore, am I? I'm homeless. Worse than homeless. *Timeless.* You think you have it bad because you drift from city to city. What do you think it's like drifting from time to time? Trying to come up with enough money to pay for Mom's treatment and now, also, enough money for my own legal defense. I'm pretty sure that my buddy who was supposed to come back for me . . . well, I'm pretty sure he—how do you say this in your time?—that he 'snitched' on me instead."

Gene's eyes widened. In the code of the streets, wasn't nothin' lower than a snitch. In the code of the streets, wasn't no one more deserving of help than a dude who'd just gotten snitched on. Gene started to feel something deep down in his gut. He knew what it was like to get snitched on. He started to feel a little guilty about making the deal for the cigarettes. He started to feel *sorry* for the little guy.

"For real, you're on the lam? Then hidin' out here in a homeless shelter is the last thing you should do. I mean, they call the Louisville-Metro Police in here all the time to arrest people with warrants against 'em."

The little guy rolled his eyes. "It's not the Louisville-Metro Police that I'm worried about."

Gene decided to play along. "Sure . . . well, um, what I mean is that the future people are studyin' what goes on in homeless shelters, right? Which means they might have eyes here."

The line moved two steps forward.

The little guy gave nervous glances to his left and his right. "No ice cream trucks. I'm safe."

"So you're damned if you do and damned if you don't. You need an ice cream truck to time travel back to 2835, but if the ice cream truck driver *sees you*, then you could get locked up."

"That's where you come in." The little guy looked at Gene all bug-eyed. "I mean, I'm scrawny but you're not. They know me, but they don't know you. *You* could give us the element of surprise, *you* could really knock them for a loop, then I could join in and, well—I don't know—kick them in the testicles or something. Two guys could take over a timeship easier than one. That's what it comes down to. And wouldn't it be better to go someplace without lines?"

How could it *not* be better in a place without lines? Right then, with his feet aching the way they were and the air itself smothering him, he felt half-tempted to help the little psycho knock over an ice cream truck, just for kicks. He'd get in the back and have a fudgsicle. Hell, even if they got caught, it might be worth it. Didn't they keep the jail air-conditioned nowadays? Didn't they keep it less crowded than the shelter on a white flag day? Wouldn't he have a bed there—a shitty bed, of course, but wouldn't it be better than a place on the floor? If he didn't have that suspended sentence hangin' over him, he'd do it. But the last time he'd gotten snitched on (for stealing some rich guy's Schwinn) the judge gave him a year on the shelf. There wasn't no fudgsicle on God's green Earth worth that.

He arched his back and stretched his arms. Decided to turn down the little guy's offer without bein' a dick about it. Decided not to call him out as a nutcase anymore, and just go along with him. "I dunno, dude. For real, it just seems like I'd be swappin' one problem for another. Microchips. Drones. Nets. That disease you mentioned, the one that's so awful you won't even tell me about it. People throwin' 'emselves out of flyin' cars."

"Buses," the little guy said. "Flying buses."

"Yeah. Whatever. Six of one, half a dozen of the other. Anyway . . . you get my drift, I think. There's never been a cool time in history to be homeless, yanno?" Gene chuckled at the thought. "It's *never been* what we'd call *stylish*. If what you say is true, then I guess it's also the case that it *never will be,* either. No matter what year you travel to, they all suck. No matter what year you travel to, seems like there's always people livin' on the streets. Always people like us around. You know, that's sad as hell. Yeah, I mean, you make it sound like they tinker with things here and there, but honestly . . . don't sound like much has changed. You might as well stop thinkin' about time travelin' and try to find satisfaction here in 2015."

The little guy got this *look*—like a balloon that suddenly lost all its air. Gene thought he might start to cry. Lord, he didn't need *that* right next to him. Not with a ways left to go in the line and the sun hovering right over him like a lamp over a suspect in one of those old crime flicks.

The little guy balled up his fists. Suddenly, his bronze tan had a red tint to it. "Oh, yeah? Well, I guess there's never been a cool *place* to be homeless, either. Did you ever think about *that,* Einstein? Chicago didn't work out for you, apparently. Neither did Buffalo. Maybe there's no perfect *place* to be homeless. No matter what city you travel to, they all suck. No matter what city you travel to, seems like there's always people living on the streets. Always people like us around. Maybe each city tinkers a little with the way they treat the homeless, but it's basically all the same . . . basically, it all sucks! Maybe, the way I see it, your drifting around space is every bit as futile as my drifting around time!" He flung the box of smokes at Gene's belly. "Here, I'm a man of my word. I've said my piece. Take the Chesterfields!"

The line moved two steps, and for a long time afterward they both stood in awkward silence. Neither, now, had the energy or desire for words. Sweat trickled down their cheeks and chests and ass-cracks. A gust of hellish wind kicked up, sending a blast of oven-hot air and the smell of piss into their faces. About ten feet ahead of them, a young guy in a wheelchair started to cry for his mother.

Yet they did not flee nor did they falter. When chimes played "Turkey in the Straw" on the speakers of a passing white truck, they both cast their glance to the ground as though chastened. As the Doppler effect took over, warping the music like water going down a drain, they let it go. They both now knew that no matter where they went in space or time, things would never be much better. So they kept walking in silence, toward the stuffy, stinking coolness of the Mission.

# THE COMPANY TOWN

**A**bout two weeks after Mom's funeral, Dad loaded up a moving van and drove us north to the company town. In between puffs on his cigarette, he tried to get me to go to sleep. "The trip will go faster that way," he said.

"But I don't want to leave Louisville," I whined. "Indiana's *dumb*. Meghan and Cheyenne are going to start middle school without me."

He let out a sigh and ran a hand through his shaggy hair. He looked as if he was on the verge of another crying jag, but knew he couldn't give into it because he was driving.

I turned on my side and tried to act as though I was taking a nap. I kept my eyes half-open, though, so I could glance at the shopping mall and Chuck E. Cheese's and skating rink I was leaving behind. I wanted a last look at each of them. I didn't want our van to cross the bridge into southern Indiana. I suspected that the only things to see out the window there were dumb truck stops, dumb junkyards, and dumb cows. At least, that's what Meghan and Cheyenne had told me when I gave them the bad news.

But cross we did. I spotted a dented, dingy sign welcoming us to our new state. A heaviness settled in my throat as I considered the fact that the entire *Ohio River* now stood between me and Mom's grave. Why were we *just leaving her* there? The whole thing felt disloyal. Having seen all I cared to see of Indiana for the day, I decided I preferred sleep. I closed my eyes completely, this time napping for real.

By the time I woke, night had fallen. The van was making an awkward, too-crazy-a-curve exit off the Interstate and I could hear all our boxes shifting and flopping around in the back. I looked out the window and tried to find the moon, but couldn't. Plenty of streetlamps brightened the roadside, though. Moths fluttered around them and *into* them, over and over. Much of this light made it into the van, but some of it didn't. I turned my head toward Dad and thought I noticed his cheeks were moist.

"You're up?" he asked. He sounded as if he'd accidentally let me glimpse something I wasn't supposed to see. "Why don't you get a little more sleep?"

I fidgeted in my seat. Looked out the window and saw a long, squat, red brick building. A white sign with black lettering announced it as PISTOL STORAGE. Similar buildings lined both sides of the road, adorned with signs revealing them to be ROPE STORAGE and PILL STORAGE.

I pointed to the latter. "Looks as though they're ready in case the whole town gets sick," I said, noting the building's size.

Dad just bit his lip the way he always did when he was trying to find a way to tell me something he knew I wouldn't like. Then he changed the subject. "Okay, let's find a motel."

"But you told Aunt Susan that we had a place to—"

"Never mind what I told Aunt Susan. Just do your old man a favor and keep an eye out for someplace to stay."

We drove beyond the well-lit warehouse district and into a shadowy block littered with deserted storefronts and one or two places that looked as if they might have been bars. On the side of an old brick house there was a flickering red neon sign that said INFORMATION. I pointed it out to Dad.

"Atta girl," he said. He pulled the moving van toward the curb with his left hand while tousling my curls with his right. Part of his palm rested on my forehead. It felt sweaty. "Okay now, let's do this."

I'd looked forward to getting out of the van. I needed to stretch my legs. But the moment my nostrils hit the company town's sour air, I dry heaved.

Dad coughed and tried to pass it off as a giggle. "Getting sick, eh? You're just nervous about seeing your new town, ain'tcha?"

I held my breath and rushed inside, tramping through the lobby's thick, maroon carpet to join Dad at the counter. A pale, wrinkled lady stood behind it. She had dark circles under her eyes and her scraggly gray hair looked as though it hadn't been combed in months.

"Where's the nearest place to stay for the night?"

Her voice cracked when she spoke. "That information's

for authorized personnel only. May I see your identification please?"

"I'm sorry . . . maybe you misunderstood. I just need directions to a motel."

"Sir, I *asked* for your identification. No ID, no directions."

Dad paused as though considering his options, then retrieved his driver's license and pushed it toward her.

Her face scrunched up into something that I think was supposed to be a smirk. "I'm sorry, sir. This just won't do. I meant, *company* identification."

Underneath the counter, Dad's hand started to tremble. "I'm . . . well I'm between jobs right now."

She began typing something into a computer. "I see. Here for business reasons, I take it? A potential customer?"

"Yes, here to make a purchase."

"For you *and* your daughter?"

He leaned forward and lowered his voice, but I could still hear him. "Of course for both of us. The girl's mother just died. You don't think I'd leave her all alone, do you? I was thinking we'd do it with a garage. That way we could both do it at the same time for one price. It'd be, well, you know, *easier* than some of the other ways, too."

"*All* the methods are easy here. Relatively speaking, I mean. That's the whole point. Once you make the purchase, there's no need to work up the courage. If I may for a moment be frank, the company specializes in a clientele of cowards. Too many folks just want to play Hamlet. But once you make the purchase, the company takes it from there. The company makes things happen. For example: on the morning of the event, they sedate you so you don't try to run. You know, in case you change your mind. A sedation fee is included with each and every method."

Dad's voice began to quiver. "Even the g-garage? That doesn't make sense. It's just . . . I mean, the exhaust carries with it all the sedation we'll need."

The lady shook her head. "Potential customers tend to come here rather out of sorts. If you don't mind me speaking plainly, sir, *you* have come here out of sorts. Sedation is required for each and every method. Therefore, a sedation *fee* is automatically added to each and every method."

Dad ran his fingers over his stubble. If he'd had a full

beard it would have looked like he was stroking it thoughtfully. He would have looked *wise*. But he didn't have a beard. He only had about two weeks' growth. "You care to tell me what other expenses didn't make it onto the website?"

"I can assure you, sir, that all the fees are enumerated quite specifically online. These are the rules. The rules for *everyone*. Is it possible that you were, perhaps, not of the most sound mind when perusing our web page?"

He began searching his pants for his pack of Camels. "So basically we drove all the way up here from Louisville for nothing."

"My word, not at all! I can't think of a single customer who's been able to pay for the service out of pocket. Even with credit cards."

Dad tilted his head like a confused dog. "Beg pardon?"

The woman leaned over to her side. She retrieved a plastic three-ring binder, flipped past a few of the dividers until she reached the section she wanted, and pushed down to break the metal rings apart. They let out a loud snap. Then she took a bunch of papers out.

"Everyone I've seen come through town ends up making arrangements to work their fee off. We'll take the money that you brought with you as a down payment, of course. And you can sell things—all but your most essential belongings—to the company store. Then you can begin working until you pay off the rest. We certainly need people to work in the warehouses. But other . . . well . . . other fields are better compensated. Are you a good marksman? Can you tie a noose?"

Dad started to stammer a response, but the lady continued.

"Of course, there will be expenses deducted. Food allowance. Tuition for your little girl to attend the company school so that she can learn skills that are in demand. So that some day she can pay off *her* part of the fee. That sort of thing."

"So how much are we talking about? I mean . . . *total* costs."

She swiveled her computer monitor around so Dad could see it.

"That's not what the website said. Nowhere *near* what the website said."

The woman nodded. "Fair enough. Then I suppose

you'll be on your way?" She handed Dad's license back to him.

He tucked it into his wallet. Then he stood there for a long time, just sort of staring at something in the middle of the wallet. This whole trip had been creepy and sad, but nothing felt creepier or sadder than that stretch of time (a minute? *five* minutes?) when he just stood there, looking at the middle of his wallet, all bug-eyed. "No," he said, finally breaking his silence. "It's a high price. But, honestly, I think it's worth it."

"We all do," the lady said. "If you don't mind my saying so, sir, it's been about twenty-seven years since I first arrived. I only need to stay hired here another six months until I've worked off the fee. Then the company will take arms against my sea of troubles and by opposing, end them."

Dad nodded and smiled and ended up signing a lot of papers that night. Oodles and oodles of them. I ended up walking over to a bench and catching some zees. I realized the whole thing would go faster that way.

# THE CHOIR OF BEASTS

"... the logic of supernatural horror ... is a logic founded on fear, a logic whose sole principle states: 'Existence equals nightmare.' Unless life is a dream, nothing makes sense. For as a reality, it is a rank failure."

—THOMAS LIGOTTI
"Professor Nobody's Little Lectures on Supernatural Horror"

I left my hut at the first sign of darkness yielding to the incursion of day. I indulged the hope that sunlight and the sound of birds might help me forget the previous night's disturbing dreams. It was a pleasant interval, in retrospect—a foggy, forgetful moment that served as an oasis between nightmare and *waking* nightmare. Then the day started in earnest, and I began to remember all the reasons I'd come to prefer troubled sleep to excruciating wakefulness; all the reasons I'd come to prefer blackness to the daytime, autumnal hues of gray and brown and—worst of all—yellow.

For better or worse, a cloud-veiled sun still rose over Sultor. But birds no longer sang there. Most of them (just like most of the dogs and crostens and lugons and chickens and people) had been slain by the Pox. Instead of birdsong, I heard the buzzing of flies hovering 'round the corpses of my fellow villagers. So littered was the grass with dead creatures—human and otherwise—that it was as though a new topography of gore had replaced the old one of rock and soil. Only one fowl remained in the village proper: a quivering, emaciated buzzard that stood, as though dazed, atop a corpse in the middle of the road. It let out raspy, coughing screeches. Sores and scabs covered its swollen eyes. Thick yellow slime drooled out of them.

Sultor had once boasted a population of thousands, but only three of us had escaped the scourge of the Yellow Pox. We were a motley assortment of men: Rontor the Blacksmith, Quintivius the Acolyte, and I, the Hunter.

The acolyte had only been a semester into his studies when all his teachers acquired their first sores. He'd come to Sultor from the countryside, so that he could learn rites of prayer and propitiation. Instead, he only learned to dig graves (so many graves, he began to lose hold of his sanity).

He was little more than a child. His young mind couldn't absorb all the sights and smells of the Plague. He eventually refused to leave his dormitory on the temple grounds. Most days, he lay curled up in a corner of his tiny monastic cell, muttering to himself. "The flies," he'd whisper, while trembling. "The flies."

Rontor took pity on the lad. This surprised me, as the blacksmith was known for his open irreverence toward the Gods and those who earned a living in Their service. Perhaps he'd come to think of Quintivius less as an acolyte and more as just a young boy. Perhaps he thought of the acolyte as a son, now that the Yellow Pox had stolen each of his seven children from him. In any event, the blacksmith spent an inordinate amount of time bringing the lad salted deer jerky to eat and trying to coax him out from the shadows of his lair.

But we were running out of salted deer jerky. The leaves had begun to dry and brown on the branch, and winter would soon be coming. We needed food to keep our strength up, and our smokehouse supply of meat had begun to dwindle.

For at least nine comings and goings of the moon, Sultor had been caught up in the Plague-induced crisis. We busied ourselves with the tasks of tending sick family and burying the dead. We busied ourselves with putting a halt to looting and, in general, perpetuating order. For as long as we could, we kept markets, temples, and academies going. We kept them going until there was no one left to run them and no one left to patronize them. In the end, dead merchants, priests, and teachers found themselves tossed into the same pile of yellow-oozing flesh as dead peasants, thieves, and whores.

We hadn't bothered restocking our food supply. None of us thought we'd live long enough to come close to exhausting it. But three of us did. In the middle of decay and putrescence, our job was to go on somehow.

And so, go on I did that day. There were no more sick to tend (aside from the lad, sick of mind, and tended well enough by Rontor). There were, however, bellies to feed, and I felt a duty to ensure we'd have enough to eat through the winter.

Before the Plague, I'd been Second-Chief Hunter. Back then, I cared about titles and honorifics. I took delight in my quick ascension through the ranks and the luxuries this afforded me. I had my pick of many a maiden, many a plot of land, and many a feast. My bow found the heart of elk and goddrel, my bow fed empty bellies and made men strong.

After the Plague, I had no more Hunter's Legion to command. The skins I'd worn as badges of honor from past kills meant nothing anymore: they were relics of a dead civilization. The bellies I'd fed had become first sunken and emaciated, and then had themselves become food for flies.

I had an aching desire to see my arrows plunge into some gamey hide. I entertained a notion that the Plague had been confined to our village and hadn't spread to the forest. I walked, that day, out toward the stable. I had a quiver of arrows slung over my shoulder, and my favorite bow in my hand. I endeavored to bring some small hope to the other survivors.

Before, I'd always traveled to my hunts on horseback, but most of the livestock had breathed their last while still confined in barns.

I commandeered an underfed, just recently Plague-stricken mule from land that had once been Gregor's. (Or had it been Martin's? It was difficult to recall the property dividing lines that had demarcated the old order.) The animal had weeping sores on its leg, but I rode him anyway. He carried behind him a cart designed to haul away whatever quarry I could find in the woods. I found myself much-delayed by the wretched animal's pace—but I felt the need to keep him. I needed him to haul the cart, in case I slew a deer too large to carry back on my own. Had he not been so scrawny, I would have just slaughtered *him* for a few days' meal.

When I reached the forest's edge, I tied the wheezing mule to a withered tree. Then I took an arrow from my quiver, armed my bow, and walked into the woods.

Sultor lay in a fertile valley, with the Halator River to our south and the foothills of the Cravenbynn Mountains to the east. The hunting grounds weren't in our ancestral lands, but had been won in the War with the Amberbynns. Nonetheless, I felt a connection to the land and its creatures—a connection surpassing even my link to the land of my forebears. I'd lived the happiest times of my life in that forest, away from the politicians and merchants. Living a real man's life, in the hunt.

Thus, when I first strode into the shade of oaks and found that the scent of death lingered there, just as much if not more than in the village, I despaired. All around me, all over the forest floor, birds and macaras and rabbits lay festering. I tried not to look, but there were just too many of them. They all bore the colors of their conqueror; that hideous shade of yellow, the hue of a pale, weak sun. The discharge seeped out of beak and snout alike. It was as though the autumn daylight itself had gone molten and malignant and leaked out of the animals' mouths.

As had been the case in the village, the flies alone had found a way to survive. Their buzzing replaced the birdsong. That's all I heard for half a day—the buzzing of flies and my own footfalls on fallen leaves.

Throughout the whole ordeal in Sultor, I had not wept. When I'd seen abandoned babies in the streets, unburied and rotting for days on end, I hadn't wept. When the Baron's messenger had come to my door with a notice that my land was to be confiscated for use as a mass grave, and the first cartload of bodies was already on its way, I hadn't wept. When a sore had formed inside Father's mouth, and he could no longer talk because the discharge had drained down his throat, then dried and hardened there, I hadn't wept.

It wasn't until I was there in the wild—when I saw that life *everywhere* had succumbed to that damnable Yellow Pox— that I fell to my knees and sobbed and wailed and screamed. I ruminated on dark thoughts. I crouched and crawled to a tree, ignoring the stinging wounds inflicted by thorns I'd trudged through along the way. Did I happen to have a rope in the cart? Could I go back, fetch it, and manage to hang myself? The idea of depriving the Pox (or Its sister, Starvation) of the trophy of taking my life offered some solace. Perhaps self-slaughter was the only solution. But slaughter of the Gods Themselves seemed an even better idea. Slaughter of Them and the entire fractured world They'd sadistically brought into being. They'd admitted me, the acolyte, Rontor, the rabbits, the buzzards—all of us—

into this gaudy festival of existence without our consent. I felt loathing and revulsion for the agonizing affair of birth, disease, and death. I wanted to sabotage the world. I wanted to bring the whole thing crashing down.

I might have rested against the tree, fuming until sunset, had I not been distracted by a sound off in the distance. The fall of heavy hooves on autumn leaves. Ever louder. Approaching.

It was a beast of great girth, whose massive shape shoved aside saplings and knocked older trees askew. I saw it had white horns, a white hide, and most unusual of all, white eyes of the sort I'd never before seen. A wild, white bull—apparently clean of the Pox. A huge beast; easily the weight of three men, I reckoned.

I dried my eyes, readied my bow once again, and hoped it didn't spot me. I stood no match against its speed, bulk, and horns. I had to rely on stealth if I were to make the kill. And, even assuming I did make the kill, I'd have to find a way to butcher him right then and there, as he might not even fit into my cart.

The bull lowered his head, and I panicked. *It had seen me,* I thought. I braced myself for his charge. But then he kept lowering his head. Lower . . . lower . . . until his snout nearly grazed the dirt. I began to see the gesture for what it was. For some reason I couldn't yet fathom, this made me tremble.

He was submitting to me.

He just lingered there in a clearing about ten paces away—waiting, cowering. I crawled out of my hiding place.

The bull did not move. He just stood there and—I swear on the grave of my firstborn son—grinned.

I drew my bow back and let the first arrow fly. I struck him in the side, from close range. I heard something like a roar and a sigh mixed together.

Then the bull was no longer a bull, but a man.

An odd, fat man with white skin, white shoes, and a white silken suit. During the course of the transformation, his white horns drooped and softened to become the silken points of a white jester's cap. My arrow gave him a wound that in time would certainly prove mortal. He bled and bled, staining his suit and the ground around it.

"I am slain!" the fat man cried. He sounded half in agony, half on the verge of laughter.

I wailed, feeling nauseated and dizzy. I sensed my pulse in my ears.

I'd not meant to murder, only to hunt. I feared that, in my grief, I was becoming as mad as the acolyte (no, madder, for even at the height of his melancholy the lad hadn't committed any crimes). I ran toward my victim and began to examine his wound. I suppose, at this point, I should have offered the man my apologies. I should have done what I could to extract the arrow. Instead I knelt by him and looked into his white eyes. "Who are you?" I said. White eyes, not merely *filmy* like those of a blind man, but *white*. Old, alabaster skin, too. Pale and thin as the clouds. "*What* are you?"

He gasped and coughed before answering in a weak, whimpering voice. "I am the Shaman of Cravenbynn, at one with all the creatures of these hills. Thank you for your kind act of murder. There is nothing more shameful than for a Shaman to outlive the animals in his forest."

He didn't look like what I'd always supposed a Shaman would look like. I'd been taught they took on the appearance of demented wild men—though they were anything but. They were sages, loosened from the constraints of customary appearance. He, on the other hand, looked like one of the itinerant stage performers who once a year traveled through our region. The kind who performed pantomime and juggling. Not a sage, but a fool.

Incredulous, I stammered. "K-kind act?"

"I heard what you'd said. About the cruelties of suffering in this world, about the way the Gods are cruel to bring us into existence. I saw the decimation of the great City of Amberbynn on the other side of these hills. All that remains are three maidens, one of whom is little more than a child. She crawls in a corner and sucks her thumb like a babe. All three, left to fend for themselves. I'd held out hope that Sultor had fared better, just as I'd earlier held out hope for these woods. Then I'd overheard your comments on the matter. It's all a— how did you put it, a garish festival? If life is a garish festival, than I am the Festival Fool, Hunter. For what else can you call someone who exists, but has no purpose for existence? I had no choice but to end my life."

I hadn't *said* a word. The Shaman had read my thoughts (as, it is rumored, Shamen were wont to do) and mistaken them for words. Indeed, he must have been a very old Shaman. It's said that once Shamen have lived to be over one thousand years old, they lose the distinction between thoughts and words altogether. To them, it is all just communication.

"So you took the form of a bull and used me for the purpose."

I looked down into his white eyes and discovered a subtlety to the coloration I hadn't noticed before. There was something of a glint to them. Somehow, the old Shaman had a twinkle in his white eyes, a shimmer not unlike crystals of ice in the midst of fallen snow.

He nodded. Smirked.

"Trickster!" I bellowed. "If you *had* to shapeshift, I can't see why you couldn't stay a bull. That way, at least, I would have had food for my people."

"I had to take my true form once again," the Shaman said. "To repay you for your kind deed. Yes, I could have stayed in the form of the White Bull and provided a feast for those remaining in your village, but that would be a mere pittance compared to the gift I'm about to provide in recognition of the great offering you bestowed upon me."

"Offering?"

He pointed to his chest and began to cough up blood. He smiled with blood-stained lips. "Your arrow. What a delightful offering it is!"

I shuddered.

"Now, while I still have time, I want to point you in the direction of your reward. In my hovel at the peak of Bloom Hill, you'll find a table. On that table, you'll find three extracts stored in flasks. One white, one black, one gray. You must first dip your arrows in the flask containing the gray potion. This will give them the power to strike God-flesh, not just animal-flesh. Then you must drink the white potion. This will make you, your clothes, and any equipment you carry invisible for as long as necessary. Invisible even to the Gods. Then drink the black potion. This will transport you to the Plain of Drau Meghena, enabling you to fulfill your wish."

"Wish?"

"To murder the Gods, and in so doing, bring the whole world crashing down."

"I'm afraid I don't understand."

"The Gods . . . what do you think They are?"

"Our Masters. We're but Their slaves, subject to Their whims, be they cruel or kind. Most often, these days, the former."

A smirk. "Typical Hunter. No imagination. What do you think They *look like?* When you follow my directions to go murder Them, what are you going to be aiming at?"

Nobody knew the shape of the Gods. It was a forbidden topic to consider. The priests taught that They were without shape, that They were beyond notions of shape. I'd never even considered the possibility that this might be a lie. I could offer no answer.

"In their native land," the Shaman said, "the Gods are a Choir of Beasts. Beasts the like of which you've never seen before, Hunter! Schrellnics with beaks, instead of snouts. Tigers the color of moss. Land-walking lampreys with fur. Each of them sings a song, Hunter. A song about each different type of creature that lives. A magick song that *brings into being* each creature that lives.

"The moss-colored tiger sings the Song of the Antelope. The hairy lamprey sings the Song of the Fish. Always, the Predator sings the song of their prey. It's the same song for each animal, actually, a little ditty called 'Nightmares Making Nightmares.' And when the Predator sings it, it creates the prey.

"They sing the magickal song to the demented, deformed giant Crastagulus, the Sleeping God of the Void. They sing it to Him in the hope that They might wake Him, so that He might take on His rightful reign over All That Truly Is. You see, to the Choir of Beasts, Crastagulus is the one true God—and They are but supplicants. They were given rule over All That Truly Is only because Crastagulus (in what one might call shrewd wisdom) abdicated it in favor of the oblivion of sleep. The Choir of Beasts resent His withdrawal and wish for nothing more than to wake Him. And so They sing horrific, magickal songs to give Him nightmares, which I suppose may have led Him to toss and turn—but haven't yet sufficiently stirred Him to arise from His slumber. Perhaps that's why things keep getting worse in Sultor, Amberbynn, and the Cravenbynn Forest. The Choir of Beasts grows more desperate, seeks to paint pictures ever more monstrous with Their wretched lyrics. *Pictures*, Hunter, *lyrics* like you and me, the surviving men of Sultor, the three maidens of Amberbynn, and the dead world all around us. We have no real substance, you and I. Our lives are not real. Our surroundings are not real. We are simply characters in a magick song, who then become characters in Crastagulus's nightmares. And we can put an end to it all by silencing the Choir of Beasts."

I shook my head, disbelieving. "Even a Shaman's wisdom is subject to the cobwebs of senility."

"Use your power of reason for something besides tracking, Hunter. Use your intuition, while you're at it. *It makes sense* that you and I and everything and everyone around us are just the characters, props, and settings for nightmares ricocheting 'round the head of a demented God. Yes, this strikes you as an odd notion. And yet, the notion resonates. It seems intuitive. Look around you. Existence equals nightmare. Unless life is a dream, *nothing makes sense.* For as a reality, it is a rank failure."

"So far you've offered me ramblings. Ravings. A good Hunter relies on intuition only after surveying the evidence. Tracks, scents, fur caught on brambles. *Evidence.* You offer me tales of dreaming giants and green tigers, and expect me to believe them."

The Shaman sighed, then reached a cold, white hand up to my face and stroked it, as a woman might stroke the face of her lover. "If it's tracks you demand, Hunter, then tracks you'll get." He moved his hand away from my face and slammed it against the earth three times.

A trail of bull's tracks glowed in the woods, as if each of his hooves had set the ground afire, but did not consume it. "Follow *these* tracks. They lead back to my hovel. There you'll find all that you need. All the implements required to murder the Gods and the nightmare-world They've sung into existence."

"If you really are in possession of these tools, Shaman, why haven't you used them yourself?"

"Because I'm no Hunter. Look at me. Old. Frail. Your chance of success on this mission is much greater than my own. Though you'd do well to mark, before your expedition to the Plain of Drau Meghena, that there are many, many Beasts there. You will not be armed with sufficient weapons to kill each God that sings a creature into existence and pain. You will only be able to kill one. *Mark this, Hunter, most of all:* The Beast you will go to slay—the Predator who sings the Song of Men and Maidens—is, in size, unlike any beast you've ever stalked before. It's a—"

I looked off in the distance at the trail of glowing hoof marks. "With all due respect, I think you underestimate me, Shaman. When there was a thriving village of Sultor, I was its Second-Chief Hunter. Not only a Hunter, but a leader of men in the hunt. To this day, the antlers of a mammoth mother goddrel I killed, six men wide—the largest ever seen by Sultorian eyes—adorn the village beer hall as testament to my prowess. I think you should—" I turned my head back toward him, to make certain he was listening.

He wasn't there. In his place sat a pile of dusty, disarticulated bones. The skeleton of a bull, smothered in a cloud of flies. I took in the sight, noting with awe and revulsion the dry-rotted arrow in the midst of the bone pile.

I followed the tracks.

At first I told myself I did this only out of curiosity. I considered the possibility that the Shaman of Cravenbynn and his tale of the Choir of Beasts were just fever-dreams—signs of desperation, madness, or even the first indication I might be sick with the Pox. I felt my flesh for nascent sores, but found none. On the other hand, I thought some good might come of believing the encounter had been authentic. It gave me a reason to go on (even if that reason was the merciful annihilation of myself and the other suffering survivors).

Daylight was wasting away. The sun sat on the horizon. We still had at least a little meat in the smokehouse. No one was starving—yet. I should have returned to the village, to come back again the next day.

But I didn't. Too much had happened that I couldn't explain, and perhaps nothing appeals more to desperate men than the hope that their plight might be explained to them—that there might be some meaning.

I thought about "Nightmares Making Nightmares," then about the stench and hopelessness awaiting me back in Sultor. When fears arose about my vulnerability in the forest (without so much as a lantern), I thought about just how little

I valued my own life. Then I put all thought out of my head and set my mind to one purpose: to follow the tracks, no matter where they led. They snaked through the woods, forming a path miraculously uncluttered by carnage. I followed it until I arrived at a swelling from the ground, bedecked with flowers bearing soft petals that grazed my bare calves as I climbed it. Bloom Hill. At the top, a dwelling.

I expected a hut, of the sort typically found in Sultor. What I found, instead, was a dwelling made entirely out of tufts of thorn bushes that had been yanked out of the ground. Mud had been used as mortar to give the structure some stability. The entrance was low and wide. Made for a bull.

I leaned my head into the all-consuming darkness of the Bull-Shaman's lair. I encountered odors both putrid and pleasant. Between the dusk and the dense, light-blocking thorns that constituted the walls, I couldn't see what caused such a commingling of scents. I knew the Shaman was a joker and feared he might have led me to his domain for some malevolent purpose, with the lure of a lie. I feared the Shaman had some grisly surprise in store for me.

I felt my innards writhe. I reminded myself I could still turn around. I could follow the luminescent white tracks back to the point where I'd met the white bull. I could then walk the rest of the way back to Sultor, through the fallen bodies of birds, the decaying carcasses of rodents.

But what would I be going back to? The blacksmith? The acolyte? Graves and flies and worms and a world with no mystery—only death?

I took my first step into the hovel.

The very moment my sandal hit soil, two clusters of illumination erupted in mid air. To my left, tiny dots of white light, rising, falling, blowing like snow in a blizzard. Next to it, a dimmer shade of white—no, not that, a *gray* light. That's the best I can describe it, though it might seem nonsensical.

I took another step forward.

The smells—both wince-inducing and sublime— intensified. So did the light. The white and gray lights grew brighter and brighter until the whole room achieved a degree of illumination not unlike that of noon.

Then and there, I finally saw the interior of the hovel for what it was. The white and gray lights surrounded flasks of the same colors that sat next to one another on an oak table. On the far side of the table sat a black flask that had been obscured in the darkness. A disembodied hand, dark as the void between stars, held it in a clenched grip. I noted that all three flasks levitated ever so slightly off the table's surface, such that a fly or worm could have squiggled underneath, but nothing larger.

I knew now that I was not Pox-stricken. I was not insane. I'd heard a description of magickal potions and then, after only a short hike, found them. Reason and intuition both spoke the same answers to me: there really was a Plain of Drau Meghena, and before me—floating over this simple oak table—were all the implements needed to bring an end to the nightmares wrought by each day's rising sun.

I removed an arrow from my quiver and dipped it into the gray flask. When I took it out, the tip glowed gray. I repeated the task ten times over. I wanted every arrow to be up to the task. Then I grabbed onto the white flask and without pause drank its bitter, foul-smelling contents (the source of the hovel's foul odor). It made me gag, but I did not retch. I watched my flesh dissipate into air—an odd, vertigo-inducing sensation. Seeing what I could of my own body provided a frame of reference, a compass and a grounding. Being unable to see my own body was a strange incident indeed.

Only the black potion, held in the grip of the obsidian hand, remained. I tried tugging the bottle away. The hand wouldn't yield its treasure. I tried prying its cold, dark fingers off the bottle, but found the hand's grip like that of tree roots in good soil. After pacing the hovel and considering the dilemma, I approached the oak table and slammed my palm against the surface three times—just as the Shaman had slammed his palm against the ground.

The cold black hand relinquished its flask. I took it, drank it, and woke on the Plain of Drau Meghena after what seemed like a fitful sleep. I awoke to the chant of the Choir of Beasts.

Time passed differently on Drau Meghena. No sun shone in the sky. The light radiated from the ground itself, and from its Beasts. While I was aware from the Shaman's statement that the Choir sang songs full of lurid lyrics, I heard only one note sung continuously. I couldn't count all the mouths, maws, and snouts the songs were sung from. They were legion.

Each Beast sang in a slightly different pitch. Rarely, a Beast would add a flourish—a trill here or there, a warble. But the overall impression forming in my mortal brain was that of a monstrous synchronicity.

The plain stretched out in all directions, and I could not see the end of it. My eyesight seemed to work differently. There was, it seemed, no horizon. When my eye found a point where a horizon should have been, I blinked and found that my perspective had rushed forward. This made me unsteady on my feet, until I became accustomed to it.

The light emanating from the Creatures' hides mixed together to give the sky purple and rose hues, while the ground was like a fallen rainbow; a free-for-all in which no shade or handful of shades predominated. I surveyed the herd of chimeras—each Beast a corruption of its counterpart in Sultor, endowed with some aspect or aspects that rightly belonged to another. A bird, sagging in flight under the weight of tiny hooves. A dog with the face of a monkey. A bear with a snake's eyes and tongue.

I considered for a moment that these were the Gods that innocent farm boys were taught to worship and appease. Families sacrificed much in the way of wealth to send such a lad off to learn from the priests how to make proper supplications to these Monsters. I shuddered, and nearly ruined my stealthy advantage by vomiting. But I managed to swallow my bile. Then I padded through the multicolored ground, again surveying the quarry, looking for a sign of that Beast that sang the Song of Men and Maidens so I could silence it and bring the Great Nightmare—mankind—to an end.

I could not, at first, detect any sign of the giant. I began to suspect the story of Crastagulus was an embellishment on the Shaman's part (after all, storytelling is another traditional Shaman craft). Then I felt a gentle rising and falling motion beneath me, as though I were in a boat on the Halator when it was calm. I then knew that what I'd mistaken for the ground beneath me was, in fact, the very torso of the gigantic God, Himself.

I crouched and tiptoed my way through the Choir, taking in the whole scene, plotting and planning how I could possibly complete my mission. After I'd walked several hundred paces, by my best reckoning, all the Beasts took on the chanting of a new note. This one ever so slightly higher. I heard Their song in this fashion, one note at a time, each note consuming vast stretches of time. Or, perhaps, my experience of time did not match that of the Beasts of Drau Meghena. Perhaps time passed more slowly for me than for Them.

I'd traveled, before, to other lands and noted the relationships of their animals one to another. If a chimeric tiger sang the Song of the Antelope and a chimeric lamprey sang the Song of the Fish, then it made sense that whatever sang the Song of Men and Maidens would be a chimera who was Predator to our prey. I searched for the bear-snake chimera I noted upon my arrival, as both beasts could be fatal to man. I looked also for something in the shape of a wolf. Or, perhaps, a wild boar.

As I surveyed the plain for the proper Beast whose slaying would bring an end to the misery of myself and my species, something wispy and slimy grazed my face. I slapped at my cheek, trying to be rid of it—as even that hint of a touch of its legs on my face felt foul. The insect offered Its own high-pitched rendition of the note sang by the Choir as a whole. It flew tight circles in the air around my head while singing, then landed atop my nose.

It couldn't see me, but perhaps this particular Beast could *smell* me.

I looked in horror at the mishmash of beasts It represented—a long, slimy midsection of white worm, covered with a sparse coat of bristly black hair, bulging with tumors crusted over by oozing yellow sores. It had the thin, membranous wings of a fly. It buzzed. Like the pestilence-bearing, corpse-corrupting flies in Sultor and the Cravenbynn Forest, It buzzed. It sang Its high note, synchronized to that of Its bestial kin.

I examined It in each of Its parts—the maggoty middle of It, skin so afflicted with disease it seemed to be boasting of it. I examined how the body was attached to the buzzing wings of that creature who had proven so inescapable since the rise of the Yellow Pox in Sultor. Whose song replaced that of the birds.

Then the recognition came.

I fell to my knees, laughing and wailing, and the Fly-Beast flew off in the air. Yes, this alerted the whole Choir to my presence, but what of it? Oh, the Bull-Shaman-Fool had played fair, all right. He'd *tried* to warn me that the Beast I had to slay was, in size, *like none other I'd ever stalked before.* And I? I'd met his warning with a boast.

I'd expected to slay a huge Monster and come to find my real quarry was a fly! A chimera of maggot, full-grown fly, and disease! *These were the Predators?* So ill-prepared was I, their puny prey.

Laughing and wailing, I abandoned all training and pursued the Creature half-frolicking, half-racing. I snapped my useless bow over my knees and used arrows only to swat at the singing, buzzing God. Nearly getting It once, perhaps even grazing Its wing as It had once grazed me, but then I found I'd been unmindful of my feet, and tripped against the webbed foot of a singing frog-boar chimera. It darted Its tusks toward me, mid-note, and it was only through the use of quick reflexes that I was able to escape being pierced as It hopped toward me.

I ran and I ran, now no longer even trying to slay the Fly-Beast. I ran to rid my brain of this new knowledge. I ran away from the herd toward the horizon—then belatedly remembered there was none. I had no choice but to listen to each note of Their melody. I covered my ears and ran through Their ranks, seeking escape but finding none. After much running, I felt a cramp in my side. My stomach began to spasm, and—mercifully—black bile (the Shaman's potion, I imagine, commingled with bile) erupted from my mouth.

My head grew heavy. I saw conflagrations of purple and rose. I had visions of the entirety of Sultor slathered in yellow effluvia. I saw two lights—one white and one gray.

What I yearned for most of all was blackness.

The next thing I saw was sunlight bleeding through the open passage into the Shaman's thorn-hovel. The next thing I heard were birds. Coughing up more black sputum, I found myself too weak to stand. I could, at most, only squat there on the dirt floor. I looked down at my leg and noticed, with some trembling, that I once again could see myself. I had, apparently, thrown my clothes off in a fit that I couldn't recall.

My flesh had been bleached white as a cloud. The Plain of Drau Meghena had absorbed all pigment from my body. Moreover, my skin had become extensively wrinkled and sagging, much atrophied. I ran a nervous hand through my hair—only to find myself without any.

For many comings and goings of the sun I regathered my strength. I rooted into the dirt floor and fed on worms and beetles, managing to snag a stray rodent now and then. (The forest animals had no aversion to entering the hovel; they came and went quite freely and showed no signs of fear.) In time, I found myself strong enough to rise. I didn't dare venture outside, for fear I might discover the birdsong had been a false noise foisted on me by madness. I hadn't the heart to glance on a world nearly picked clean by pestilence.

Instead, I lingered like that in the hovel, naked and reclaiming the use of my senses. I discovered the Shaman's scrolls hidden away in clay canisters and found him to be a grim scribe, indeed. Some scrolls told of the conspiracy inflicted against men and maidens by the priests (among others), to keep from them the truth of the Choir's existence. Some scrolls provided instruction in a hideous branch of chymistry. Some were works of poetry and fiction (after all, storytelling is another traditional Shaman craft)—songs for dead dreamers and tales of a Great Black Swine that is All That Is.

Had I stumbled upon such scrolls before my voyage to the Plain of Drau Meghena I would have considered them the world's worst abominations. As it was, I found in them the ability to create nightmares outside of the Nightmare. A sort of magick the Shaman had used to out-dream the Nightmare. Perhaps that's how Shamen managed to live so long.

Yes, he dwelt among the animals of the forest and built a kinship with them. But not because he ventured out among them. Rather, *they* must have come to see *him*, through the open door of his hovel. He must have been a recluse. Staying there, writing on his scrolls until he ran out of them. Only venturing out to slay a deer from whose skin he made new scrolls (or to play the part of a Bull for a hapless Hunter).

I read and I read the Shaman's scrolls until I succumbed to a pristine, dreamless sleep unlike any I'd ever had. A slumber that lasted lifetimes.

It was the voice of a maiden, shouting outside my hovel, that awoke me—the first voice I'd heard since the Shaman's. "Is anyone there?" she said, with a manner and an accent I could barely understand. "Show yourself. Friend or foe!"

Pale, naked, and wrinkled, I was in no condition to greet a young lady. I'd not yet lost respect for that convention of society. I walked past the oak table and found a wardrobe I'd never bothered opening before (for the animals hadn't found my nakedness at all offensive). Inside, there hung a white silken suit, shoes, and jester's hat. I hastily put on the attire, then crouched down to exit—for the first time in so long—the hovel.

She wore black boots and a strange, green gambeson and trousers that made her blend in well with the lush leaves of the forest. A helmet adorned her head. She wore a belt that held various and sundry devices, the likes of which I'd never seen before.

Her eyes widened at the sight of me. They were tired, vacant, suffering eyes. I discovered I now had the ability see inside her head, to see the hideous tapestry and hear the chaotic cacophony hidden in her brain. The whole world on fire. Villages the size of a thousand Sultors destroyed in the blink of an eye. Iron rods that one man could use to spit fire into another. Only tiny pockets of survivors here and there. In her thoughts, if not her words, she wished the death of the world and the deity who fashioned it. If she listened to me, perhaps I could help. Could make things right, after my failure at Drau Meghena. All I'd need was an offering, that most special of offerings. The one I'd given the Shaman before me.

"Who are you?" the lady warrior said. "*What* are you?"

It was then I gave words to the new truth. "I am the Shaman of Cravenbynn."

*—for Thomas Ligotti*

# ALL I REALLY NEED TO KNOW I LEARNED IN PIGGY CLASS

## I. Piggy Class

We'd made the papier-mâché Piggy masks in art class, all the way back in middle school. It had been career day, and we'd just taken a vocational aptitude test. My cousin Cheyenne's results had told her that she'd make a good Hen. Daniel (my older brother), who'd taken a similar test five years before me, had been told he'd make a good Bull. The butcher who prepared his body for market sent a kind note informing us that he'd proven a fine specimen and had not so much as flinched before entering the abattoir.

The treasure of our family, though—the one who made us all proud—was my *eldest* brother, Dylan (at fifteen years my senior, he always treated me more like a niece than a sister). His aptitude test had said he'd make a good farm hand. And so off he went one day, to a farm up around Cherry Hill. He consoled us by pointing out that they mostly grew feed corn and soybeans up there, with a few goats thrown in as a hobby. So the chances of his being put in the awkward position of farming a sibling were remote.

My aptitude test said I'd make a good Piggy. As soon as I'd received the results, the Enforcer escorted me out of the principal's office to join the other Piggies in Ms. Tinsman's art class. That's when we made our masks.

It didn't make any sense to me at the time that Ms. Cafferty (our principal) confiscated them before we could try them on. "Not yet, my little Piglets! Wallow in summertime before you don your masks," she'd said.

That didn't make any sense at all. Not until the first day at Lagrange High School, when I opened my assigned locker and discovered the Piggy mask I'd made three months before dangling from a coat hook, awaiting me. A mimeographed sheet read: *Wear This Now! Be This Now! If You Are Not Piggy*

*Enough, You Will Be Expelled!*

I'd never known anyone in school who'd been Expelled, but one heard stories over the years. Rumor had it that the school system liked to dissect The Expelled to find out just what had gone wrong. Rumor had it they started the procedure when you were alive. I can't imagine why, unless one's response to the dissection was part of the data collected. The school system did so love testing.

To be Expelled meant you had failed to fulfill your niche in life—a fate most people in town considered worse than death due to the dishonor it inflicted on the entire family. If I were ever to join the ranks of The Expelled, I would bring great shame to my mom and dad.

So I put on the Piggy mask and went to visit my new homeroom teacher (and, it turned out, my new everything-else teacher), Ms. Landres. She'd been in the employ of the school system for decades and had all the mechanical add-ons to prove it. Gears in her eyes. All the better to see us with. Gears in her heart. All the better to hate us with.

When I tell people about it *now,* I'm told I shouldn't be surprised I got Expelled. Maybe it all started on September 1st, the day of our first class inspection (right after lunch and a fire drill). The first day I saw Ms. Landres's *Scaramouch* mask. The day I pissed her off by calling it a Bird mask.

"I'm not a filthy animal like you, Swine. Now repeat after me: Scar-a-mouch," she'd snarled, glaring down at me with those gear-eyes of hers.

"Sc-scare-a-Moose," I'd stammered, my voice muffled under the papier-mâché Piggy mask.

"Close enough, you worthless Piggy!" she'd said just before she hocked an oily loogie onto my new school dress. The rest of the Piggy Class broke out in a chorus of condescending snorts and squeals.

After that, I did everything Ms. Landres said and limited my communication with the other kids to a stray whisper every other day or so. "Stop looking at me," I'd croak.

I'd learned my lesson, I thought. I wasn't about to call her *Scaramouch* mask a Bird mask anymore. I would just do my best to be a good Piggy and blend in. On inspection days, in particular, that was the best strategy.

It happened on November 1st. The first of the month, just a couple of weeks shy of Fall Break. Ms. Landres hissed directions for us to line up for inspection, boy-girl-boy-girl, same as always this day of the month, at high noon. Each of us stood in queue, struggling to project the aura of the quintessential papier-mâché Piggy.

Ms. Landres's gear-wheel-eyes churned with deliberate machination on such days. They made slow, safe-tumbler sounds. *Click-click-click-click-click*—each "click" an indication of her sensation, her perception, her *judgment* of us. Each click rendered the true status of our souls harder and harder to hide.

"Scara-you-scara-me-scara-mouche!" the braver, less browbeaten Piggies had whispered to one another at the bus stop that morning. Although they seemed well on their way to Pigginess, I took solace in thinking that they must have had at least *some* human kid still in them (to defuse their dread with a lame joke). After all, Piggies don't whistle past the graveyard.

If we passed inspection, Ms. Landres would shriek that we were (in her singular but sufficient opinion) "Piggy!"

"Piggy!" Ms. Landres hollered with approval as she stared into the soul of Natalie Simmons. Then Natalie smiled and snorted and skipped off to her seat.

"Piggy!" Ms. Landres yipped as she took a quick glance at Aiden Addison—a Piggy so brimming with Pigginess that inspection itself seemed an unnecessary formality. He squealed long and longingly, crawling back to his seat.

Then she got to me. That mean old hag placed one gnarled arthritic finger under my chin and brought my reluctant eyes to hers. I looked up, past the Scaramouch mask, into her eye-gears. Gears that started to go faster. Gears that seemed able to ground up my soul.

"Not Piggy enough!" she wailed, reaching her claws into the holes of my mask and nearly scratching my eyeballs with her ragged, untrimmed nails in the process. Her gears clicked away faster still, like a roller coaster approaching the plunge. *Click-click-click-click-click-click-click.* "No! No! Not Piggy enough!" *Click-click.* "No! No! Not Piggy enough!" she roared. She yanked for all she was worth, unmasking me.

For a few moments I just stood there, adjusting to the odd, unwelcome kiss of air against my cheeks. Just stood there, not understanding the implications of the unmasking.

"Expelled! Expelled!" Ms. Landres screeched, her eyes clicking with manic judgment. She pushed a red button on her desk.

My face flushed. My face ached. My face must have expressed, at that moment, all the aggregate horrors encountered during my days in Piggy class. I don't know how long I stood there, stunned still, until I heard the first slap of the Enforcer's boot against the linoleum floor. That reminded me of all the agonies (both of the flesh and of the soul) awaiting me.

I ran.

Ran out of the high school, pulse pumping, arms pumping, my face ablaze with the wince-worthy pain induced by air rushing onto it. Air hitting raw nerve. The extra weight I'd put on since September jiggled around my midsection.

I ran past the ball field, past the tree line, and splashed into the shallow creek nearby. I'd heard somewhere on TV that if you did that it would make it hard for someone to track you; that your scent would disappear. And disappear is exactly what I wanted to do.

I ran along the soft creek bottom, splashing for a bit, nervous that what the Enforcer's hounds couldn't smell the Enforcer himself would plainly hear. I decided after more running that I'd best make it to land. There was a cemetery nearby, and then some woods past that. Where I'd go after that, I did not know.

I made a leap out of the creek onto the waiting bank and slipped. My new girth pulled me backward, and I fell into the water. The splash of water onto my face stung like a hundred bee stings. I yelped. My fall kicked up a vomit of sediment from the sandy creek bottom, and minnows scattered in its wake. As the water stilled, I caught a rippling reflection of myself.

My face was scarred and deformed, with nerves and muscles visible (and throbbing) under my eyes and cheeks. But even with that mess, I could see a few suggestions of Pigginess. My nose had become more upturned than it ever had been before, and it had grown in length about half an inch. I could see that it had begun to resemble a snout. Likewise, my ears possessed a suggestion of pointedness. I'd gotten a double chin.

But it struck me that there was something about my transformation that had gone awry. That Ms. Landres had been right, if not in her pedagogy then in her perception, that I *was* "not Piggy enough!" It was as though the mask had suggested the change to my facial features, but my face—by some vestigial sense of fixed identity—had compromised. Had talked back to the mask. Had said "This far, no further."

Looking down at my reflection, I felt the whole world wobble. The aptitude test had said I'd make a good Piggy, but there I sat, looking into a reflection that at best seemed like some sort of Piggy-abortion. I began sobbing. I'd failed. I'd been Expelled. This meant disgrace for my family. Mom had already told me that if I washed out and didn't fulfill my potential, I shouldn't bother coming back home. She said that if I did come home, she'd have no choice but to turn me in.

What could I do? If I could have found a way to drown myself right there, in the foot or so of creek, I would have.

Instead I crawled up the creek bank and ran. Past the cemetery, past the woods, darting behind one house and another to catch my breath and evade detection. It was this way, sleeping in cornfields and stealing melons, that I survived as I found my way out of town. To the city.

## II. Freak-Catcher's Modeling School

When you're young, Expelled, and of ambiguous species, you end up surviving in some of the worst possible ways. You are, after all, a fugitive. Even worse, you're naïve and willing to glom onto any facsimile of family. You're willing to set aside gut feelings about people you'd ordinarily see as shady because you are, after all, a freak.

You buy into society's hype about The Expelled. You learn to stop trusting yourself. You trust clichés instead ("beggars can't be choosers," "any port in a storm").

So it was that I ended up with Freak-Catcher.

He fancied himself an underground artist. He taunted the authorities by taking grainy photographs of The Expelled and posting them on telephone poles in the arts district. Freak-Catcher and his wife (Freak-Watcher, they called her) "discovered" me scrounging through the trash outside a trendy artist's restaurant. They offered me a free meal and a place to stay the night if I'd participate in a photo session.

By then fall had turned to winter. The temperature had plunged to ten degrees, and the thin, calf-length sweater I'd recycled from the trash wasn't cutting it. Meals recycled from the trash weren't cutting it either. Still, the idea of trusting Freak-Catcher to photograph me and simultaneously keep my location a secret from the authorities gave me pause.

After all, Freak-Catcher wasn't a freak. That is, no matter how much of an affinity he had for The Expelled, he wasn't one. He liked to tell us (over and over) that his aptitude test had told him that he was to be an artist, but I doubted that the aptitude test told anyone to be an artist. Aptitude tests just weren't like that.

Besides, he didn't exactly dress the way I expected an artist to dress. He wore a black leather jacket over top of a grease-stained NASCAR T-shirt. He bragged on having been a sailor once, and he wore his salt-and-pepper hair in a mop top. He said he could be my new dad, and that Freak-Watcher could be my new mom. Together, they'd take pictures of me.

After hearing his proposal I stood there, paralyzed.

"Trust him—he won't turn you in," a voice said from behind me. "He never snitched on me or Huck." The voice sounded young and deep, exuding confidence. Confidence was a commodity in short supply in my life, so I turned to meet it.

The boy was maybe a year or two older than me. He had a long face with big teeth, prominent nostrils, and bulging eyes. Bulging eyes that just kept *looking* down at me from a height of about six-foot-four. Eyes that wouldn't let go. At that moment, I felt relieved that poverty had taken off the weight I'd gained during my brief time in high school. From the moment he opened his mouth, I liked this Horse-abortion-boy (even if his face didn't exactly conform to universal standards of handsomeness). I liked that he'd noticed me.

"Freak-Catcher rescues us," the tall Horse-boy said.

A much-shorter dude with a bushy, blood-red Mohawk and sagging jowls emerged from behind the Horse-boy and made a coughing, crowing sound that I thought might have been a laugh. "He recycles us," the Rooster-boy said.

Huck the Rooster-boy, Champ the Horse-boy, and I

only spent three months with Mama Freak-Watcher and Daddy Freak-Catcher before they kicked us out. I know it sounds mean, but I don't think they meant it that way. I think they just got bored with us. I think that the entire city got bored with us. We were overexposed. We weren't even newsworthy anymore (Freak-Catcher had showed us the clippings back when we'd been the talk of the town). Even an *underground* artist had to introduce enough novelty to keep the audience interested.

A month or two after he evicted me, I noticed that Freak-Catcher had moved on to using transvestite hookers in his photography. Champ had to explain to me what a transvestite hooker was. We didn't have those in the country. Once again, Freak-Catcher's art was the stuff of headlines. One day, when I glanced up a telephone pole and saw Freak-Catcher's grainy rendering of a transvestite's meaty man-foot in a high-heeled shoe, I had to stop and wonder: Had the transvestite's aptitude test *told* her she'd be a transvestite?

Anyway, three months wasn't a lot, but it was enough time for me to learn the ropes of life in the city. Champ and Huck seemed to know what to do when we got kicked out. They'd heard of an acting troupe that sometimes hired creatures like us to portray burn victims, ghouls, and other monstrosities. The pay wasn't much, of course, but between the three of us we could afford a shabby one-bedroom apartment within walking distance to the theater. We had just enough left over to buy the cheapest store-brand bread and eggs at the market.

## III. Industrial Arts (Today)

We've lived this way for about three years now. During that time, I've played every variety of disfigured monster the theater has to offer. I've had every combination of wild, half-bestial sex with Champ, Huck, and any other Expelled creature I've run into.

I think the only reason I've never gotten pregnant is that I like to party pretty hard. Okay—*extremely* hard. I've tried every flavor of liquor (in copious amounts, each and every night) and have sampled enough pills to start a pharmacy. Whenever I pop one into my mouth I tell myself that I'm taking the cure for my freakishness and I pretend—for a half-second—that the pills undo the work of that high school mask. Sometimes, if I take the right combination, I get high enough that they seem (for a few minutes) to do just that.

I try to not show my face during broad daylight, and that's why theater—the ultimate second-shift job—works for me.

Yeah, I know it's not the greatest life in the world. But I'm pretty sure that it's better than live dissection.

I mean, I *do* want more than this hand-to-mouth existence. I think I want Champ's baby someday. But that will mean changes. I'll need to stop drinking and pill-popping. We'll need more than bread and eggs to feed a child. Champ knows all this. He wants to ditch Huck and get a place for the two of us, but it's awfully expensive and dangerous for two Expelled folks like ourselves. I'm convinced, though, that we finally need to drop all pretense of being artists and redouble our efforts to find the niche we never did in high school. Maybe we could even find more than just a niche. Maybe we could find redemption.

Champ agrees with this wholeheartedly. Today he brought home a brochure for a local industrial arts college. "No more struggling, babe," he said. Promises abounded amidst the brochure's glossy pages. New careers. New vistas.

One could be a piston, a spark plug, crank shaft, or rod. One could even aspire to be an entire wheel onto oneself (someday). Perhaps a gear, or whole collection of gears. Our education will require multiple surgeries, the transformation of some aspects of our bodies into a liquid state, and the pouring of those parts into molds.

There will be sacrifice (but then again, no worthwhile calling is without it). I just have to keep in mind the end result: a future in which Champ and I would have parts to play in the real world. A future for *just* Champ and me (no more Huck), with our shiny gears intermeshed with those of our offspring. Usefulness and prosperity for all three of us.

Only time will tell. The industrial arts school seems quite promising. The possibilities are limited only by our scores on the entrance aptitude test.

# THE LAST KID SCARED BY LUGOSI

On February 12, 2031, Margie Dale of Clarksville, Indiana, exhumed the remains of Béla Lugosi. It was a balmy night at the cemetery in Culver City, California—so much warmer than she was used to. That helped. Gave her creaky body the stamina to hide in the shadows until the coast was clear of security guards. Gave her resilience to dig for hours with shovel and hoe. *I must look like the grave robbers at the start of* Frankenstein, she thought to herself. *Or maybe one of the angry villagers, holding her farm implement aloft, eager to use it to strike the creature.* She sighed. *Good movie, that one. Better, even, than* Dracula. She looked down into the dark maw of the grave and whispered to her not-yet-revealed quarry, "No offense, Béla."

She would have preferred to exhume Boris Karloff's grave, but there wasn't one. Not really. He'd had himself cremated, and his ashes were all the way in England. Ashes just wouldn't do for her purposes. And England—yikes! The Greyhound was expensive enough. She'd also briefly considered trying this with Lon Chaney, Jr., but his body had been donated to science. So it was either Béla or no one.

She'd chosen this night because the psychic in Louisville had told her that this is when the energy would be right. It was the one hundredth anniversary of *Dracula*'s release. If ever there was a time when the spirit of Lugosi would want to come back and re-inhabit his body to walk among us, this would be it. The Louisville psychic had worn slacks, a purple T-shirt, and a gazillion rings on her fingers. She'd spoken with a deep Southern accent. Margie didn't find her at all impressive in either her appearance or speech. She wasn't like Maleva, the gypsy fortune teller from *The Wolf Man. That* chick was the real deal.

She dug and she dug until her shovel hit something hard. It took nearly an hour to bust open the vault and another half-hour to bust open the coffin. She bit her lip, swallowed a lump in her throat, and gazed at the remains of a Hollywood legend. There wasn't as much to glance at as she'd like: poor Béla was just bones, adorned in the tuxedo and Dracula cape he'd been buried in. But even though the flesh and its ichor was long gone, their stink lingered. It was a good thing she'd gone to Home Depot beforehand and picked up a filter mask that (mostly) blocked out the stench.

"I'll raise you," she promised in between dry heaves. "I'll raise you from the grave and *then* you'll be scary again."

That was the whole point of this resurrection: to restore Béla Lugosi to his rightful place in the pantheon of film gods. He'd been slipping into obscurity. This couldn't be allowed to continue.

There had been one particular evening when it all crystallized for Margie, that this was what she had to do. She'd taken the bus into Louisville to see *Dracula* shown on the big screen at the Palace Theater during a day-long event highlighting antique black-and-white films. It had been a poorly attended showing—open to the public but truly intended for a handful of film historians in the area who had heard of this curiosity and wanted to see it exhibited in person, in a theater of the sort that would have shown it at the time of its original release. She'd cringed in her seat when she saw hands creeping out of coffins—cringed as she had when she'd been a child and first seen those hands and those coffins on the Saturday afternoon horror show. But the scholars hadn't had the same reaction: they'd started laughing! And they'd just *kept* laughing after that! Laughing at Béla's accent when he slowly enunciated the word "evening," laughing at the exaggerated stage-play-style mannerisms he used when avoiding Dr. Van Helsing's mirror. If she had been outside of the theater, listening to the commotion, she'd have thought the film was a comedy.

The question-and-answer session afterward had been even worse. One young film student—little more than a child, really—had raised his hand and asked why Tod Browning had elected to forgo CGI. Another one had asked where Dracula's fangs were. All the discussions had focused on what the film was *missing* (fangs, blood, gore) instead of what was *there* (restraint, chills, atmosphere). That's when Margie had made the decision to embark on this most desperate of maneuvers. If Béla Lugosi needed to be disgusting to trigger a scare again, then she'd show the world a Disgusting Lugosi. She'd make Béla scary again. Unignorable. She would take his reanimated corpse to one of the news channels. Given that there were literally *hundreds* of them these days, there had to be *one* that would show off her grotesque miracle. And when that happened, he would be famous again.

But when she looked at the fruits of her labor, she wondered if even *this* would be grisly enough. Yes, the remains were rank—that would lend Béla a certain repulsion, but all the flesh was gone. He'd have no gruesome decay to show off, no wounds, no maggots. His half-decayed cape would look cartoonish when seen draped over the bony shoulders of a skeleton. Moreover, poor Béla would only be *a single* zombie. Such threats had been out of vogue since the turn of the century, at least. Audiences in the thirties—the *present-day thirties*, that is—were only frightened when faced with an *army* of ghouls, rendered by the computer graphics that reminded them of the video and holography games they so enjoyed. One creature, however desiccated and uncanny, was insufficient to arouse more than—*dare she think it?*—pity, if not outright laughter.

But she had not come all this way for nothing. She'd endured thirty hours on a bus for this opportunity. She'd violated laws. She'd spent a small fortune (by her standards, at least) on the potion. She wasn't about to forgo using it. She wriggled the vial out of her pocket, took a deep breath, unscrewed the lid, and poured the contents into Lugosi's gaping teeth. (True, he had no esophagus left with which to swallow, but where else was she to pour it?)

Defying all laws of science, the skeleton spoke. "I vas een a nice place," it said. "I vas asleep. I teenk I have been asleep a long time. Vhere em I now?"

"You're in your body, Mr. Lugosi. It's the one hundredth anniversary of your most famous film."

"Lu—go—si?" the skeleton said. Then it groaned. "Feelm?" It shifted around in its coffin. Its skeletal fingers grazed its cape. *"Dracula?"*

"Yes, of course, *Dracula!* I've brought you back on the one hundredth anniversary. So you can be remembered again. So you can frighten again."

"Pardon me, madame, I had forgotten who I vas. I had forgotten vhat it vas like to be human; forgotten, indeed, vhat a 'human' vas. Forgotten vhat *fear* vas. I have been now sleeping the sleep of the dead more years than I vas avake and among the living. Zees is who I em now. Zees is who I vunt to be. Dead . . . asleep . . . not even dreaming . . . at one veeth the dirt and the creatures of the dirt. Vhy must you remind me of zings past? Vhy must you call me a name I have not been called een seventy-five years?"

Confused, Margie could only stammer. "W-what is your name now?"

"Notheenk," Lugosi said.

"But, Mr. Lugosi, your fans—"

And then it happened, the moment she'd been waiting for: he stood up in his coffin. Stood there, by the light of Margie's flashlight, majestic. Imperial. But that sight lasted only a moment. The skeleton had stood up for only one reason. Its right hand grabbed its left leg and gave a hard tug. There was a scraping, popping noise as bone came unjoined from bone. When it had fallen, the hand did the same with ribs. With teeth. With skull. The Lugosi Skeleton was tearing itself apart.

His voice was now marinated in anger and bitterness. "No memory. Let me sleep. I don't vunt zees vorld. I vunt only the dark. I had forgotten who I vas. Vhy can you not do the same?" And there was a loud rattling as bone slammed against bone. There was a splintering. A cracking. And the rattling . . . oh, the terrible rattling, as something like a seizure overtook the skeleton, as it slammed itself against the bottom and sides of the coffin, bent on bodily self-destruction. It wanted nothing more than to turn itself to dust, so that it might never again have to be summoned away from an eternity of consciousness so dull and fuzzy that it was practically unconsciousness. Nothing.

Margie huffed to replace the coffin lid, winced with back pain as she replaced the lid of the vault. They were not put back on perfectly, but good-enough had to do. Then she stood on the vault and, with as much athleticism as she could muster, half ran, half climbed up the incline of the hole she'd dug. Stinging pain lit up her knees, and when she arrived at the top she collapsed on the grass to catch her breath.

But the rattling . . . oh, the slamming and rattling and cracking and splintering . . . the noise of a sort of *suicide* could still be heard. How small must the pieces of bone be now? How small would they be before Béla felt satisfied? She didn't know. She only did what she could. Took her shovel and her hoe and filled in the hole as best she could. Even then, she felt goosebumps rise up on her arms as she heard the faint churning of bone against bone, like rocks in a tumbler.

She felt ridiculous even going through the motions of filling in the grave. What good was it? It would fool no one. Someone—a groundskeeper, a family member—surely *someone* would see it had been disturbed. And then there would be questions about *who* did the disturbing. What if there were security cameras tucked away somewhere and she hadn't noticed them? It would be odd, in some ways, for a cemetery to be equipped with such devices , but *what if?*

On the bus ride home she was always looking over her shoulder, wary of the presence of police. There were none. When she arrived home, she used her remote to flip past each and every news channel to see if there was even the briefest mention of the disturbance at Béla's grave site. There was none. For months afterward, she scoured the Internet, looking for signs her misdeed had been noticed; for indications of the start of an investigation. There were none.

She felt relieved. She felt heartbroken.

# I Am Moonflower

**S**unshine isn't all it's cracked up to be. Just ask the flowers. Ask the bees.

There once was a gardener who only planted morning glories. He was a well-meaning, devoted old man who treated flowers as he would have treated his own children (if he'd had any). He knew that flowers were more than just stems and leaves and petals. He knew they had a soul, like you and me.

He liked the idea of flowers that closed up their petals at sunset, so they'd never have to look at the night. He knew that flowers—like children—were afraid of the dark. He wanted to protect them. Better to have them go to sleep at sundown and only wake up in the morning. Part of him may have suspected that they were, in a sense, cheated because there was a whole half of the day they'd never get a chance to see. But if he ever *did* harbor that suspicion, he didn't think about it for long.

Now in this garden there was a bee who pollinated the flowers. Late one afternoon, while she was hard at work, a shrew invaded her hive and killed everyone it found there. Even the Queen. This bee didn't realize the attack had occurred until she flew back toward the hive and saw the shrew devouring three of her brothers. And as she saw the manic mammal tearing apart her family, she grew fearful and bitter, and hid deep inside the petals of one of the morning glories.

The daylight hadn't protected anyone.

The bee didn't know what to do. From having lived in this garden a long time, she knew the morning glory would close around her at sunset, trapping her inside. But she also knew that if the shrew saw her fly out of the flower, it wouldn't rest until she was dead.

She had no place to go.

The bee despaired—not trusting her safety to the outside world and its shrews, nor trusting her ability to survive within the petals without being crushed or suffocated. She didn't move. The flower had no choice but to close its petals when the sun went down. In mad rage the bee flailed her stinger into her captor.

The morning glory had never before seen a bee act like this. Before the shrew's attack, the bee had always been so pleasant. They'd worked together, harmoniously, for the well-being of the garden. But after feeling the bee's stinger in its petals, the flower knew about grief and rage. Knew alienation and panic. Knew, for the first time, *betrayal of trust*—as the light had failed to keep the bee safe. No longer could the morning glory endure its name, for in that name was a lie that valued the light over the darkness.

In the very core of its soul, the morning glory wailed and cried and *cursed* its name, and in that curse there was magick.

It found itself able to open its petals and embrace the night, allowing the bee to come and go as it would (and protecting itself from her stinger in the process). It found itself able to look up to the moon and knew it had become a new creation. "I am Moonflower," it said in its soul.

The bee found herself changed by all this, too.

No longer was she a bee at all; she had been transformed into a lightning bug of such brilliant luminescence that the Firefly King took her as his Queen. And it is said that Her Majesty still lives, a force of nature who will not die until the Earth itself dies. Such is the gift that Mother Darkness, the Goddess of Night, has bestowed upon her out of pity for all the great suffering she endured in the daylight.

And she loved black skies ever after.

# The Meaning

Entry in the *Encyclopedia of Obscure Video:*

*Witchfinders vs. The Evil Red* (Unrated)
Year of Release: Unknown (Possibly early 1970s)
Country of Origin: Unknown

*Introduction*

As far as anyone can tell, *Witchfinders vs. The Evil Red* isn't even this unusual twelve-minute film's real name. It has no title or credits, and has been attributed to everyone from David Cronenberg to David Lynch.

A group of film historians estimated the year of *Witchfinders'* release based on the wear and tear evident on one of the surviving prints, as well as from the testimony of various Greenwich Village residents who recall seeing it as a short (shown before midnight screenings of Jodorowsky's *El Topo*). However, special effects professionals who have watched the film declare that its visual effects are state of the art, even by today's standards. The riddle of how such a technologically advanced piece of cinema could have been made so many years ago remains a significant motivating force behind the effort to identify the creative team behind this project.

*Witchfinders vs. The Evil Red* is just a name the underground film community has, apparently through consensus, given this short. If there's one single man or woman who originated the title, the identity of that person remains lost to the annals of cinematic history.

*Plot synopsis (including spoilers):*

The film opens with a panoramic shot of a raging river of blood. Viscera float in it like seaweed. Crimson waves crash against a muddy, peninsular coastline.

A man rises up out of the muck of this muddy shore. A man *made* of mud. He doesn't so much walk as waddle. He makes an awkward march toward the river bank and takes a gander at the sanguinary tide. The soundtrack amplifies the squishy sound of mud separating from mud as his lips break away from each other to speak. He points to the river. "Sorcery!" he snarls. "Sorcery!"

The bloodwaves begin to break against the coastline more quickly, the tide rises, and before you know it the river's gotten to the level of the Mud Man's knees. He makes no effort to flee. "Sorcery! Sorcery!" he repeats, as though that's the only word he's ever learned. Eventually, the tide rushes into his mouth. But he continues on, gargling "Sorcery!" over and over until the bloodtide has its way with his body, until his head and neck and torso and appendages lose definition from all the erosion. Near the end you hear only the faintest wheezing of a residual pocket of air in the mud, then the loud crash of waves swallowing the Mud Man's body whole.

The final shot zooms in on a section of the muddy shore several yards inland from where the river has crested. A head, made of mud, erupts from the ground, like a molehill. Neck, shoulders, and arms emerge. A new Mud Man struggles out of the muck and points to the red river. There's a squishy sound as his lips separate from each other to scream "Sorcery!" Then the screen fades to black.

*Interpretations:*

In his essay "Witchfinders at One with the Evil Red," American Buddhist scholar Ben Tillen suggested an interpretation founded on the Zen ideal of non-dualism. "The film is rife with images of opposites in confrontation. The individual against nature, life against death, river against coast. Ingeniously, it resolves these conflicts by revealing that they're all illusions. The individual *is* nature. Life *is* death. The river is in the coast, and the coast in the river."

Schopenhauer disciple Max Maxfield, Ph.D., has instead focused on what he calls "the agony of repeated death and resurrection." According to Maxfield, "the image of the sentient being emerging from the muck must give one pause. I found myself yelling at my television, yelling at the poor mud fellow the way Burgess Meredith yelled at that boxer, Rocky Balboa: 'Stay down,' I found myself yelling. 'Stay down! Don't rise from the muck. There's no so-called 'sorcery' to be found in the blood-ocean, or—if one is brutally honest with oneself—anywhere else!'"

But the most well-known commentary on the film comes from the YouTube video series "100 Ordinary People React to *Witchfinders vs. The Evil Red*"; specifically the now-infamous Video #58 ("The Woman from Kentucky"). Although YouTube removed the video due to inappropriate content, one could (as of the writing of this entry) still view it on other, more obscure websites.

A brief summary follows below for those who have not yet watched it.

The woman from Kentucky has bleached-blond hair, and a cigarette dangles out of her mouth. She has the burnt-brown look of a Caucasian who visits the tanning bed far too often. For no apparent reason, she's sweating heavily.

We see her watching *Witchfinders vs. The Evil Red* on a television. She grins, stamps her cigarette out in the ashtray, and momentarily moves off-camera. When she returns, there's a razor blade in her hand.

She positions the blade vertically, so that the cut will run parallel to the vein (or, if she's lucky, actually strike it). She closes her eyes and digs the razor into her wrist, wincing when it makes contact but getting a good anchor a half-inch under the skin. She drags the blade upward, eviscerating dermis, vein, and muscle alike—all the way to the crook of her elbow.

Somehow, in the midst of this madness, the woman from Kentucky maintains the presence of mind to move the webcam so that we see a close-up of the wound. A tide of blood rises up from the slashed veins. We hear, over and over, the accusation—"Sorcery!" Most viewers assume this is coming from the television in the background. But a significant minority swear it's too loud and clear to be that. Those are the same people who insist they can see a tiny humanoid figure rising like a welt from the woman's dark, damp upper arm.

# THE SUFFERING CLOWN

**B**lack greasepaint—the vacuum of space. A half-dozen white asterisks painted, pox-like, atop the darkness—stars. When the suffering clown smiled, they stretched.

He sat on a chair in the middle of the supermarket parking lot, fidgeting with the tassels of a flannel blanket draped over his lap. It could only have offered token protection against the cold.

My four-year-old couldn't resist the temptation to investigate. We'd just spent a tense half-hour in the store, butting heads over his compulsive requests for any plastic trinket or box of junk food that crossed our path. When he discovered the clown in the parking lot, what else could he be expected to do but walk over and introduce himself, dragging me all the way? Children here in Hanswurst, Indiana, and the surrounding environs are used to such oddities in parking lots. Here in Hanswurst, parking lots serve much the same purpose as a European town square. Anyone—politicians, performance artists, or even recruiters for armies or cults—can set up impromptu engagements there. The clown was obviously ready to put on a show for passers-by.

The flickering parking lot lamps provided an effect not unlike that of strobe lights, facilitating and impeding sight with equal measure. When the clown smiled his lips curled back, revealing twisted yellow teeth and bumpy gums. When the clown smiled, he stared at my son for too long, too wide-eyed. A full minute passed with his face frozen in that overly congenial grin.

If I were the sort of man who watched horror films, I might blame the clown's creepiness on some diabolical nature intrinsic to his profession; but, after absorbing the entire scene, I realized his stilted, awkward manner owed more to illness than to any character defect. Indeed, he was as frail a specimen of buffoonery as I'd ever the misfortune to behold.

I doubt he could have tipped the scale at three digits. The

loose fit of his silken yellow costume implied recent, significant weight loss. Clear plastic tubes delivered oxygen into his red rubber nose. A minivan was parked behind the clown's chair. Its hatchback was open, and I spied beverages and snack food inside (as though he were at a Hanswurst High football game, tailgating). To my chagrin, I also spotted a package of adult diapers alongside the food. The thin plastic grocery bag wasn't tall or opaque enough to obscure it.

The clown shouldn't have been out on a night like that—the sort of night I made my son wear a jacket and hat, whether he wanted to or not. Rain glistened the cracked asphalt. An unseasonal thunderstorm had passed through less than a half-hour before. The wind howled, sending clouds blowing through the night sky as though tugged by an unseen hand. Their departure unveiled the full moon first, followed by the multitude of stars in all their twinkle-twinkle splendor.

A potbellied man wearing a blue, grease-stained mechanic's shirt and threadbare trousers threw his calloused hand out for me to shake. The name patch sewn on his shirt announced him as "Butch." He looked up at the clearing sky. "Weather's breakin'. The show must go on! Just one dollar, mister."

My son craned his head up to mine. "Please, Dad? Pleeeassssseee can I see the show?"

I turned to Butch. "You'll have to pardon us, but it's pretty cold and getting late. The boy's only a preschooler. His bedtime's soon." It was as polite a refusal as I could muster. What I *wanted* to tell this man was that his clown was in no condition to work. What sort of entertaining little show could he be expected to perform while incontinent and demented? I didn't say that, though, because some clown promoters take it personally when you refuse their services.

"Please, sir, have a heart. This fella—König's his name— hasn't had the pleasure of performing for a single customer tonight, with it rainin' so hard."

"What's his act have to do with the weather?"

"The rain smears his makeup. We can't have that. Besides, for the audience to appreciate his powers, the night sky has to be clear. You see, this here ain't no ordinary clown— nosiree."

"That's what they all say."

Butch scowled. "This act is absolutely one-of-a-kind. No one else in all of clown history has attempted it, sir. This clown can kill stars (and I ain't talkin' about the Hollywood kind)."

"Beg your pardon?"

"I don't know any better way to explain it, mister. If a kid comes up to this clown and smudges one of the white stars on his face into the black base coat, a corresponding star up there in the sky dims and dies. It's easy enough to show you — all it takes is a dollar."

"But I like stars," my son said. (I had to confess to feeling a swell of paternal pride when he said that; I could see that my boy had internalized the appreciation of nature his mother and I had worked so tirelessly to instill in him.)

Butch sighed. "Look, it's not like there's any real shortage of 'em out there. We got more of 'em than we know what to do with."

I never could keep a poker face. My skepticism must have been obvious. I tried to let out a hearty laugh, but all that escaped was a raspy, nervous giggle.

Butch tried a new approach. He took a glance at my casual attire, apparently sizing me up as just another of Hanswurst's rednecks. "Hey," he said, "you hunt deer?"

"I can't say I have. I own a gun for self-defense, of course. I just don't feel the need to fire it at a dumb animal."

"W-well," he stammered, "I was just going to say that killing stars is a little like killing deer—it's mercy killing. You see, the problem with both of them is overpopulation . . ."

"The only thing I see overpopulating Hanswurst these days is parking lot performers. Now, if you'll excuse us, my son needs to go to sleep. We don't have time to watch this invalid attempt some cheap parlor trick."

König let out an incoherent, mournful wail. His awkward smile had been replaced with an even more awkward grimace.

Butch clinched his fists and cleared his throat. His face flushed. He started hollering. "Jeez, mister. What do you wanna do, make him *cry*? Don't you see the risk he takes on, coming out here like this? In his condition? I mean, do you even *care* what his condition is?"

Caught off-guard by the severity of Butch's anger, I had no words to offer in my own defense. König's oxygen hissed. The lights teased us, staying on for several seconds before returning to their flickering ways. Finally, Butch continued ranting to fill the ugly void.

"He has *cancer*, mister. In his esophagus, his lungs, his brain, his liver, his pancreas, and his blood. Each day this little guy struggles to tread water in an ocean of pain. But he doesn't whine. The only time he gets pissed off is when he runs into an unappreciative audience. Don't you realize that this show is the only thing that keeps König from dying?"

My little boy looked up at me, eyes wide and glistening at Butch's disclosure. I felt like such an insensitive jerk. It all made sense. Hanswurst, Indiana, was too remote a location to host a circus of any size. All the clowns in our region worked freelance for whichever promoter would be willing to take them on for a few weeks. Therefore, none of them had health insurance. If König wanted to afford even the least promising cancer treatments, he'd need cold hard cash; thus the extreme measures—courting pneumonia on a cold night just to snag even a handful of customers.

I took out my wallet and gushed apologies. "I'm so sorry. I, well, I just didn't know he was *that* sick." It was a lie that didn't convince König or Butch, but I didn't care all that much about them. At this stage of the game, I was just trying to preserve my reputation with my son. I was just trying to role model sympathy for the less fortunate. I didn't want him to go away from tonight thinking it was okay to humiliate a cancer patient (even if he set himself up for humiliation with that bizarre outfit and those grandiose claims).

"Look," I continued, "I know that the show only costs a dollar, but seeing as it's been a rough night—and considering all that your clown has been through—what do you say I give you a five?" I presented the bill to the promoter.

Butch smiled and snatched the Abe Lincoln away. The money seemed to calm him down. "Getting paid's nice, but the most important thing for König is performing. The immune system is a funny thing, you know, mister? Nothing puts more pep in this guy than pickin' off a star or two before bedtime. For real, it does his body good."

I smiled. Nodded.

"The show will start in just a couple of minutes. Let me get it set up."

König let out a high-pitched gurgle and shook his

gloved fists.

"Awww," my son said. "What's the matter, Koonig?"

Butch bent down to my little boy. "Oh, don't you worry, kiddo. Mr. König's okay. I know him well enough to be able to tell that this noise he's making now is a *good* thing. That's just his way of showing he's excited and happy that he'll be able to perform for you!"

Butch opened the back seat of the minivan and pulled out a tripod. Once it stood erect, he retrieved a series of metal tubes and went to work putting them all together. "It'll just take a few minutes to get this here telescope assembled before the show, so you can verify my clown's the real deal."

My boy and I looked at each other, then at König. I had to do a double-take. His face paint hadn't changed, but something in the structure of the visage underneath had. His chin had become longer, his forehead higher. His ears had grown bigger. My son didn't say anything, but he took a step back.

König himself just stared at us and flashed his creepy little dying man's grin.

Butch clapped his filthy hands together. "Okay, now we're ready for some clownin'! Ordinarily, I'd go into my whole carnival barker routine building excitement about König's amazing powers, but we sort of covered that part earlier and we're not likely to get any more foot traffic around here until the cashiers on second shift count out their tills. So let me just tell you how this works. Earlier today, König sat quietly—all by himself—and *meditated*. This is what gave him intuition as to which patch of the night sky needed weeding. Then he took his magic clown paint and decorated his face in the manner you see before you."

"It's magic?" my little boy asked.

"Yup," said Butch. "Just like I said: If a young child places his or her hand on König's face paint and smears away one of the stars, a matching star disappears from the sky—never to nuisance us with its light ever again."

"Like killing lightning bugs," my youngster said, smiling and clapping.

I cringed. Did my boy really take that much joy in destruction? Maybe he hadn't internalized a love of nature after all.

Butch smiled. "Yes, that's it. Exactly like killing lightning bugs. So are you ready?"

"Boy, am I!"

I looked at König again and was rendered uncomfortable by the inescapable perception that his skull had yet again undergone transformation when I wasn't looking. Now his face was heart-shaped, with high cheekbones. His chin was pointed—almost dainty.

My son approached the clown on tiptoe, trying in vain to reach his face. "Which star should I kill, Dad?"

"Whoa," Butch said. "Wait . . . Before you touch a star on König's face, I want you to see the matching star up in the sky." He gestured toward a stepladder he'd brought in front of the tripod. My son jogged toward it, climbed up the steps, and began to look through the telescope.

Butch smiled. "See all those stars?"

"Uh-huh!"

"Which one do you want to kill?"

"There's a real bright one. Let's make that one go 'way."

"Alrighty, then . . . with the help of König the Clown, I think we can do just that!" My boy jumped off the stepladder, and Butch moved it away from the tripod and put it in front of König's chair. "Now climb up that ladder again and see Mr. König."

"How come I have to come over there? How come he can't come see me?" A bright child, my boy, asking such an observant question.

"Well," Butch said, frowning, "if you want to know the truth, son, König the Clown is *so sick* that he can't even walk anymore." Then, with a single twitch of his meaty paw, he tore the flannel blanket off the clown, revealing the rust-pocked wheelchair in which he sat. The wheels looked low on air. Several of the spokes were fractured. It was a contraption from another generation, perhaps purchased for a few dollars at the local Goodwill. It should have been in a medical museum, not a rain-slicked parking lot.

My son looked as if he was going to cry. Even *his* brain—so new to the world—could detect that something was amiss with the wheelchair. He couldn't place the antique medical device as something that was *old*, because his life experience stretched only a few years. But he could definitely intuit that it *didn't belong*.

Butch spoke up, shaking both of us out of our daze. "If you want Mr. König to feel better and be able to leave the wheelchair, you have to hop up there and help him kill stars. It's the best medicine in the whole wide world! König, do you want to point to the star on your face that matches up with the one the little boy wants to kill?"

The clown raised a trembling hand up to his right cheekbone, fingering the appropriate star.

"Okay then, son, all you have to do is smudge it out with your fingers."

My boy climbed the stepladder and reached up to the clown's face. But the star wouldn't budge.

Butch sighed. "The bright ones are sometimes a little harder. I'll tell you what to do: Why don't you spit in your hand and use that to wipe the star away?"

I felt the need to intervene. "Sir, pardon me but this *really is* unusual—"

My son spit in his hand.

"Stop that right now, mister! That's not how we behave!"

Ignoring me, the boy wiped his slobbery palm over König's cheekbone. A single white asterisk melted into the black background. When it was over, the marred makeup looked like nothing so much as one of the finger paintings adorning our refrigerator back at the house. Five stars remained, and by the smile on my son's face I could tell that they might also be endangered if I didn't immediately hoist him away from the stepladder.

Butch looked through the telescope. "And . . . it's gone! Wanna come see?"

I set down the lad, then hunched over and looked. Black emptiness occupied the space previously allocated to the bright star. I pulled my eye away from the lens. "It's just a trick," I said. "While our attention was focused on the clown, you must have moved the telescope to a different section of sky."

König wailed with newly plump lips.

Butch sneered. "Tell you what, buddy: If by sunrise you *still* think we've bamboozled you, we'll give you back your money. Deal?"

Had I been a wise man, I would have asked him then and there just what he meant. As it was, I turned my back to him, grabbed my boy with my left hand, and steered our grocery cart back to our car with the right.

That night had simmered with unease. The following morning, this boiled over into terror. My boy was nowhere to be found. A sticky, smeared, gore-colored residue stained his bedsheets. It was as though he'd melted and a cosmic finger had reached down to make a swirly, preschoolish finger painting out of the remains. His mother balled her fists and shrieked.

My first call was to 911. For some reason they sent an ambulance. We felt just as puzzled as the paramedics were when they arrived at our house. It took another half-hour for the Hanswurst Police to arrive. They asked questions. Trying not to sound crazy, I let them know my concerns about König the clown.

The sergeant taking my report rolled his eyes. "You expect me to believe that a wheelchair-bound cancer patient did *that* to your son?"

"So you know him?"

He stroked his walrus mustache with his chubby thumb and index finger. He took a too-long pause. When he finally did speak, his voice was tremulous. "Y-you shouldn't ask the law a question like that, mister."

"What's that supposed to mean?"

His face took on a sheen of sweat. "Who do you think is the most likely suspect in this case? Who had access to the boy during the night?"

"You really think my wife or I could do something like *that?* We have no motive. That's our son!"

He walked closer up to me. Almost belly to belly. "No," he whispered. "Off the record, sir, I *know* you didn't do it. But if you call 911 and the police come, then *someone* (someone *human* and *only human*—someone who's just one *discrete* human, I should add) has to be arrested and tried. You should have just pretended this didn't happen, like the rest of us. As it is, I'll have to ask you to place your hands behind your back, sir." He took out his handcuffs. They were riddled with specks of rust, but appeared to still have enough sturdy steel left in them to restrain me.

"But you've no probable cause. On what grounds am I being arrested?"

"On the grounds of having reported a crime! A crime implies a criminal, and the only criminal the laws of nature allow us to identify in this case is either you or your wife. My choice of you, in particular, was admittedly arbitrary—*c'est la vie*. Now, if you'd rather skip the tedium of incarceration and trial, I suggest you recant immediately. If you tell me that you made a gigantic blunder, perhaps mistaking your dog's vomit for the remains of a child, I'll forget that all this ever happened and merely issue you a citation for making a false report. In most cases they'll plea bargain that down to a lesser charge. You'll pay a fine, perhaps perform some community service."

My wife sobbed and shook me by the shoulder. "J-just do as he says. Just make it stop! Just make it all *stop!* Recant, for God's sake, just as the good officer asks, sweetheart."

"But what about our son?"

The policeman answered. "If you recant (which I strongly suggest that you do), then you must never again speak of him. For all intents and purposes, he never existed. The same goes for that clown and his promoter. For the sake of your very sanity, you must convince yourself that they were just nightmares. This may sound harsh, but it's the way everyone else in Hanswurst has dealt with this kind of thing. It would be snobbery, on your part, to expect anything better."

I looked at the cop. I looked at my wife. "Then that's what I'll do. I-I'm sorry. I was mistaken, officer. Please forgive me." I trembled.

Maybe I was a snob. Maybe that's what led me to expect better answers than those offered by the authorities. Maybe that's what led me to defy the conditions of my arrangement with the police and investigate the grocery store parking lot by day, looking for any sign of the clown and his handler. Maybe that's why I took my pistol along.

Sunlight bleached the eeriness out of the place. Active commerce made it feel less haunted. Nevertheless, my pulse raced. I couldn't imagine that they would have traveled far, given the advanced stage of the clown's cancer. I discovered that, in fact, their minivan was still parked in the same space it had been the night before.

By daylight, the vehicle looked old and decrepit. Its blue paint peeled. A handful of dents (some incidental, others disfiguring) suggested it might be ready for the junkyard. Rust afflicted its wheel wells.

Looking over a broader swath of parking lot, I saw that rust afflicted every car and truck within a six-foot radius of König the Clown's minivan. All the vehicles outside that perimeter were newer, or, at least, had been spared that particular state of decay.

The sun cast a glare on Butch's windshield. To catch a peek inside, I had to squat down to just the right angle. A gaudy, beaded curtain separated the front seats from the rear. Butch reclined in a tilted-back passenger seat. His fat stomach and legs were visible, his upper torso and head hidden behind the beads.

I knocked on the windshield. Butch scrambled his hands through the beads, then tilted his chair into a sitting position. He rubbed his eyes with his fists, getting the sleep out. Then he turned a crank and his window lowered. An odd smell wafted out—a nauseating mix of the artificial scent of clown makeup and all-too-natural body odor.

"Still think we cheated you last night?"

I hunched farther down so I could look him in the eye. "What did you do with *my son!*"

"Son? You have a son? I'm afraid I can't help you out there, mister. When I met you last night, you were alone."

"You filthy liar! What the fuck *did you do?*"

He sighed. "Me? I didn't do anything. Now König, on the other hand . . ." He ran stubby fingers through long, unwashed hair.

"What did *he* do?"

"Look, mister, I think you'd do a lot better for yourself in life if you just took things on faith instead of asking so many questions. I'm sure that if there were really any foul play involved, the cops would have been on it like white on rice!"

"They won't do anything. I don't know what your angle is with them. Maybe you're second cousin to the police chief, or maybe you have photos of him in a compromising position. I don't know what game it is you're playing that lets you murder preschoolers, but I promise you I'll find out!"

"You don't know what you're saying."

"Where's König? He's in there with you, isn't he?"

Butch grabbed a pack of Marlboros from his shirt pocket. Took out a zippo and lit up. "There are some things better left unknown."

I leaned forward, grabbed Butch's shirt collar with my left hand, and put my pistol to his temple with the right. "Look at me, you little two-bit clown promoter, you're going to show me where König is right now, or else he'll be required to seek out new representation."

"You don't want to know, not really. You don't *need* to know."

I applied pressure with the pistol, pushing it harder against his temple. "And maybe *you* don't need to live."

Butch sighed. "You're doing it. You're really making me show you König in the morning. Do you have any idea how many parents have shoved guns in my face? Do you know how many of them take those very same guns and stick 'em in their own mouths, once they see König the morning after a show?"

"Enough yapping," I said. "Show me the clown. Now."

He reached back and pulled up a small nob, unlocking the door. "You asked for it."

Yes, he was only a frail, sick clown—but I nonetheless found it necessary to brace myself for the need to shoot. At least, what I *expected* was a frail, sick clown. When the door opened, this is what I saw in the backseat: a bald, *buttery* man. Heavier than Butch, even. He wore the same yellow silk suit König had worn the night before. It billowed out at odd intervals, as though there were small animals racing around underneath, climbing around his torso. A series of muffled squeaks and high-pitched growls seemed to confirm this observation. The buttery man looked unperturbed by the ruckus. He sat with his legs folded underneath him, his eyes closed. Meditating.

"Where's König?"

The man fluttered his eyelids, as if waking. Then he spoke in a voice that was more than one voice. "Everywhere. In rising mountains and sinking islands, new worlds and dead ones. In any place that comes and ceases to be. Which is (if I may repeat myself) *everywhere*."

Not human. Not *only human*.

I began to feel my pulse in my jugular. "Who are you?"

"Everyone," said one hundred-voices-in-one.

Not one *discrete* human.

No merciful dark night or face paint obscured the hideous sight of the buttery man's skull rearranging itself. Bones flexed and contracted, and his buttery skin flexed with them. They made popping and cracking and clicking sounds. The buttery man's head transformed from the thick, broad noggin I'd first seen to something more slender—but by no means emaciated. "Anyone or anything that is born and dies. Even you."

I studied the visage of the buttery man in the back seat until I discovered that his new face was my own. But the buttery man's body was still fat—far fatter than mine. "Not exactly to scale, is it? Hey, you like comedy? I do impressions. No charge, since you've come all this way."

I whimpered.

The buttery man was enjoying himself. "Abra Cadaver," he shrieked (intentionally, I think, twisting the magic words into morbid ones). His face stayed as *my* face, but grew thinner. Bony. Likewise, the barks and howls under his clown suit quieted as the girth of his body dissolved. When he finished his metamorphosis, I was sitting across from myself, in a clown suit several sizes too big for me. My frame—the frame I was looking at—was frail. I could not have tipped the scale at three digits.

"Here's my impression of *you* dying from cancer ten years from now!"

"Stop it," I said, backing away from the minivan.

"Awww," Buttery-König-Cancer-Patient-Me-Man said in his voice that was more than one voice. "Don't leave. You haven't even asked me about your boy. Don't you want to see him?" He tucked his withered hands at his costume's collar and stretched it out from his body so he could see inside. "I know he's in here somewhere. He might be that melanoma that just showed up today on my tummy tum-tum."

As if to verify the clown's claim, I heard a squeaky, lisping voice coming from his (my) belly. "Help me, Dad. Please, Dad. Pleeeeassssee! It's dark in here!"

I took a step back, took a deep breath, and said the words that damned me. What other choice did I have? Who among us has resisted the urge to give up asking questions and just go with the flow? Who among us hasn't painted a surrendering smile over an inquisitive smirk? We've all volunteered for the part of the fool, going along with the conspiracy of happy delusion that keeps all Hanswurst (and if König was to be believed, much beyond our little town) in its grip. It would be snobbery to expect anything better.

"I'm sorry to have troubled you, sir. There's no need to show me your anthropomorphic melanoma. It turns out I was mistaken. You and I have never met before. Perhaps that's someone else's boy. I have no son."

# FUNHOUSE MIRRORS

# EULOGY TO BE GIVEN BY WHOEVER'S STILL SOBER

**M**ervyn Guestwhaite wasn't dead yet, but that didn't stop him from sitting behind a table just outside The Electric Lady Gentleman's Club in Corbin, Kentucky, and taking money from those of us about to attend his funeral.

I avoided strip clubs for all the reasons good feminists did, but, of course, I made an exception for Mervyn's funeral. After all, this wasn't about me; it was about him. If this was the way he wanted his colleagues, fans, and hangers-on to remember him, I was powerless to stop it. No one could dissuade him once he had an idea planted firmly in his head. Especially if he thought it'd earn him headlines in *Publishers Weekly,* or maybe even a place in horror history.

I avoided bars, in general, for all the reasons good recovering alcoholics did. A.A. had hammered a billion slogans into my head about the dangers of going to places that served liquor, even if my intention was to abstain. ("If you stay long enough in a barber shop, you're going to get a haircut"; "We avoid slips by staying out of slippery places.") I'd been sober for about six years at that point. Six years.

Question: Why did I risk getting drunk again by venturing out to the Electric Lady in the first place?

Answer: My old friend Mervyn Guestwhaite was going to die that very night. I could white-knuckle it through any stray gin or rum cravings that might stir once I found myself assaulted with the smell of the stuff. Or, at the very least, I could try to. And if I couldn't take it, I could just leave. And if it got to that point, I would. Whether Mervyn had died yet or not.

But I had to try. I owed the man that much.

Two thin, breast-implanted girls wearing white ghoul

makeup, pasties, G-strings, and a few strategically placed fake scars took my twenty and gave me change. I took the resulting cash and paid Mervyn himself five bucks for the right to sign the guest register.

Of course, like everyone else in the horror genre, I'd heard that the funeral was going to be something of a circus. The rumor mill had been working overtime ever since Guestwhaite's first cryptic tweet about planning his own services a fortnight ago. Supposed portents of the author's imminent demise passed from Twitter to Facebook to message boards and back again.

The gossip proved inescapable. I'd heard that he planned to sell books and sign them all "Dead Man Walking, Mervyn Guestwhaite." I'd heard about the raunchy locale, and about the guest book. Had I not been besieged with anticipatory grief, I would have taken the time to conjure up a pithy bon mot to scribble in the guest book. Instead I just wrote this:

MERVYN: BE CAREFUL WHAT YOU DRINK,
LOVE, ANGELA

He'd blogged that the doctors had recently told him his cirrhosis was advancing. He had maybe two or three years if he laid off the whiskey.

Mervyn wasn't about to lay off the whiskey. He was drinking himself to death, more or less intentionally. The funeral festivities hadn't even begun, and he already looked shit-faced.

He looked down at what I'd written and winked. "Darlin'," he said in his Dixie drawl, "I'm always careful what I drink. Nothin' but Woodford Reserve for this reprobate!" He smiled, baring lustrous yellow teeth (almost the same shade as his jaundiced skin). Sweat beaded over his bald head and dripped into his dyed-red ZZ Top beard. The smell of stale liquor oozed out of every pore, mixing with a stench of body odor that only Guestwhaite himself seemed not to notice (or care about).

"You know it doesn't have to be like this. You could—" Right in the midst of my attempt to tell Mervyn about how good sober life had been to me, one of his fans elbowed me out of the way. He screamed something about Mervyn being "The Man." Mervyn hollered back, insisting that, to the contrary, the fan was "The Man." In any case, I was (without a doubt) *not* "The Man," I found myself nudged out of the way, shoved to the side of the line, my one-to-one time with my old friend diminished to a swap of one-liners.

A tall, Scandinavian-looking dancer with a pixie hairdo seemed to notice my distress. "Do you have a service leaflet, ma'am?" the stripper said. She sounded as if she came from up North, but the jerk of her chin and the darting of her eyes suggested that I was supposed to glance South. I looked down and found a dozen funeral programs stuck in the girl's milky white cleavage. I went ahead and took one. She made a cooing sound, as if I'd just felt her up.

I'd never blushed at a funeral before. I did that night.

"Don't forget your wristband," a Katy Perry lookalike said. She put a fluorescent orange paper band on me.

I moved over to the side of the line to get my bearings and found that Mervyn's fans had flooded in to the place I'd just vacated. It looked as though it would be standing room only. I pulled out the perfumed service leaflet and looked at the liturgy for this evening. It set a new standard for poor taste. It read something like this:

*8:00 p.m.* Benediction—Mervyn Guestwhaite Drinks Whiskey & Prays

*8:01 p.m.*—Mervyn Drinks Whiskey & Watches Strippers

*8:30 p.m.*—Mervyn Drinks Whiskey & Gets A Lap Dance

*9:00 p.m.*—Mervyn Drinks Whiskey & Reads From His Legendary Zombie Novel, *Renegades Against Necrotic Killers (R.A.N.K.)*

*9:30 p.m.*—Mervyn Drinks Whiskey & Answers Your Questions On How To Break Into Publishing

*10:00 p.m.*—Mervyn Drinks Whiskey & Signs Copies of His Last Zombie Novel Ever, *Renegades Escape the Corpse Horde (R.E.T.C.H.)*

*10:30 p.m.*—Presentation, Mr. Benedict Brown from Brown's Funeral Parlor, "You, Too, Can Have A Pre-Planned Funeral Just Like Mervyn's"

*11:00 p.m.*—Mervyn Drinks Red Bull So He Doesn't Pass Out, Then Drinks More Whiskey

*11:30 p.m.*—Mervyn Writes His Will

*12:00 a.m.* (?)—Mervyn Drinks Himself To Death

*12:00 a.m* (?)–*4:00 a.m.*—Mervyn's Body Is Taken To A Private Room For Embalming

### <u>Deluxe Membership Guests Only</u>

*2:00 a.m.*—Panel Discussion: Mervyn's Death & Its Impact On The Collectible Market

*4:00 a.m.*—Panel Discussion: Who Will Be The Next Mervyn Guestwhaite?

*6:00 a.m.*—Eulogy (To Be Given By Whoever's Still Sober)

*7:30 a.m.*—Sunrise Burial At Pleasant Meadow Memorial Garden

At first, I didn't believe all this could be happening. Was Mervyn really *that* eager to throw in the towel? Could the local authorities be *that* laissez-faire about what amounted to exhibitionist suicide? But here I was, holding a funeral leaflet in my shaking hand—having just seen how ill Mervyn looked, knowing that Mervyn was, well, *Mervyn*.

It sounded like *exactly* the sort of thing he'd do. It was, after all, the same sort of high-gamble publicity stunt that he'd built his career on.

I'd always envied Mervyn's career, but had grown to pity his life. It didn't seem so much that he had success as that success had him. The industry trampled him underfoot. He himself was just a grape. All that his publishers were interested in was the wine of his words.

How, you might ask, do I dare say these things? How can I tell you things that imply a knowledge of Mervyn's personal life?

Years ago, before he made it big (when we were both just unknown writers), I knew him pretty well. Back then, I drank just as much, if not more, than he did. I threw up in hotel hospitality suite sinks. I passed out at book release parties. But I ended up crashing, burning, and not writing for several years—not until I finally got clean and sober. It had only been recently that I had returned to the game. The clear mind yielded rewards, and I found myself writing better stuff—and finding more success—sober than I ever had drunk.

But anything more than a superficial connection with Mervyn was gone. While I went away and got sober, he ascended the ranks and got famous. And so whenever I ran into him at conventions, I felt a chilly distance that hadn't been there before. After some soul-searching, I didn't hold it against him. He'd always had a lot of people in his life. In the years I left to get sober, though, his following increased exponentially. Almost everyone wanted to be close to Mervyn Guestwhaite; if only so they could leverage their closeness for career advancement. He had to draw the velvet rope someplace.

I came to regret staying away from writing for so long, but I found that the mind cannot create when it's closed down for repairs.

Yet if I had myself been cursed with the disease of alcoholism, Mervyn had been doubly cursed. He suffered the worst variety of that disease: the functional kind. The kind of alcoholism in which the alcoholic is still able not only to stay employed and put food on the table, but also to produce some of his best work; win awards, contracts, and fans. Tens of thousands of fans. The type of alcoholism that preserves the brain while destroying the body. The type that doesn't give you any reason to stop drinking, until the body ups and quits.

As Mervyn's appeared to be doing lately.

The first several items on the evening's agenda proved unremarkable. One of Mervyn's newer fans might have been more impressed, but I'd known him long enough to have seen him pull this shtick before. Mervyn ridiculing organized religion during the course of his belching "benediction," Mervyn getting to second base with the strippers, in front of several hundred onlookers, Mervyn reading the alternate ending to his first novel. Call me jaded, but this was all old hat. Things didn't get too interesting until the question-and-answer session.

A girl with purple hair and dark circles under her eyes asked the first question about breaking into publishing. "Mervyn, I know that zombies are hot right now. And no doubt you have a lot to do with it—you've carved out an impressive career by writing *nothing but* zombie books. But, as we all know, you're drinking yourself to death. You seem miserable. Is your zombie-fame a curse? How do you recommend that a newer writer avoid getting pigeonholed in one subgenre?"

"Look, I'm not a dilettante scribbling away just for the fun of it." He badly slurred the esses in "scribbling" and "just." "I'm selling the shit I think *you* want to buy. The fans are my bosses. I'm just doing as I'm told." Mervyn grimaced. For a moment I thought he was going to cry. But he seemed almost too far gone for that.

The next question came from a short, husky man sporting a series of piercings arranged over his face in the shape of a beard. "Mervyn, if I can tell you a dirty joke and make you laugh, will you stop drinking yourself to death?" Polite laughter erupted from the crowd. At that moment, I suspected that the majority of them must have still thought that all this was an elaborate hoax.

"Do you think this is all a show? Do you think I'm faking it all?" Mervyn roared with a phlegmy voice. "Would you ask that question of Poe or F. Scott Fitzgerald or Ernest Hemingway?" He staggered toward the fan and took a swipe at him with ragged, unkempt fingernails.

Maybe the fan fell. Maybe Mervyn pushed him. In the low light it was hard to tell. All anyone knew was that he'd landed on the floor.

Many in the crowd gasped, but a handful giggled. The *nervous* giggles from those who were concerned mixed with *snarky* giggles from those who still saw all this as nothing but theatrics—the sort of over-the-top Friday night antics that were tailor-made for Monday morning blogs.

Beard-of-Piercings-Dude came to realize Mervyn wasn't playing, though. He crab-walked away as swiftly as his own tipsy, uncoordinated legs could take him. In his haste, he knocked over some of the shorter, thinner women like so many inebriated bowling pins.

More people laughed, but I didn't see the humor. This just confirmed the worst rumors that I'd heard about Mervyn. Stories had leaked out that, outside of a handful of public appearances, he'd gone Howard-Hughes-reclusive over the years. One of his personal assistants (a pale, nervous hipster named Jake Togg) quit last year—ostensibly because he "was tired of cleaning up Guestwhaite's puke."

It took no more than a week after resigning for the erstwhile servant to write a stunning series of blog entries running Guestwhaite's name through the mud, entitled "Slave to the Redneck Master: My Life Behind the Scenes with Mervyn Guestwhaite."

Tales were told of the great Guestwhaite pissing all over himself the morning after a particularly egregious bender; of the author not even bothering to take a shower (much less change clothes) afterward. "Mervyn could handle losing control of his bladder," Togg had blogged, "but he couldn't stand the idea of losing a train of thought. Clean underwear and a shirt free of b.o. could wait. The muse could not."

The blog was, however, most famous for this single paragraph, an artsy creative nonfiction composition that turned the heads of a not-a-few editors recruiting new talent:

"For Merv, the smell of body odor was the smell of writing. Which was the smell of cash. Which was the smell of Woodford Reserve. Which was the smell of work getting done. Which was the smell of body odor. Which was the smell of writing. Which was the smell of cash."

It wasn't long before a micro-press publisher approached him with the idea to mash up his muckraking blog with a fictional zombie apocalypse tale of his own. That was how the 2014 Rotting Austen Award Winner for Best Mash-Up, *Slave to the Redneck Master & His Zombies Which Turned Out to Not Be Fictional But Really Real*, came to be.

After Mervyn's question-and-answer session freakout, the entire evening derailed from the schedule. Shortly after that débâcle, I saw Meryvn and a couple of strippers groping one another while sauntering off to one of the club's private rooms. Then two hours passed without any sign of them. Benedict Brown, the mortician, was ushered onto the stage ahead-of-schedule to give his spiel. I wasn't in the mood for a morbid sales presentation. Luckily, while pinballing around the crowded club I happened to run into my old friend Katie Winslow.

Katie went by "Kathryn" on her book covers, but went by "Mistress" at conventions. I didn't get the whole S&M thing, but didn't let it stand in the way of our friendship either. Katie wore a black leather version of the outfit donned by Xena: Warrior Princess. Only Xena never juggled a whip, handcuffs, and a mixed drink.

Even with the depressing circumstances of the evening, I couldn't help ribbing her. "I know it's traditional to wear black to a funeral, but . . ."

She mumbled something I couldn't hear over the heavy bass of the stripper-music.

I pointed to my ear. "Huh?"

She leaned forward. "I *said* my sackcloth is at the cleaners." I didn't think that was very funny, but I smiled and nodded, getting a whiff of Katie's breath. Rum. Rum *and mango juice.* One of our old favorites. We used to sit out on my deck in the springtime and drink them while talking about which anthologies were open to submissions.

My mind started to play tricks on me. Earlier in the evening, Mervyn had reeked of liquor. But by this time of night, it seemed that *everyone* did. Even Katie. I felt myself start to get a vague contact buzz, just from the smell. Sounds washed together like the inside of a seashell. My forehead tingled.

"Hey, do you mind taking this off my hands for a second?" She put the drink in my hand. "There's a submissive male—he says he's going to be one of Guestwhaite's pallbearers—that's expecting me in one of the back rooms."

I looked at her. *Stared at her.*

"Oh! I'm so sorry. I forgot you still . . . I mean, you're still not drinking, right? I just thought . . ."

I looked at the pink stuff in her goblet. I remembered the taste. Sweet with a kick. A nice change of pace from my old drink-of-choice, gin and tonic.

"I'm not drinking. Why don't you go ahead and just have this *guy* hold it for you? I mean, if he's all into serving you, then that seems to be the way to go."

She smiled and grabbed her glass back. "Good idea. You know, you could be a dominant yourself. There's this slave in our kink group who gives the *best* pedicures . . ."

I felt my stomach start to slosh. My head start to buzz. My ears start to tingle. Just like before. *It's just a contact buzz.* I told myself. *Just a contact buzz.*

"Look, maybe another time . . ." I stood on tiptoe, trying to spy on Mervyn. He'd just emerged from the private room with the strippers and had been mobbed by fans. I looked down at my cell phone. If this were really on the up-and-up—if Mervyn really planned to die by midnight—then he had less than an hour to live. I excused myself and decided to get out into the night air. Away from the smell of rum and stench of cigarettes.

Outside, it felt better. *Cleaner.* The starry sky offered a sense of wonder, awe, and reassurance. It all looked so sterile and orderly. As if someone was in charge. As they say in A.A., a Higher Power.

Such a Higher Power appeared to hold no sway over the macabre events inside The Electric Lady, but here, outside, looking up, I had faith again. Faith in the fixed bodies of the cosmos. Stars *appeared* to move across the sky over the course of months, of course—but that was a mere illusion of position. It was the *Earth* that did most of the moving.

Perhaps that's how it was with Mervyn and myself. Maybe it only *looked* as if he'd changed over the years, when *I* was really the one who had done all the changing. I was the one who checked out of writing to go to rehab. I was the one who hadn't bothered keeping in touch—mostly out of envy. Thinking of Mervyn made me think of everything I'd lost. So I tried to stop thinking of him, but even *in absentia* he still influenced my thoughts, in a roundabout way, by motivating the conscious effort to stop thinking about him.

He was a big, brilliant star. I was just one of the bodies revolving around him, whether I wanted to or not.

But what happened when a star imploded? When the denseness of its gravity collapsed it onto itself? I tried to remember the little bit of astronomy I'd learned from Carl Sagan. Carl had said on his TV show, *Cosmos*, that a star that imploded into itself would become a black hole; that it would suck in everything around it.

Just as an alcoholic does.

I decided to call my sponsor. I wasn't sure if attending this funeral was such a good idea.

My sponsor (a kindly real estate agent who was ten years sober, but who knew nothing about Mervyn Guestwhaite) insisted I drive home immediately. "You're in a slippery place," she said to me. "Slippery places lead to slips."

I explained that I wanted to determine if Mervyn was really going to drink himself to death that night.

"Good Lord, girl, you need to get that man to a hospital. I don't have to tell you to call 911, do I?"

"B-but this is just a little hick town down here along the Tennessee border. They're not taking this seriously."

"Then make them take it seriously. Call them."

I called 911, but thought I got the wrong number. It sounded as if I'd gotten a hold of a busy bar by mistake.

"Bristol County 911," I heard amidst the din, "where is your emergency?"

I looked around, frantic, and realized I had no clue of the street address for The Electric Lady. So I just blurted it out. "The strip club. I'm in the parking lot outside the Electric Lady strip club."

The redneck guy on the other end of the phone giggled. "I'm sorry, ma'am, but there's no listing for 'Electric Lady Strip Club' in your area."

"Look—you have to know the place. What do they call it? A Gentleman's Club. 'The Electric Lady Gentleman's Club.' It's here in Corbin. There's a big party here tonight."

The door to the Electric Lady swung open. Two men—muscular EMTs in full rescue squad regalia—strutted out, gravel growling under their every step.

"911 is getting forwarded to my cell tonight. Now what seems to be the problem, missy?"

"What do you mean, what's the problem? Have you been inside and seen Mervyn? He's dying!"

"Actually," the blond EMT said, "he's running late for that. It's midnight now, and he's still breathin'."

The brown-haired EMT snickered. "Pay up, cuz! You said he'd croak early! But I knew that tough son of a bitch wouldn't die that easy!"

The blond one huffed. "I'm never bettin' with you again.

It's like you're psychic or somethin'."

"Look—both of you—you're emergency medical technicians, it's your *job* to make sure he doesn't die."

"Lookit this," the brown-haired one said. "A troublemaker! Comin' in here from the city and tellin' us what our job is!"

The blond gritted his teeth. "I don't like that. No, not one bit."

"There's a man in there who's going to die. Maybe not right at midnight, but probably tonight. If not tonight, probably *soon*. All because you goons aren't doing your job."

"Actually," the blond said, "we are *exactly* doing our job. We're working two gigs tonight. We're taking calls for 911, sure, but The Electric Lady hired us as bouncers for this event." He grinned. "Guess who pays more?"

I cringed.

The blond guy continued. "And so, in our capacity as bouncers, we're issuing you a warning. Mr. Guestwhaite has made it abundantly clear that he wishes not to be disturbed by interlopers during this evening's event. If you hassle Mervyn Guestwhaite during this performance, then I will be forced to call the cops to arrest you under the same state law that punishes customers for hassling strippers."

Exasperated, I raised my voice. "He's not a stripper!"

The blond's muscles flexed as he grabbed my shoulder. "Calm down, ma'am! If you can't calm down, I'm going to ask you to leave."

I didn't want to leave. I wanted to stay; to do what I could to help Mervyn. And, if I was honest with myself, I didn't want to talk to my A.A. sponsor either. If I was *really* honest with myself, I just wanted to get drunk. All for a good cause, though, of course.

I wanted to get drunk and summon up the courage to tell Mervyn he should stop all this right now. Only a drunk could tell a drunk he was too drunk. And a former drunk just wouldn't do. I'd lack street cred if I didn't smell of booze when I shared my recovery with him.

The only thing left to do was march back into the strip club and belly up to the bar.

It took a long time for me to actually work my way through the line at the bar. Long enough for me to have second thoughts. I decided I'd order a virgin strawberry daiquiri.

The topless bartender shook her white, ghoulish head. "No virgins allowed here," she said. "You need to be good and drunk for the crazy shit goin' down tonight." Then she went ahead and poured copious amounts of rum into the drink. Less than a minute in the blender, and it was ready to go.

For a few moments I just stood there, gawking at the drink in my hand, swirling my straw in figure eights around the icy froth of the daiquiri. A girl with gray skin sat in the closest bar stool. All the other stools were taken, too.

"Need to sit?" the gray girl said in a perky voice. She started to get up from the bar stool, revealing the fact that she, too, had been made up to look like a zombie—but not hastily made up the way the strippers had been. Made up in a way that made me wonder if she dated Tom Savini.

"Oh, it's okay. I don't want to take your place."

"I don't need to sit," the gray girl said. She got up with an awkward, shuffling motion. "I'm a real zombie, you know. My limbs will never tire again. I could stand all day."

I'd heard that Mervyn's fans could become unhinged. And this, apparently, was a prime example of the phenomenon. Mervyn had cranked out zombie novels by the dozens during his career; but he never mistook fiction for fact. The novels were just a way to make a living telling stories. But to readers like the gray girl, the books provided a new cosmology, a new ethics, and so much more than that: a *raison d'être*.

"I really am a real zombie," the gray girl said. "And I'm not the only one here who is."

I nodded and smiled and just thought about leaving my drink there with her. Maybe it would calm her down.

"Mervyn's a real zombie, too, " she said. "I saw it on his message board. His avatar clearly shows him in undisguised zombie mode."

"I think you misunderstood a publicity photo. That was just Mervyn clowning around with some makeup people on the set of the *R.A.N.K.* movie. He's really not a zombie."

"He is too a real zombie. He almost began feeding on that one guy during the question-and-answer session. He's like me—without a soul. Lost in the automation of his own flesh. Just a skin puppet."

"I'm still not convinced. Extraordinary claims require extraordinary evidence."

The girl smirked. "The evidence is right in front of you—he's not dead."

"Exactly. But I'm a little confused. How does that prove your point? If he's *not* dead, how can he be a zombie?"

"He's not dead because alcohol poisoning won't kill a zombie. But this misery of his has been going on for too long. He deserves release from his pain, and the only way to kill a zombie is to shoot him in the head." That's when she dug into her purse and showed me the gun. She took it in hand and strode away toward Mervyn.

I looked around for the off-duty EMTs. She lurched through the crowd with her lithe little body. I slapped the bar with my palm. She disappeared from sight. I began to scream and point to where I'd last seen her. "She has a gun, she has a gun!"

I heard something that sounded like a firecracker going off.

The wound in Mervyn Guestwhaite's head looked like the mouth of a wheezing baby. Tiny. Spastic.

A hush came over the crowd, and I heard the gray girl shouting. "This is the way—the *only* way—for a zombie to die with honor!"

Blood began gushing out of the hole in spasms. It fell on his cheeks and dripped onto his teeth. Mervyn looked more awake than he had at any point during the evening. He let out a hoarse moan and staggered about.

He did not fall.

And so the gray girl kept shooting. She demonstrated decent marksmanship for a "real zombie," landing most shots on Mervyn's forehead but missing once in awhile—blowing off Mervyn's left ear or piercing the arm or leg of a bystander.

Whoops rose up from the crowd. The topless bartender climbed atop the bar to get a better view. But that only lasted for a minute. In the end, she decided to rush into the crowd—she and all the others who were feeling their booze consumption by this part of the evening. They surrounded Mervyn and the gray girl like kids at a birthday party, waiting for the blow that would pierce the piñata.

Fear nailed my feet to the ground, so I stood apart from the rest. I watched. I watched without helping Mervyn live or die. I stood by the bar and just watched.

I don't know how many shots it took to blow Mervyn's head off. Smoke and bad lighting obscured some of these particulars from my vantage point near the bar. I only know that there was a chorus of demon-screams one moment, and someone shouting "Brains!" the next.

"Brains! Guestwhaite's brains!"

I saw the crowd fall to the ground, searching for a gray matter souvenir of the wildest night of Mervyn Guestwhaite's life. "I need to eat it. Eat Guestwhaite's brain! By consuming it, I can absorb his writing power," I overheard someone say.

"I can be at one with him," a hipster goth girl said. "Like sex, without the sweating!"

They picked over the body, looking for whatever shred of cerebellum might have flown off in this direction or that, and they did that for hours. Until they passed out. On the floor. In their vomit. In pools of Mervyn's raspberry-red blood.

I turned to my melting daiquiri. By then, it had become sloshy. I tried convincing myself that the melted ice would dilute it. That it wouldn't be like drinking at all.

But I couldn't.

I shuffled away from the bar. Out the door. Into the night. I gripped my cell phone tight, knowing my sponsor wasn't up this late but contemplating calling her anyway.

I'd tell her I'd come close to drinking, but hadn't. That I'd learned that now, more than ever, I couldn't. I'd tell her I'd learned my lesson: that if I drank I'd end up like Mervyn. Or perhaps, even worst, his fans.

I never read or wrote another word of fiction.

# Youth to Be Proud Of

REVIEW OF THE RILEY HIGH SCHOOL
LITTLE THEATER GROUP'S FRIDAY NIGHT
PERFORMANCE OF *OUR TOWN*

by Narvin Glasgow

If this is the best our children can give us, then our children's children are doomed.

Even when compared only to other student productions, Friday's performance of *Our Town* left quite a lot to be desired. A student director—Natasha Ogden (daughter of Riley Funeral Home owner Oscar Ogden)—perverted Thornton Wilder's masterpiece with the use of various special effects bells and whistles which the Director's Notes indicated were intended to make the play more relevant in the era of text messages and Twitter.

Originally supposed to take place nearly a century ago, Ogden set the play in the time span between the late 1970s and the mid-'90s and dressed her cast up in white leisure suits, gauzy Stevie Nicks–style dresses, and cords of corduroy. In scenes where there is a death or (SPOILER) where the dead speak, she had that character climb a stepladder and spin a suspended disco ball ("to symbolize the shining brilliance of each and every soul," her notes said). She then had a squad of stage mothers hoist the actors into the air using a system of pulleys and very thin stage wire. "That way the audience knows they're in heaven," the notes explained.

As if this wasn't horrendous enough, pandemonium broke out during intermission. The actress playing Young Emily (Meghan McElroy, daughter of Buddy's Pharmacy owner and operator Buddy McElroy) wriggled past the closed curtain, burst onto the gymnasium stage, and announced to a soda-sipping, cookie-nibbling audience that a pee test had just confirmed her pregnancy.

The few students who bothered attending (all weirdos—boys wearing eyeliner, girls decked out in combat boots) failed to restrain their laughter at this ill-timed disclosure. But a fair number of the farmers, bikers, waitresses, and hospital maids in the gymnasium that night assumed the speech was part of the show, and had no clue Ms. McElroy was breaking character. This changed when she hollered how she suspected Mr. Richardson, the sensitive—and honestly, hitherto-assumed-homosexual—guidance counselor, to be the father. A close review of the program verified there was no presumably gay school guidance counselor in *Our Town*, let alone one who meandered across boundaries with enough gall to impregnate a student. And speaking of homosexuality, when Meghan McElroy spilled the beans about her pregnancy, Todd Blankenship (son of Superior Court Judge Howard Blankenship) and Joey Bancroft (son of Grace Presbyterian Church's junior pastor Craig Bancroft)—both youths of fifteen—began tongue-kissing each other right next to her. In between slobbering gasps, they announced their undying love and threatened to elope.

At that point Luke Emerson (son of Riley's only private practice psychotherapist, Emerson Emerson, Ph.D.) walked up next to Young Mr. Blankenship and Young Mr. Bancroft and explained to the audience that he'd long been an aficionado of self-mutilation. He then removed his shirt to reveal a torso criss-crossed with scars and a cavity of crusty muscle where his belly button should have been. He screamed he had eradicated his navel in an attempt to erase every trace of evidence that a connection ever existed between himself and his "controlling (expletive)-mother."

Emerson Emerson reportedly expressed relief afterward that his son "at least wasn't like those two kissing boys."

It took some time for Ms. Ogden to settle down her charges and get the second act going.

But the damage proved irreparable. The special effects (that is to say, the pulleys and the wire) did their job well enough, allowing the "actors" (a term I use loosely for this gaggle of maladjusted youth) to float in mid-air, inducing a sense of crude wonder. Director Ogden deserves the mildest of kudos for at least making sure the machinery worked well enough. And her inclusion of musical effects—such as how the first bars of *Thus Spake Zarathustra* played whenever a character died and began levitating off the stage—kept things interesting.

But even that success was not enough to overcome the deficits of the actors and their transformation of a classic piece of American stagecraft into a tawdry confessional. The only "drama" in Riley High School's production of Thornton Wilder's *Our Town* was of the trite, histrionic rumor-mill variety. There is no place for this sort of thing on the Riley High School gymnasium stage.

This production is pollution.

I call on all Rileyite parents to come together and take a stand against this onrush of oddity. I call for our youth to once again be guided by the wise steering of their elders. I call for consequences: immediate and severe.

## RILEY REBOUNDS FOR SATURDAY PERFORMANCE OF *OUR TOWN*

by Narvin Glasgow

Like many of our readers, I have heard the rumors of rampant drug use on the set of Riley High School's production of *Our Town*. How else can one explain how things fell apart, how the center would not hold? Fortunately, our own Riley Police Department has apprehended nineteen-year-old Maxwell McElroy (see page A1, "Pharmacist's Son Nabbed for Pill-Pushing"). Authorities arrested McElroy-the-younger for distribution of unprescribed Xanax and Oxycontin to the rest of the *Our Town* cast. An initial hearing before Superior Court Judge Howard Blankenship has been scheduled, and a cash-only bond set at $10,000.

Perhaps Young Mr. McElroy only pushed the pills in an innocent attempt to "mellow the troupe out" (as my own daughter, Katie, a box office volunteer and *in no way involved in Friday night's scandal*, informed this journalist Saturday morning). If that were the case, Max McElroy should be informed that by Saturday night the cast apparently lost their case of stage fright without pharmaceutical assistance and pulled off a sensational—one might even say thought-provoking—performance.

If the Tonys gave out awards at the high school level and

one of the categories was "most improved performance," I'd be the first to nominate Riley High's production of *Our Town*.

For starters, the play suffered none of the embarrassing, character-breaking confessions that marked Friday's show. One had the sense the actors felt dutifully ashamed of their missteps. They were, in fact, as quiet as cornstalks throughout the entire evening.

This was to be a night at the theater like none ever seen. Even before the performance, one had the sense that the evening held a certain . . . gravity. A low, musky, sweet-sick scent permeated the air. As Riley's most influential critic of the arts, I have to admit that I am catered to and spoiled by venues that reserve a seat in the front row for me. However, at this performance I discovered no reservation was necessary as the chairs in the Riley High gymnasium were devoid of parents. The only other audience members were a handful of young people—the most garish and awkward of the proto-freaks who had attended the show the night before. They sat in the back of the gym, snickering and whispering to one another as I walked past them. I paid the ruffians no mind and placed my camera and notepad in the empty seat next to me, settling in for what I assumed would be another long evening.

As with Friday's show, pulleys and stage wire were an integral part of the production. Even more so Saturday than Friday, come to think of it. As noted in my previous review, there were moments Friday night when the actors moved about freely by foot. On Saturday, however, the pulleys animated the cast throughout the entire performance. Wheels squeaked overhead, and the wire lifted the youths to just the right height so their legs seemed to gallop across the stage. The actors were at ease with the arrangement, and I could not detect any sign of discomfort, even when the pulleys sometimes jerked to and fro with a bit too much force.

Given the actors' Friday night debauchery, it makes sense that they appeared not-quite-themselves on Saturday. One couldn't put one's finger on it. They looked more pale and waxen than when I'd last seen them. Riley Funeral Home makeup artist Sarah Ogden (noted in the program as a last-minute addition to the crew) did a splendid job, though. The youths had none of the untamed nastiness that had been on outrageous display Friday night. They looked, in fact, rather at peace. As though they were all in a better place now, both mentally and morally.

The lips of the actors did not move, but I could hear lines of dialogue nonetheless. They were bellowed by voices residing in the rafters above the stage. The voices were not those of the teens, but instead a more haggard—some might say, more mature—echo of those voices. Older voices, but similar enough to the youths themselves. More skillful voices, delivering the dialogue in a far more snappy, even melodic, fashion when compared to the stammering and giggles on Friday.

There was no sign of the corduroy, the leisure suits, or the nipple-suggesting gauzy dresses that had embarrassed the entire town of Riley on opening night. Each youth wore classic black. The boys wore black suits adorned with a white carnation, white shirts, and black neckties. The girls wore calf-length black dresses, adorned with a white bow at the neckline and a white carnation pinned to the chest.

There was no sign of the disco ball; but there were flowers in many places, and a guest book had been set next to the box office. There was no more *Thus Spake Zarathustra.* Instead, old Ma Ogden sat at an organ I'd never noticed in the gymnasium before. At the end of each scene she played a few bars of "Amazing Grace." I don't know about you, but *this* Rileyite will take "Amazing Grace" over *Thus Spake Zarathustra* any day of the week.

Whereas those in attendance on Friday night had noted that the allegedly "dead" characters could be seen flinching—even smirking—I could not observe even a stray breath among that very same cast on Saturday.

I found myself moved by the Riley High Little Theater Group as they'd never moved me before. At the performance's end, one of the ushers (I think Zeke Ogden) must have noticed the tear rolling down my cheek. He offered me a tissue, and I gratefully accepted.

While momentarily distracted I took the opportunity to glance back at the other members of the audience seated in the rear, to see if they shared my appreciation for the Little Theater Group's 180-degree turn.

It seemed as though they were at least as moved as I'd been, if not more so. Even in the dimly lit theater, I could see them lurched over, shaking and sobbing. They must have felt self-conscious (they looked more nervous than cats in a room full of rocking chairs). As soon as they became aware of my backward glance they made a beeline for the exit.

The premature departure of so many audience members created some awkwardness, but at least there was none of the nonsense from Friday's performance—none of the missed cues or sloppy costume changes. Only cold precision.

At the show's end, the curtain fell. Modest to a fault—and perhaps gun-shy about breaking character as they had on Friday—the cast did not take a bow. Theater veterans may find this to be the one inexcusable breach of etiquette, but I considered this newfound reserve a welcome change. There was no unscripted chaos in Saturday's performance. There was only *Our Town*.

After the show concluded and the last note of "Amazing Grace" was played, I asked Ma Ogden if I could have a word with her granddaughter, Natasha. I wanted to know how she'd pulled off (literally overnight) such a swift revision in so many areas of production.

Ma Ogden paused for a second and looked embarrassed. But when she realized I wasn't going to let the matter drop, she looked up to me and smiled. "The difference, Mr. Glasgow, is prayer. You can go back and see her, but I wouldn't expect her to be too talkative. She's still praying. We convinced Natasha to pray long and hard about what she'd done last night, about letting all those unspeakable things be said and making a nice student play all weird. After some time speaking to the Man Upstairs she accepted our suggestions without talking back."

I went backstage and verified this was, indeed, the case. In the green room, Natasha Ogden wore the same black dress the actresses had. She knelt rigidly on the floor with a tattered family Bible resting on a chair in front of her. She looked expressionless—as if she'd somehow fallen asleep in that posture—so I called out her name. I tried, oh, I don't know, three or four times with no response. I can only reason that she was in deep contemplation of the scriptures. Her eyes were shut so tight, as though they'd been *sewn* shut. If only we could all remain that focused on God's word, the world would be a better place. This Rileyite rests assured our community will stay in good hands.

Yes, if Saturday's show is any indication, Riley can

look forward to quite the bright future. One day made all the difference, it seems. On Friday, the cast was the most undisciplined array of fringe freaks our town could ever assemble. But by Saturday, they were youth to be proud of.

# SUBCONTRACTORS

**I**n the eighth month of the plague (the month all the pills stopped working) the funeral homes started deputizing subcontractors. This was a great boon to Mama and me. It allowed us to afford little extras, like ice cream.

Morticians still insisted on doing the embalming themselves. They weren't about to give away any of their trade secrets. They divulged no details about the incisions and drainings and infusions and makeup tricks that preserved the appearance of the dead (and, more importantly, preserved their monopoly, their *raison d'être*).

No, the only aspect of their services they bid out to subcontractors was the hosting of various visitations, viewings, funerals, and memorial services. With all the bodies streaming into them, they no longer had room for such affairs. Areas of funeral homes previously reserved for the accommodation of these events were remodeled into additional embalming facilities. Only the very wealthiest citizens of our small Rust Belt city were afforded the luxury of a service held "on location" (if you will) at the funeral parlor. The rest were farmed out to any member of the populace who took a one-hour certification course in "grief management," and who was willing to encumber the risk of taking a body that died from God-knows-what into their home.

(I say "God-knows-what" because fibbing about the cause of death was rampant, as no one wanted the stigma and shunning that followed the revelation that a family member, friend, or acquaintance had been infected. Our local coroners, in fact, were rumored to falsify death certificates if they'd had even the most fleeting association with the body. After all, they too had wives and mistresses who would have bolted if they'd known the truth. As a result, reports of death from "heart attack" and "stroke" skyrocketed. Surely, a sizable number of these cases were actually plague victims.)

Despite all the risk, my mother rushed at the opportunity and signed subcontracts with not only one funeral home, but three. It mattered little to her (or to the funeral homes) that we didn't own any of the biohazard suits that had been mandated for handling the plague-dead (and had become requisite, indeed, for simply navigating the post-plague world). "I already work at a laundromat," Mama explained. "And I ain't got sick yet. Don't you think that's somethin' special? All my co-workers keep comin' down with somethin' or other and havin' to stop work. Some people even think we should just close the business. But me? Totally unaffected. You see, *I think* it's all in the Good Lord's hands."

To her, it mattered little that we lived in a two bedroom apartment with only a small living room and smaller kitchen, possessing barely enough space to house the deceased themselves, let alone any mourners. I brought this to her attention. "If you think there's not enough space in here," Mama countered, "why don't you stop takin' it up and go off to the park? Pick me some wildflowers. People expect bouquets an' shit at a funeral. Here, take these scissors with you and cut some for Mama."

So I grabbed the scissors, tucked them away in the little plastic purse I took with me everywhere in those days, and jogged out of the house to the park. Whenever I'd gone to the park in the past, the only threats I had to brace myself against were bumblebees. But that day I took scissors to cut flowers — the worst day of my childhood, I suppose, not counting the day Dad left — I faced the tinny taunts of older, wealthier kids bullying me through the speakers of their designer biohazard suits. The boys' suits were gray or blue, squarish and simple, the girls' were pink or purple and tight in the butt and where boobs would have been if they'd been old enough to have much in the way of a bosom. The sun made a glare across the plastic face shields, making it difficult to identify my tormentors at first.

"I've heard your mom's turned into a body-borrower," one of the older boys said in his metallic-speaker-voice. (It took me a while, but I eventually placed him as Joe Pipken, a charismatic bully from one block over. He must have only recently acquired the biohazard suit. When he'd last teased me, a week before when we'd passed on the sidewalk, he'd been without one. He'd also been suffering a terrible case of "allergies" and had been coughing up a storm.) "Body-borrower! Body borrower!" his lemmings chanted, joining in with the teasing. Then Pipken let loose with a volley of sneezes. I heard a stray cough from one or two of his followers. A metallic sniffle rang out over the park, followed by more put-downs. "How many bodies is your mom going to borrow to pay rent this month?" Pipken hollered. "What are you doing out in the open air with decent people? Don't bring your death-cooties near us!"

They may have had biohazard suits, but I had scissors. I furtively slipped them out of my purse and hid them behind my back. I walked up to the bully-boy and feigned defeat so that I would have the element of surprise. I forced my face to look sad, my spirit broken. "Don't say that about me," I whimpered.

"Aww . . . look at the little white trash body-borrower," one of the girls said through her speaker. "I think she's gonna cry!"

"And I think you're going to *die!*" I yelled. I brandished the scissors and lunged at a place on Pipken's calf, a flap of biohazard suit that offered itself up as the perfect target—far away from defending hands and sturdy boots. The suit was made of a rugged plastic that resisted my scissors' intrusion. I made a dent. With a second effort, I pushed the scissors harder. The plastic yielded, stretched.

But it did not tear.

The boy grabbed me by the shoulders and shoved me to the ground. The scissors flew from my hand. One of the girls bent over (with some effort, as her suit was fashionably snug) and grabbed the shears from the ground. She then waddled forward. "You like scissors, eh?" She then started to succumb to a coughing fit. When she regained her composure, she reached for me. "Come here, body-borrower, and let me give you a haircut, if you like scissors so much."

I didn't like the idea of losing Mama's scissors to Pipken and his gang, but I liked the idea of public humiliation even less. I rose to my feet and decided to abandon the scissors and run home. My little legs worked away at the ground and my little arms pumped hard and fast, until a cold plastic glove caught up to me. It clasped onto my right upper arm and threw me back to the ground. Hard.

This second crash knocked the wind out of me, and I lay there not even able to grunt when I saw the blades coming; I lay there not even able to protest when I heard the first whine-grind-chirp of the shears doing their work. Wispy brown locks were caught up, like dandelion seeds, in the breeze. By the time I had enough breath back in me to mount a struggle, the deed had been done. My curls, butchered.

I ran back home, bawling. I ran awkwardly, covering my head with my hands (as though that would be effective in hiding my shame). I ran to tell Mama about the mean kids in the park who'd hurt me. But when I arrived home, Mama was busy. She was out in our apartment complex's parking lot, signing some papers given to her by a man who'd just gotten out of the driver's seat of a hearse. After she'd finished signing them all, the hearse driver used a gurney to remove a body from the back. It was (that is, it *had been, in life*) a man.

"Not so fast," Mama said to the driver. "That gurney won't work too good—we're on the second floor."

He sighed. "No elevator?"

"Nope."

A crowd of neighbors started to gather around the scene. Only a few owned biohazard suits (many, in fact, looked feverish and boil-ridden), but they all came out to sell their services as body-haulers. About two dozen gathered around the body and started carrying it up the stairs, without Mama even giving them permission to do so. So numerous, in fact, were the helpers, so *persistent and excited* were their mumblings and whispers and coughs and giggles and sneezes and gossips, so *chaotic* (I might even say "festive") was the scene around the body, that it was difficult to concentrate and remember just who was there, actually lifting the corpse, and who had merely *accompanied* the procession up the stairs.

They all had their hands out afterward.

Mama settled up with them as best she could, offering to take ten percent of her payment from the funeral home and divide that up twenty-four ways to pay them all. There was much grumbling among the newly minted sub-subcontractors at this news, and a few particularly disgruntled types actually tried to lift the body off the living room couch (where it had been placed) and take it back downstairs in protest. The more practical among them, though, knew that this would only make it easier for Mama to retract her offer when the funeral home's payment arrived. In the end, the cooler heads prevailed, and everyone agreed to the terms offered.

# THE MIRRORS

Mama shooed them all out of the apartment, but the scent of sweat from the exertion of the body-haulers lingered long after they'd gone. When combined with the smell of formaldehyde coming out of the pores of the deceased, it created an unbreathable atmosphere. Our little apartment had been made into an inhospitable, alien world.

Mama rested her hands on her hips and surveyed the situation. Despite having been worked on by the embalmers and makeup artists, the dead man's face looked swollen and disfigured. Pockmarked, as though someone had taken great effort to lance boils and had unconvincingly covered up the resulting scars. A tag on his toe announced the cause of death ("heart attack") and several statistics about the deceased ("Age: 52; Height: 5'11"; Weight, 155 lbs."). It did not, however, specify the dead man's name. She looked at him, then she looked at me. "What did you do to your hair?"

I told her about the bullies in the park. I told her I never wanted to go there again. I told her that I hated anyone who owned a biohazard suit, and that I wished they all were dead.

She embraced me for the first time in a long time. Squeezed me tight, and whispered to me. "Don't say such things. Why do you think I've started to take in the bodies? This shit *pays*, honey. Pays enough so that, someday soon, you'll have the cutest little biohazard suit you could ever *dream* of. So don't go wishin' rich people dead. We're gonna work so hard at this that *we're* gonna be rich. And you wouldn't like it if someone wished *you* dead after you got *your* suit, now would you?"

She had a point. "No, Mama," I said. "I suppose I wouldn't."

"Of course you wouldn't. You see, you shouldn't hate them. You should try to be *like* them."

I pointed to the dead body on the couch. "But . . . I mean . . . we'll never be like them. I mean, not really. They made their money working in banks or law offices. You make yours doing other people's laundry and borrowing bodies!"

She smacked me hard in the face. "That's for sassin' me!"

I whined. "What?"

"You know damned well 'what.' That sass-word. 'Body-borrower'! I never want to hear that in this chapel again, young lady!"

I wanted to point out to her that the living room of our shabby little apartment wasn't really a "chapel"—that, in fact, it was no more a "chapel" than it was a "stadium" or a "courthouse"; but I didn't think it was the right time. I feared she'd give me another walloping if I opened my mouth. So I kept quiet, but she seemed to be able to discern what I'd been thinking.

She sighed. "Here's somethin' I'm gonna tell you about this world. Names have power, and we have to choose the very best names and titles for ourselves these days. Sometimes stretchin' the truth is the best way to be *kind* to ourselves (and we need, now more than ever, to be kind to ourselves). So let's not think of this as a livin' room any more. From now on, it's a funeral chapel." She grabbed paper and pencil, then looked at the clock. "And let's think of this time right now not as a mother-daughter argument, but instead as this nice gentleman's visitation. I think the funeral home pays for visitation by the hour, so I'm officially declarin' this poor ol' soul *visited*, if you know what I mean. And, seein' as the funeral home shipped him over to us without the benefit of any paperwork sayin' who he is, let's not just think of him as some random gentleman—let's give him a name." She walked over to the couch and examined the dead man. "He looks like a Frederick to me. Frederick Keys, I think we'll call him. Has a ring to it, don't it?"

Hadn't she considered just calling the man "John Doe"? Had she forgotten that the Frederick Keys were the minor league baseball team up in Maryland that my dad had left us to play with?

"You see, honey, if I decide to call this man Frederick Keys, well, damn, I'm sure as hell that *he's* not gonna object. Somethin' tells me his *people* ain't gonna track him down here and object. We has us some power then, you see. Power to give names to the dead."

"But the funeral home must have his name somewhere. They must have just lost track of it."

"I'll bet you five dollars right now that I'll be able to submit a bill to the funeral home for the visitation and funeral of a certain Frederick Keys, and I'll bet you they'll pay. You just have to have some imagination now, girl. The funeral home is just workin' a business like anyone else. Do you think they care what happens when that body comes off the gurney? Hell, no!

If they did, they wouldn't have started subcontractin' in the first place!"

I gave voice, weakly, to my objection. "But his name isn't *really* Frederick. It's a make-believe name, it's not *real*."

"When you do a job no one else wants you *make* real— at least as far as that job goes. Remember that, and you'll go far in this world." She yawned and stretched. Her flabby arms wobbled when she raised them, like rising flags in a breeze. "I'm gonna go lay down," she said. "It's been a long day and I'm plum wore out. Now you stay here with Mr. Keys and have a good visit. Go ahead now and mourn him. Mourn him good."

Mama decided that the visitation and funeral for Frederick Keys would last three whole days (it made good business sense, given that we were getting paid by the hour). Mama and I took turns staying in the so-called "chapel" with him, lest anyone from the funeral home stop by to inspect the premises to make certain we were legit.

No one from the funeral home or the state funeral home board or the city health department stopped by, though. Our entire city, in fact, had lost its prior aura of creaking-clanking industrial busyness. The road outside our street took on the same forsaken appearance it had early on Christmas morning. The park, too, was abandoned. (A pity, since it was such a lovely day. Alas, only the bumblebees seemed to be enjoying it.)

"This is creepy, Mama. Where is everyone?"

Her eyes darted back and forth, assessing the situation. "I'll be damned. I betcha a whole bunch of people signed up to be subcontractors. They're probably all tucked away in their own personal chapels, visitin' the dead. I betcha *that's* where everyone is—tryin' to barge into *our* business!"

I went on the Internet to see what explanation I could find for all the quiet, but the local newspaper hadn't updated its home page in two days. The big headline at the top of the page made reference to the soaring number of heart attacks and strokes, and provided helpful tips for good cardiovascular health ("Exercise at least three times a week, for at least a half an hour each time," the website advised).

Mom nudged me out of the seat. "Move," she said. "I

need to use the Internet to submit our bill to the funeral home."
And that's exactly what she did. Two days later, the money was
direct-deposited into our bank account.

Mr. Frederick Keys had begun to smell of something
other than formaldehyde. I asked Mama whose job it was to
bury him. She scratched her head and started thumbing through
her contract. "You know, that's a very good question! Doesn't
seem like that's covered here. A loophole, it seems. We might-
could do it ourselves, and tack on another charge. But before we
do, let's see if the home has another friend ready to visit us!"

Mama took out her cell phone and called Higgenbotham's
Home for Funerals (the folks who had provided us with the
body that now lay moldering on our sofa). She got voicemail.
She left a message asking when a new body would be ready.
Then she hung up. The same thing happened when she called
the other two funeral homes she'd signed on with.

A day passed without getting a return call. A handful
of houseflies circled the deceased, periodically landing on his
nostrils and eyes. Mom shrugged and submitted another bill to
the funeral home. Twenty-four additional hours of visitation.
She got an email telling her the claim had been rejected. The
reason given was as follows: "You have already reached your
maximum reimbursement for this transaction."

"We should just bury him," I said. "It can't go on like
this."

"The first rule of business is not to do anythin' to put
yourself *out* of business! I mean, you're right about things not
bein' able to go on. I sure as hell ain't gonna keep him here
without gettin' paid. But you know what? I think this doesn't
look like Mr. Keys, layin' here." She shook her head dramatically.
"No, no, no . . . This looks like someone else entirely, don't you
think?"

It took me a few seconds to get what she was driving at.
But I was starting to become sufficiently accustomed to Mama's
shell games and shams to know that she was suggesting we
introduce a more ballsy fraud into our business repertoire.

"This man here, I think this doesn't look like Frederick
Keys at all. I think you must've gotten a new body from the
funeral home while I was in the kitchen. I think this here is
none other than . . ." She paused, mulling over her options.
"Mike Mussina." (Again, she should have picked a different

name. Mike Mussina was the name of a starting pitcher for the Baltimore Orioles that my dad had worshipped when he was growing up.)

She found, however, that when she entered the name into the online claim form, the automated system accepted it for up to three days of visitation/funeral time. In a matter of days, more money had been direct-deposited into our bank account.

"Now we have enough to re-stock on groceries," Mama said. (Our routine was to make one single, large trip at the first of the month.) "Looks like we might even be able to splurge a little."

"But Mama," I said, "no one's out and about. The newspaper hasn't updated their website. Do you think the store's even still . . . well . . . you know, *open*?"

Mama looked at me, scowling. "There you go again. Always the glass-half-empty type, ain'tcha? Well, you'll find out when we get there that you worry too damn much!"

I'd looked forward to getting out of the apartment because I'd looked forward to getting away from all the flies. But there was no getting away from the flies. They swarmed in abundance in our second-floor hallway, and Mama was forced to gag at the pungent, fetid odor that lingered there. Even in the best of times, mind you, that hallway always smelled musty. (And it didn't surprise me when Mama tried to attribute the odor to "that mold the landlord never gets around to cleanin' up." But I knew better.)

I'd feared the streets would have no cars on them at all. This fear, at least, was unfounded. Cars littered the road here and there. Some had crashed into telephone polls. Some had pulled over onto the median. The drivers of all the vehicles were slumped over the steering wheels. Even from a distance, you could see their disfiguring boils.

"My, my," Mama said. "Looks like those drivers had heart attacks behind the wheel! Or, you know, it could have been strokes."

I wanted to point my finger at each of the bodies and shout "Plague! Plague!," but Mama's denial was simply her way of being kind to herself. (And who was I to rob her of that kindness?) So I nodded. I even joined in. "They should have exercised," I said solemnly.

Mama brightened when she realized I wasn't going

to take away her self-delusion. "Yes, we need to start doin' calisthenics, you and I, together out in the park. That way we won't be like them."

Of course, I knew that we would never be like them. Mama had worked at the laundromat all that time and had never gotten even the slightest sniffle. Perhaps, as Mama said, the "Good Lord" had loaded the dice in our favor, but I judged that line of thinking to be just another of her ways of being kind to herself. Kinder, indeed, than believing that the answer to the riddle of our survival rested in the unfathomable depths of our genes. Kinder, still, than believing that the riddle *had no answer*.

The grocery store parking lot was packed. The cars were festooned with corpses, either sprawling over their hoods or seated within. All bore a series of boils—sometimes purple, sometimes black.

"They're all dead," I said to Mama. "Every last one of them."

She took a deep breath, put her hands on her hips, and darted her eyes about. "Not dead," she said. "They're all just *in a coma*. Didn't you know that can happen when people have heart attacks and strokes?"

Mama had to nudge one "stroke victim" aside with her shoe (his fallen body had gotten in the way of the supermarket's automatic door). Once inside, we grabbed a cart. Mama took her shopping list out of her purse, just as if it was any other trip to the store.

We didn't loot. In order to loot, Mama would have had to admit to herself that chaos had descended on us. She couldn't find it in herself to do that. So we simply loaded up the cart with our usual goodies (and a few extras, like ice cream). None of the cashiers were left standing (although I did catch a glimpse of one, on the floor, still moving—she trembled and writhed behind her work station, her arms and legs getting entangled in thin plastic bags). We didn't go into her line.

We didn't go into any line, in fact, staffed by a cashier. We went through one of the automated cashier lines—the kind where you scan everything yourself. It took a long time, because we had more than fifteen items in our cart and the way it's set up, it's only supposed to work like an express lane. We had to put stuff on the conveyor belt a little at a time.

While I was there, helping Mama put things on the belt,

I realized I'd forgotten something. I went back to the school supplies department and picked up a pair of scissors, then hurried back to the line. (Why did I hurry? No one stood there behind us, tapping her shoe or giving us the hairy eyeball. Some habits even managed to survive civilization.)

Mama raised her eyebrows when she saw I wanted to add scissors to our order. "You need those?" she asked.

"Yeah. I think I want to keep my hair this way," I said. The automated cashier told us the cost in a pleasant, calm, automated voice. Mom inserted her check card, and everything went smoothly. We bagged our own groceries and went home.

That was the first day of our new life.

I remembered having seen one of Mama's favorite TV preachers talk about how people in Old Testament days had shaved their heads in mourning. I decided that my butchered hairdo was the closest I could come to that, for now. I wouldn't make Mama deal with the epidemic and its aftermath; I wouldn't make her grieve. I wouldn't even give voice to *my own* grief — because to do so would burst the bubble of kind delusion she'd created around herself.

But with my shorn hair, I could *silently* observe it. And that's how I've handled it, for all the years since then. I guess, in retrospect, I actually should be thankful for the bullying of Joe Pepkin and his friends. If they hadn't ruined my hair, I might not have gotten an idea of how to mourn. And if I hadn't mourned, I would have gone mad. And if I'd gone mad, the only remnants of humanity would have been a couple of lunatics with a rotting body on a sofa in their little two-bedroom apartment. It's meant something, then, for me to stay both alive and sane. It's meant that sanity, itself, still exists.

I've never gone for more than three days without a trim.

Boudoir Mirrors

# The Peculiar Salesgirl

One way to avoid the peculiar salesgirl is never to shop at the North Vernon Skin-Mart in the first place. Avoid the store proper. Avoid the entire dingy, crumbling outlet mall if you can. Avoid the walls festooned with unimaginative graffiti scrawled by white trash pseudo-gangstas. Avoid the fractured pavement of the parking lot, overgrown with weeds sprouting in between the cracks and littered with beer cans and condoms. Avoid, even, the Rust Belt town (just a few miles up I-65) itself. You won't miss much. It's less a town, really, than the fossil of one. Avoid it and you'll be safe.

When I offer this advice to my old friends from high school, they accuse me of "overkill." In context, it sounds like this: "You snob," they say, rolling their lined, mascaraed, shadowed eyes, "that would be overkill." Sometimes they remark that I have changed too much since I went away to college in Chicago. They're still "down home" but I'm not, they claim. They cite, as evidence, the big words I use now, my "dykey" short hair, and my newfound tomboyishness. They point out the way I shrug off the summer 4-H Fair with indifference, while they see it as an opportunity to flirt with potential beaus.

Sometimes they scoff at me for other reasons altogether. They accuse me of objecting to Skin-Mart out of some general resistance to fashion and joke that I should join one of the stodgier religious sects—the ones that prohibit women from wearing pants, the ones in which the ladies volunteer for coerced modesty.

"Longskirts," such ladies are called—for obvious reasons. "The trailer park Amish," they're called—for pejorative ones. You can see them in the grocery store, their long hair drawn up in buns, their denim skirts revealing nary a hint of calf, or even ankle. Their dollar store blouses cover sagging breasts that have suckled too many too long. For you see, no less than five children follow behind the average Longskirt. The youngest of the brood might only be a toddler, but the mother's hair is invariably streaked with gray, her face prematurely wrinkled, her expression stuck fossil-like in a raised-eyebrow grimace of despair.

They drive ancient minivans adorned with bumper stickers announcing that:

## IN CASE OF RAPTURE, THIS VEHICLE WILL BE UNOCCUPIED

*These* are the sort of ranks my friends say I should join, just because I object to Skin-Mart in general and harbor a deep distrust about that one peculiar salesgirl in particular. Their mistake is a natural one. Truth is, the church folks object to Skin-Mart the strongest. They say that Skin-Mart is "of the world" and therefore unwelcome. One would think that their message would find traction, given the region's reputation as a haven for Christian fundamentalism.

But even here, where the Midwest and South meet in a confluence of piety, the numbers of the churchgoing faithful are dwindling. The influence of organized religion wanes when it comes to loggerheads with the promise of new jobs for unskilled labor. It may be true that neither man nor woman can live by bread *alone*, but neither can they live with bread *absent*. I suspect all the locals now employed at Skin-Mart had reservations at first. But what can they do? McDonald's left town years ago.

I try to assure my friends that I object to Skin-Mart on *humanitarian* grounds, not puritanical ones. "Have you," I ask, "ever read the tags to see just where the skins come from?"

At this, the other girls just sneer. "Julie and her 'skin tags,'" they say, giggling. Once, for no less than two weeks, that was my nickname. "Hey, Skin Tag," they'd say over the phone, "want to join us at the bar? It's ladies' night. You *are* still interested in *men*, ain'tcha?" We're all underage, but the only number that matters to the bouncer at the bar is your bra size.

I don't think that the "Skin Tag" joke is funny. I think it's just their way of minimizing any concerns that the skins for sale at Skin-Mart come at the expense of donors who may have been pressured into the arrangement. A cursory glance reveals that the skins come to southern Indiana by way of some infamous locales. "Made in Chechnya," one says. "Made in Reno," says another. But my old friends don't know (or care) what goes on in Russian rebellions or Nevadan brothels. They only know that when they wear a skin more fashionable than their own, they feel pretty. Men ask them out. They feel treasured.

The most popular skins are those that come already tanned, tattooed, and pierced. Don't get me wrong—they're exquisite products. Lovely. Soft. Smooth. For all my objections, I'm as guilty of window-shopping at Skin-Mart as the next girl.

"Skin is in," my friends remind me, parroting a recently aired advertisement. Tempting me into going along with the fashion. It's a hard slogan to argue with, seeing as I'm the only one in our crowd who hasn't given in to getting an F&G (flaying and grafting) even once. Many of the girls I graduated Beckettville High with have patronized Skin-Mart more than three times in the past year.

There's a rumor that shopping at Skin-Mart is addictive (after all, some girls have reported "getting off" on the pain of having the old epidermis removed and replaced). But I think the frequent purchases have more to do with the way the skin gets, well, *damaged* sometimes. The domestic violence shelter says wife-beating prosecutions have much declined since Skin-Mart came to town. The evidence of injury disappears too readily, they claim. I suspect they're onto something, because it's not unusual to see a gentleman escort a lady with a black eye or bruised throat into the store, presumably to rid himself and polite society of the evidence of his misdeed.

Distributors furnish Skin-Mart with a wide variety of products from throughout the world. Black skins ("Made in Nigeria"), brown skins ("Made in Chiapas, Mexico"), yellow skins ("Made in China"). Perhaps they mistake the outlet mall for a true, vibrant center of commerce that attracts traffic off the Interstate, and therefore a more worldly clientele. As it is, foreign skins remain on the racks collecting dust. No one in this part of the world wants them. In fact, my friend Mindy swears she saw some of the blacks from down in Jeffersonville drive up one day to get F&Ged into white skins. She tells me this as if it was a point in Skin-Mart's favor. "It's a miracle," Mindy says. "It's not their fault they're black. Everyone *should* have the right to be white, and now they *do!*"

I remain unconvinced that Mindy really saw what she said she saw (and if she did, I'm even less convinced that it was for the best). That's the thing about Skin-Mart, all of us see different things there. Take the peculiar salesgirl, for example.

Some of my friends say they've never even heard of her, while others say they're all too familiar with her.

I can tell which of my friends have really seen her (instead of just humoring me and *claiming* they've seen her) by their inability to look me in the eye when they talk about her. Sometimes there's a quiver in their voice, too. They tell me that if I would only take the proper precautions, knowing just what sort of skin I want *before* going into the store, I would never have to worry about the peculiar salesgirl. The trick, they say, is to get in, make your selection, and then go get F&Ged. Don't dawdle.

If you linger too long, the staff at Skin-Mart will think that you want to buy something special order. Something for those with *peculiar* tastes. That's when they dispatch the *peculiar* salesgirl.

You may, at this point, rightly ask *what* is so damned peculiar about her. The answer is . . . everything. She is, for one thing, too tall. Well over six feet. Her height is not graceful nor statuesque. It gives her, rather, the appearance of a scarecrow. There is something too soft, almost molten about her skin—as if, perhaps, she started out as a customer of the store (many times over) and ended up as staff. She is clumsy. Awkward. Hunched over at an angle much more fitting a ninety-two-year-old than someone of her apparent youth (and yet, still, she towers over me). It's almost as though walking on all fours is her natural posture, and she only maintains a bipedal stance with some effort.

But the most peculiar thing about this particular salesgirl is that she isn't from around here. No one knows her, personally. No one knows her kin, either. There's some suspicion (among those who acknowledge her existence) that she moved here from Skin-Mart's home offices; or, at least, from a larger store.

When the peculiar salesgirl finds you, she takes an interest—a clumsy, too-eager interest, "You, miss, look like a discerning customer," she says to me each time she sees me. "I reckon I've done seen you here at least a half-dozen times before, but I haven't yet seen you make a purchase."

"Oh," I say (shuddering), "I'm sorry, I can leave if you'd like."

"Oh, no, no," she says. "You're all right, babygirl." There's something about her demeanor that distresses me; the way, perhaps, she tries to take on the local accent and vernacular. It's awkward. She's trying too hard to sound like a country girl and it's clear to anyone with half a brain that she's not. "It just strikes me that you haven't yet found the right product. You might-could be better served by perusing our back room. It's for those with more *sophisticated* tastes."

This is the point in the conversation at which I demur. "No," I say, "that's quite all right. For now, I just want to browse."

She doesn't take rejection easily. I see an emotion (sadness? frustration?) creep onto her otherwise emotionless face. I begin to wonder if she might not work on commission. But that is *her* problem, I tell myself, *not mine*. Most of the times I've had an encounter with the peculiar salesgirl, it ends right there. She leaves, disappointed, and I get the hell out of there. But not today.

Today I start to leave and she scurries—almost *jogging*— to the back room. She comes back with three skins wrapped over her forearm. She is tall enough that they don't drag on the floor.

There's something wrong with them. They look jaundiced. They're dotted by scars, sores, or growths of undetermined origin. There's a liquid seeping from the skins, dampening the peculiar salesgirl's pantsuit. It reminds me of the way my grandmother's bed sore weeped when she was dying of lung cancer. One of the skins looks charred. Another looks as though it boasts an unnatural plethora of appendages.

I have no poker face. I cringe.

"You don't understand," she says. "Skin is in." She points to a duo of far-less-peculiar salesgirls—locals who I remember from Beckettville High—hanging a banner printed with that very slogan. It's a slick piece of promotion that bears the pedigree of corporate PR (and, thus, seems odd when juxtaposed against the general atmosphere of rural decay in which the store is suffused). They look like soldiers raising a flag over conquered territory.

In that moment, I reflect on some of the arguments used to counter the criticism Skin-Mart gets when it moves into small towns and displaces mom-and-pop businesses. "What alternative is there?" the store's boosters sometimes ask. "Who else is going to come into towns like this one and hire unskilled labor?" I look at the two girls hanging the banner. They're missing at least three teeth between them, but smile anyway. They have wages, two fifteen-minute breaks, and a half-hour lunch. Their kids' fathers came into town on a tractor trailer and left the same way. No forwarding addresses. No child support or promise of it coming.

Skin-Mart puts food on the table.

Skin-Mart is closed on major holidays. Skin-Mart obeys laws pertaining to the minimum wage. One imagines that the employee lounge at Skin-Mart is adorned with all the announcements the Occupational Safety and Health Administration requires Skin-Mart to post there.

Skin-Mart provides opportunities for moving up in the world. If the girls work hard enough, one of them might, in time, find herself promoted to assistant manager. I contrast this with my suspicions of what their lives would be like without their jobs. Would they have to resort to working at an adult bookstore and doing, well, *what you know girls have to do there* to make ends meet?

Despite my wish to support the local economy, I can't quite find it in myself to buy what the peculiar salesgirl is selling. I look at her selections from the back room and shake my head. "No thanks," I say.

Her eyes widen. Her garishly painted lips contort and she lets out a snarl. I see (for the first time, in any detail) her jagged, too-small, coffee-stained teeth. Her face is flushing and she's clinching her fists. She huffs, and the congestion in her throat gurgles. It takes her much coughing to clear it, and when she does she lets out a single high-pitched, raspy word that sounds a little too much like a dog's growl. "Dyyyke . . ."

An accusation that cuts to the quick. Not the first time I've heard it, but somehow this time it hurts more than ever. It's one thing for my old high school friends to toss around such an epithet when remarking on my change in hairstyle or lack of interest in fashion; it's quite another to hear it snarled by a relative stranger like the peculiar salesgirl. For some reason, the accusation takes on additional weight coming from a representative of Skin-Mart. From a representative of a *corporation*. For some reason, she strikes me as an authority figure who knows what she's talking about.

She takes a deep, wheezing breath, then growls once

more. "Mannish dyyykkkkeeeee!"

I scramble to rebut her claim. My heart beats like the hooves of a Kentucky Derby racehorse, and I begin to sweat. The racks of skins seem to hover over me like high stalks of corn in late August. I must convince her she's wrong. I must prove I'm not what she says I am—that I'm every bit as feminine as any other nineteen-year-old.

I find all my anti-Skin-Mart principles cast aside in self-defense. "Don't misunderstand me," I say. "I'm a girly-girl, just like all my friends. I just let myself get a little hippie-chick in my first year of college." I stammer. "I-it was just a phase. But don't worry, today's the day that I will get F&Ged. It's just . . . I think I'll start with something less—well, less *severe*. Do you have any skins that are pre-tanned, with tattoos and piercings?"

Just as swiftly as anger overtook her, it leaves. Her demeanor isn't what I'd call cordial, but it at least retreats from the prior hostility. She looks at me with a condescension she's probably cast toward hundreds of other girls my age. "Our most popular item. I don't handle those jobs. But if you wait until Bobbie Sue is finished hanging that banner, I'm sure she'll be able to assist you." Then off to the back room she goes.

The flaying hurts. The grafting hurts. The only thing I can compare it to is the time I lost most of my right thumbnail. Imagine that, but about ten times more painful, all over your body.

But when I see the excitement on my friends' faces afterward and then hear the approving honks of men in passing cars in the parking lot, I feel (for once) included. More so than I ever did up at college in Chicago. In the days after that first F&Ging my friends and I share all kinds of fun. Nights out at the bar. Trips to the hair and nail salon.

I consider transferring to Clark County Community College. I could study there with my friends. The only thing that stops me is a large envelope I receive in the mail one hot, hung-over morning in late-July, postmarked Chicago.

It's from the Chicagoland Chamber of Commerce. A letter tells me that Chicago looks forward to seeing me (and all the other college students) again for the fall semester, and encourages me to patronize local businesses. Enclosed with the letter, I find coupons and sales circulars of various degrees of glossiness. One (the glossiest of them all) announces the arrival of a new Skin-Mart opening in late August in a strip mall adjacent to campus. Perhaps there's a new pool of cheap labor available to staff the store, now that the college let go some of its cafeteria and janitorial staff. Or maybe that pool of cheap labor comes from recent graduates who haven't been able to find a job in their field quite yet.

Or maybe the city just isn't as different from the country as it's made out to be.

"Skin Is In!" the announcement declares.

I know that the Chicago Skin-Mart will have my patronage. I know too (somehow) that I will never see the peculiar salesgirl again. Her work with me is done.

# Non Evidens

**W**hen they did the sonogram and there wasn't even the vaguest fetal blob to show for it, Janet assumed the doctor had been mistaken. The missed period, the tenderness in her breasts— perhaps they were psychosomatic. Perhaps her body knew that her mind wanted a baby, and so tried to go through the motions.

"No," the doctor said, pointing to a grainy black-and-white image on his computer, "if you look right there, you'll see the umbilical cord. Your mind can't conjure *that* out of nothing! I suspect this is merely a case of *fetus non evidens*. Extremely rare, of course, but more likely in women like you, that is, approaching forty."

"*Non evidens?*"

"You're carrying an invisible baby. This means we'll need more frequent prenatal visits, of course. We'll have to do certain tests that will take a gander at the little tyke indirectly, through studying the movement of the amniotic fluid *around* the fetus. But it's nothing to be alarmed about."

"Nothing to be alarmed about!"

"Mrs. Pruitt, let me assure you that hundreds of mothers in the United States alone are raising *non evidens* kids. There are support groups, there are—"

But she couldn't listen to it. Tears welled up; she felt a lump in her throat. She wanted to break down and sob, but she wouldn't permit herself to do so in public. What would the doctor think of her if she had a breakdown right then and there? What would all the young, radiant women in the waiting room think? Janet thought they'd think something like this: *That poor, older lady must have just been told about a birth defect.*

Janet spent a lot of time guessing what other people thought (not just there at the doctor's office, but at the grocery store, the gas station, and at her cubicle). She suspected *lots* of people all across town looked down their noses at her, but that didn't make it any easier to bear the *particular* criticism of those who had a better knack than she for this pregnancy stuff. So she walked briskly out of the doctor's office without saying a word, ignoring his calls after her. Her shoes clip-clopped down the shiny linoleum tile of the hallway, into the lobby, and out the door. She kept her glance downward the entire time to avoid eye contact with everyone in the waiting room.

It wasn't until she shut the car door that she allowed herself to mourn the loss of visible offspring. "A freak . . ." she muttered to herself mid-crying-jag. "They'll stare at us!" She dreaded the oddity of the prospect. She'd be pushing a stroller that would, to all outside appearances, look empty except for a onesie and some blankets and people would still, no doubt, *stare* (even though there would be literally nothing at which *to* stare).

She let herself give in to the emotions for about five minutes, then dried her eyes before driving home. The word *freak* still echoed through the nooks and crannies of her brain. It took on a life of its own up there.

She waited until Greg was reading in bed to tell him the bad news. He was perusing the catalog of a company that sold model trains and accessories. He had a small set down in their basement, which he always wanted to expand but could never afford to.

"I went to the doctor today," Janet finally blurted out. "He says I'm pregnant with a monster."

Janet's husband's mouth dropped open. Words eventually skittered out. "Honey, you mean we did it? We're really preg—"

"What part of 'with a monster' did you not understand?"

He placed his hand on her belly. He grimaced. "No. You mean something's wrong?"

"The baby . . . well . . . it didn't show up on the sonogram."

He shook his head, pursed his lips. "Hrmm?"

"I'm carrying a *fetus non evidens*."

"What in blazes does that mean?"

"An invisible baby, that's what. A monster, straight from an old horror movie. A zygote-Claude-Rains."

"You're assuming it's a boy," Greg said. The corners of his mouth crinkled in a little smile. "It could always be a little girl. I was sort of imagining we'd have a girl, for some reason. Anyway . . . wow. Just. Wow."

"I know we've been trying so hard, honey. But do you

think this is worth, well, *continuing*?"

"How far along did the doc say you were?"

"Eight weeks."

"Wow," Greg said. "Just . . . *wow*."

"I just want the best, you know. And invisible isn't the best."

"But what if we try again and invisible is *our* best? I mean, I'm not saying I *want* an invisible baby, but if that's what we end up with, well, I could certainly love the child."

Janet cringed, as all the implications became more apparent to her. "We wouldn't have baby pictures. We couldn't watch over it at night to make sure it was still breathing. And what if it gets the measles some day? There'd be no way to tell."

Greg sighed. "I don't know what to say, hon, except that I love you and I want us to have a family together. But I don't want you to carry a pregnancy you're not one hundred percent happy with. Why not take some time to think it over? Maybe go to a therapist and talk over the pros and cons. We can go together, if you want. I'll even call to make the first appointment."

Janet mulled it over for a moment. *Yes,* she thought, *let Greg go about doing that. That'll keep him busy.* She told him she'd mull over her options.

Then, the next morning, instead of going to work she went to the nearest abortion clinic. She felt bad for misleading her husband, but felt even worse when she saw the protesters outside. Did she recognize one of them? Was that the lady from two doors down? The one who sold her Avon? She decided to drive past. She even honked her car horn, as requested by their signs, pantomiming support for their cause. She tried to make eye contact with the lady, who might have been her neighbor, to be sure the gesture hadn't been in vain. Perhaps then her neighbor would recognize her. Think well of her. It was about time *someone* did.

That night after dinner, Greg presented her with a scrap of paper bearing the name of a marriage counselor and the date and time of their first appointment. "We'll talk it over. We'll think this through real good to make the right decision."

So they went to marriage counseling. The counselor tried to focus their attention on what having a family really *meant* to them. All abstractions, never getting down to brass tacks. She went to the sessions every Wednesday at 5:30 P.M. and stayed awake until 11:00 to check the news to see if the clinic was still being protested. Yes, the newscast verified. In fact, the matter had escalated and out-of-state groups from both sides of the argument marshaled forces in what seemed to be a siege to rival that of Leningrad. The rare woman who made it through the ring of protesters had to be accompanied by a gang of counter-protesters. So much for privacy. If she had an abortion, she'd be exposed to her Avon-selling neighbor (if that *was* her neighbor). She *might* be exposed in front of the whole city on TV. This wouldn't do. No, not at all.

Coincidentally, it wasn't long at all into therapy (maybe just the third or fourth week) that she "had a breakthrough" in which she agreed to have the child. "Wow," Greg said. "I never doubted that you'd come around, I just thought it'd take longer. Um, *wow*."

Once they stopped going to counseling, she avoided the subject as much as possible. Eventually, at Greg's prompting, she did return to see her doctor, and he had her undergo another sonogram at twenty weeks. It just confirmed the diagnosis: *fetus non evidens*.

She endeavored to keep the news of the baby's birth defect quiet for as long as possible. It wasn't as if she had many friends to confide in, anyway. But the women in the cubicles surrounding hers felt it necessary to hold her a baby shower, and she indulged them.

One asked her about sonogram pictures. She mumbled something about misplacing them. That certainly caused a stir, and it took some doing to convince them that, really, she was okay waiting until the baby's birth to see it again. "I'm sure if you call the doctor's office," one of her co-workers said, "they'll print another out for you."

Janet nodded. Shrugged. She didn't want to seem like anything other than a jubilant expectant mother, but she could only stretch the act so far. The other ladies in the office would gossip about her all-too-apparent lack of enthusiasm; of that she was sure. But what of it? Nothing positive could come from talking about sonograms.

But moments like these were few and far between. For much of her pregnancy, she found it possible to ignore the problem altogether—to pretend that she was just like any other expectant mother. After all, her belly bulged just as with any other expectant mother. In time, she felt the baby kick as any other expectant mother did.

All that self-deceit ended, though, when her doctor referred her to a specialist, a teratologist. She asked what in the Sam Hill a teratologist was. The doctor didn't say. She looked it up in the dictionary and discovered it was a doctor who specialized in birth defects. The word came from the Greek word *teras* (meaning "monster").

So the normal-doctor sent her to the monster-doctor. She'd known all along that she was carrying a monster. This just confirmed it. She had to drive well over an hour to get to this monster-doctor's office, and she didn't like the anxious, dread-filled waiting room. But there were some good things that came from it. For example, the specialist was able to tell her the fetus' sex. (So meticulous was his study of the flow of amniotic fluid around the various nooks and crannies of her baby's body.)

She was having a girl.

They painted the nursery pink. Some women in the office insisted on holding a second shower, just so they could provide gifts designated for the correct sex. Pink, pink, everywhere pink. It all made the whole thing feel more normal.

As they rounded out the eighth month, she began to worry about the inevitable disclosure. One day, after several months of sullenly and passively accepting whatever care the monster-doc had to offer, she actually decided to confide in him about her worries.

The doctor tried to comfort her. "Mrs. Pruitt, let me assure you that hundreds of mothers in the United States alone are raising *non evidens* kids. There are support groups, there are—"

If she wanted to hear that, she could have stayed with the normal-doc. She interrupted him. "This invisible kid thing. It's just—how can I say this?—it's not an option."

"Well, you know . . . there are cases. A *small number of cases*, mind you, where *non evidens* kids grow out of it. In an even smaller number of cases, the children oscillate between stages of being *evidens* and being *non evidens*. I mention that just to inform you that there is a *possibility* that you'll see your child some day."

"But you're saying that these things only happen rarely."

"Yes, ma'am, that's what I'm saying. They're rare— but, I should add, not unheard of. The data we have on the course of this condition suggest that there's a twenty percent chance of it going either into sustained remission or this sort of oscillating remission I mentioned. Both variations from the usual prognosis typically emerge around puberty. Seems as if there's some metabolic changes in the body around that time that throw the disorder a curve ball."

"You said only a twenty percent chance?"

"Yes, ma'am."

"And I'd have to wait at least ten years, probably more, to see if that twenty percent pans out?"

"Well, yes, Mrs. Pruitt, that's one way of putting it."

Janet sighed. "Then, like I said, this isn't an option."

"You mean, you want a late-term abortion?"

Mental images of the Avon lady (if that *was* the Avon lady) protesting at the endless clinic-siege flickered through her head. "No, what I guess I mean is . . . there has to be something that can be done. Some sort of intervention. Something?"

"Well," the monster-doc said, "most parents of *non evidens* kids just sprinkle some baby powder on them for the first year or two. Some families jack up the wattage of all the light bulbs in their house so that the kid's shadows are more noticeable. There are all sorts of tricks to keep track of them. When they get older, you can go with various sorts of makeup, too."

"Makeup?"

"Sure," the monster-doc said. "I think I even have some literature here from a man in Indianapolis who specializes in this sort of thing." He handed her a glossy brochure. It had slick color photos of *non evidens* kids of various ethnicities on their graduation day—all of them sporting an obviously fake, overly made-up look more appropriate for embalmed corpses from particularly nasty car wrecks. A close look at the company logo revealed that, indeed, the business was "a subsidiary of Hecht's Home for Funerals."

Janet had many objections to taking this approach, but focused on the least unpleasant. "But . . . I mean . . . surely the makeup would wash off."

"Well, of course . . . that is . . . obviously. It's more the kind of thing you'd do just for a special occasion."

She began weeping (yes, she tried to hold it in, but the pregnancy had eroded her self-control under a tidal wave of hormones). When the monster-doc tried to console her with Kleenex, she took the entire box out of his hands. She whipped out a handful of tissues and presented them back to him. "Here," she said through a stuffy nose, "you'll probably need a couple of these for someone else." Then she walked out of the office with the box and drove home.

She spent the night on the Internet, barraging search engines with any one of a hundred variations on "*non evidens* AND." At two in the morning, she came across the website of Max Harper, a plastic surgeon in California. "The *evidens* is in!" the site proclaimed. "Children should be seen, not just heard!"

The more Janet read, the more she liked. Dr. Harper's artist would draw a composite sketch of what your child *should* look like, based on the most attractive outcome of mixing the parents' features. He'd use computer scans to create a plastic mold matching this sketch, from which an incredibly lifelike skin could be manufactured, to be worn as a tight-fitting suit over top of the actual skin. The child could wear it for days, weeks even, before it would need to be washed. It even had a degree of elasticity to allow for the growth process, and if you purchased a lifetime contract they would periodically adjust the skin to reflect the maturing of features. Once the child got old enough, colored contact lenses could be used to complete the anatomical ensemble.

She woke Greg up. Fetched his glasses for him, put them onto his face, and pointed at the screen. "Look," she commanded.

It took a while for him to clear the cobwebs. "What's wrong? What's wrong?" he said. He kept repeating "What's wrong?" right up to the point he seemed to get what she was driving at. "You woke me up for this? I thought you were going into labor!"

"I'm not due for another two weeks."

"You damned sure could go early. It happens."

"I won't *let* that happen," Janet said. "This baby isn't coming out of my womb until I have a way to fix it."

"I'm going back to sleep. You're obsessed!"

"You're not even paying attention to the pictures. Take a look at those before and after shots!" The before pictures showed *non evidens* kids adorned with inferior treatments, like baby powder or makeup. *Pathetic*, Janet thought. In the afters, the children were practically normal. Hell, better than normal. Downright telegenic.

Greg took off his glasses, rubbed some sleep from his eyes, replaced the glasses, and studied the screen. "Jesus. This has to cost . . ."

"We have a house, Greg. We can always take out a second mortgage. You could always take a second job. This is our child's *appearance* we're talking about! I can't believe you're making price an issue."

"We're cubicle-monkeys, honey. We're not poor, but we're not rich either. We get by. This—this is just . . ."

"Look," Janet said. "We're only going to need $5,000 to book a consultation."

"Sheesh. Doesn't insurance cover any of this?"

"An initial fitting at delivery is only $50,000. We could come up with it. We have credit cards. We could sell the house, probably in a matter of weeks, for that."

"Wow," Greg said. "Just . . . wow. I can't believe you'd suggest that. Our home is worth three times that much."

"And how much is your baby's happiness worth, Greg? Have you thought about that? Do you want your baby to have to be seen by a *teratologist* because it's a *teras*? Or do you want her to have a decent appearance?"

Greg frowned. Hung his head. "Wow," he said. "We're really gonna sell this place, eh? Just . . . man . . . *wow.*"

They named the baby Harper, after the plastic surgeon. They'd gone to California for the delivery. Special heat-sensing contraptions were arranged so that the doctor could tell how much of the newborn had made it through the birth canal. (Indeed, delivery itself was the most perilous aspect of a *non evidens* pregnancy.) The baby made it through, though, with flying colors.

For Janet, this was one of the oddest moments of her life. The agony of pushing through all that concentrated pressure sure felt excruciatingly real, but the end result seemed to imply it had all been in her head. No writhing baby. Just the infant's shrieks, telltale splatters of newborn-gunk everywhere, and an empty space in the medical staff's arms where she surmised they held her.

At least she had the shrieks. She reminded herself of that. When ladies at the office asked what childbirth was like for her, she would have to focus on the auditory—or else make up a story of what it was like to *see* her child for the first time, extrapolating from having seen such events dramatized on television.

The obstetrician and the nurses cut the cord and put the baby in an incubator for special monitoring. "But the visible skin! My baby needs her visible skin!"

"All in due time, ma'am," one of the nurses said. "Doctor Harper usually doesn't put the skin on until the second or third day."

She scowled. "Then take it out of here. Don't bring it back until it's good and ready!"

"As you wish, ma'am," another nurse said.

She tried to keep as stoned as possible on the painkillers until her baby was rendered normal. After the plastic skin was applied, she held her. *So this*, she thought, *is what the big deal is all about.* The plastic felt cold on her breast as she tried to get Harper to latch on to feed. She didn't like how there was nothing but shadowy hollows where the baby's eyes should have been. She couldn't wait until she got old enough for cosmetic contacts that would provide the illusion of visible pupils, irises, and scleras. She asked the nurse about it, and she said some moms were able to train their kids to handle them as early as four.

Janet convinced the plastic surgeon to let her try them when Harper was three and a half. The kiddo *needed* them, after all. She couldn't expect her daughter to go off to preschool without them and creep everyone out with those vacant eye-sockets. And her daughter *needed* to go to preschool. Ever since the birth, Greg had to work two jobs to support them, while she stayed home full time with the kid. They weren't able to afford a very nice place yet. Everything was so much more expensive in California than it had been in the Midwest. Janet reminded herself that it was all worth it, though, to be this close to Dr.

Harper in the event the girl fell on the sidewalk or encountered some other catastrophe that tore her skin.

The contacts gave Harper blue eyes, just like her dad. They were the final piece of the puzzle. They completed the look. They made the little girl normal. Janet explained this to Harper over and over, but the toddler somehow still had the insolence to lose the contacts, accidentally tear them, or ruin them trying (for some reason apparent only to the three-year-old brain) to put them in the eyes of the stray cat they'd taken in. This was a problem.

Janet thought through her options. Preschool was out of the question. What could she do—drop Harper off in the morning wearing contacts, then come to pick her up and find the girl had blinked them out, revealing empty spaces instead of blue eyes? But another income was needed. Pronto. She had to find child care so she could get to work.

One afternoon Greg came home for his usual two-hour break between his first and second jobs and made an announcement she never thought she'd hear. "I, um, left work a little early, honey, to swing by the food stamp office. I have some papers to fill out. Wow, I just, you know, didn't think our family would turn out this way."

It had been four solid years of adversity for Greg and Janet. Four years, Janet told herself, without much of a break. Their luck had to change—and it did. It started in a rather unpromising way. Harper had put her contact lenses in the cat's eyes again, necessitating yet another trip to the veterinarian that they couldn't afford. While Janet and Harper sat in the vet's waiting room (the cat tucked away in a carrier, yowling his head off), a lady with dreadlocks and a fashionable leather purse made conversation. She'd brought with her a dachshund wearing a huge plastic cone around his neck. It stared into the cat caddy, trying to make eye contact. The cat curled into the farthest back corner of the carrier, having none of it.

"Your little girl looks like quite the movie star with those sunglasses on," the lady said. "My goodness, she's . . . she's just *beautiful!*"

Harper beamed.

Janet smiled, grateful that the lady didn't have a clue as to the real reason she'd made her daughter wear shades inside. She nudged Harper. "Did you hear that, sweetie? That nice lady complimented your appearance! What do you say to her?"

"Thannnnk youuuuu," Harper crooned. She flashed an overly dramatic grin.

"Oh my, she does seem to have lost quite a number of teeth, though. Yikes, does she even have *any* choppers in there?"

Janet felt her pulse quicken. The *teeth*. How could she have forgotten them? She'd been isolated for far too long, that's how. Out of practice in carefully thinking through and pre-planning each aspect of Harper's appearance. It never occurred to her that when she went out in public the issue of teeth might come up.

She took it for granted that her daughter's teeth had come in. She'd poked around in her mouth herself, every now and then, when Harper was younger. She'd *felt* them. But she hadn't thought of it in well over a year, and now that was coming back to bite her (so to speak). How could she have been so careless!

"You know," the lady with dreadlocks said, "I'm a casting agent. I need a kid to work in some commercials. One's a public service announcement about child dental care. Your daughter looks like she'd be perfect!"

The cat's yowls increased in frequency and intensity. It was always a nervous wreck when going to the vet anyway — even more so when it had to endure the visit while afflicted with contact lenses that had veered off into the corners of its eyes.

The casting agent frowned. "Awwww . . . poor little puddy tat. Whassa matter with him?"

Janet frantically thought through how to best explain things. "Eye problems. Maybe an infection."

"That's strange," the casting agent said. "I never even knew cats could *get* eye infections."

"I think it's a weird genetic thing," Janet offered, trying to defuse the subject. "Anyway . . . this commercial thing. It pays?"

"Oh yes, of course. I mean, not much. Your daughter isn't a professional actor. But I'm sure she'll do fine and we will, of course, pay her *something*. Tell you what, here's my card. Give me a call and we'll talk specifics."

"I sure will," Janet said.

Then the dachshund was summoned back for its

appointment, followed in short order by Janet's cat getting summoned back for its. The veterinarian wasn't pleased.

"How the hell does your daughter get a hold of contact lenses, anyhow?" He looked at the chart. "This is the third time the cat's been in for this in eighteen months. Your daughter seems . . . well, frankly, ma'am . . . *obsessed* with this."

"It's just a phase," Janet said. "Isn't it, Harper?"

"Uh-huh," Harper said. "Just a face!"

The vet took out a variety of instruments and began his examination with grave earnestness. "Mrs. Pruitt, you might want to have Harper step out to the play area in the lobby for a moment. The receptionist can keep an eye on her. There's some things—well, grown-up things—we have to talk about."

The cat yowled.

Janet walked Harper back to the lobby. She knelt down next to her and whispered in her ear: "Remember, never take your sunglasses off unless Momma says it's okay."

Harper offered an exaggerated nod, indicating she heard and obeyed.

Then Janet walked back to the doctor's office.

"I'm afraid this time is far worse than any of the others. It appears that the contact lenses have lodged in quite a deep recess of the cat's noggin. I think your cat will have to live like this forever. There's no way for me to really *get them out*."

Janet bit her lip. Clenched her fists. "Surely there's *some* way."

The veterinarian gave her an anxious grin. "Well . . . that is, what I mean . . . The only way I can possibly imagine getting them out would be to euthanize the cat, cut it open, and *take* them out."

The cat began yowling more than it ever had before.

"A smart man, doctor. A very smart man, indeed."

"But . . . this is an otherwise healthy cat."

Janet couldn't afford to purchase new contacts from the plastic surgeon's office. She needed those two little discs ASAP. "But surely it would be inhumane to let the creature suffer so, don't you agree, doctor?"

The veterinarian sighed. Arrangements were made. Needles were filled. Lethal injections given. Autopsy instruments employed for a very non-autopsy purpose. The veterinarian only agreed to do all this if Janet paid cash up front, and promised never, ever to darken to the doorway of his office again.

Little Harper waddled toward the cat carrier Janet held in her hand and frowned when she noticed that (aside from a white plastic contact lens case) it was empty. "Where's kitty?" she asked.

"You killed it," Janet said.

The good news was that Harper was an absolute hit in the commercial. The blue contact lenses proved as good as new after getting salvaged from the dead cat's eyes. They just needed an extra day to soak in some solution. The combination of those sparkling blue eyes, telegenic skin, and an apparently toothless mouth wowed the masses, who were used to seeing far less telegenic toothless kids on those commercials. She only earned two hundred dollars for the filming of the dental care PSA, but the job attracted the interest of a talent agent. Janet had wanted there to be another income in the home and now that Harper was acting, there was one.

Greg had objections at first. (Shouldn't Harper be keeping a low profile? What if everyone found out she was a *non evidens* kid? Would she be publicly humiliated?) All these protests evaporated the day he saw his little girl on TV. "That's her . . . oh, gee . . . She's actually there on the screen. Oh man . . . *wow*."

Eventually, they went back to the plastic surgeon and explained their problem with the teeth. "Yikes," he said. "I can't believe we didn't think of that." And in short order he created a fiberglass "dental edifice" that Harper could wear over top of her own invisible teeth. They seemed to fool everyone.

In fact, the edifice expanded Harper's marketability so much beyond the realm of dental care PSAs that she was now working five, six, seven times a week, in all sorts of commercials. It was increasingly difficult to find times to remove her plastic skin, wash it, and give the kiddo's invisible body a bath. Her behavior at bath time didn't make matters any easier. She shrieked whenever Janet revealed the carefully hidden zipper and pulled it down. "I'm really nothing," the little girl said, sobbing. "I'm really, underneath, nothing."

Janet didn't like seeing her daughter cry, of course.

It annoyed her. But she was glad that Harper understood the importance of keeping her skin on. During those tear-filled bath times, Janet would comfort Harper by reminding her that, with her plastic skin on, she was something. *More* than something—an *actress*.

Commercials led to bit parts on sitcoms, which eventually led to the lead on a sitcom. Harper played the role of a plucky orphan who hung out all the time in the lobby of a police station in the hit show *Pigs & Pigtails*. Janet began to worry that millions of viewers would find Harper's performance so convincing that they'd assume she was a real orphan, so she badgered the publicist into getting a puff piece written for *Parents* magazine entitled "The Loving Real-Life Mom Behind America's Favorite TV Orphan."

In less than a year, the family moved out of their lower-middle-class digs and into upper-middle-class-digs. After two years, they lived in a mansion. With the paparazzi stalking Harper at every turn, they couldn't afford the risk of going to the plastic surgeon's office for checkups and skin-maturing-adjustments. So they paid double the usual rate for him to come in and make house calls. Janet had to make certain she gave all the servants the day off on this day, once a year, lest they become aware of Dr. Max Harper's presence in the home and leak the information to *TMZ*.

*Pigs & Pigtails* ran for seven years. After that came the movie deals. Travel to film in Prague, in Vancouver, and, rarely, in New York. Harper blossomed into a stunning young lady. Many a lecherous older man had her eighteenth birthday circled on his calendar, in bright red ink. Her publicist tried to convince her to date one of the several teenage boys she was paired with in the movies, as this would give the tabloids something to talk about, but (to Janet's relief) she always nixed the suggestion.

In the midst of all this, Janet hesitated to give Harper the typical talk about the birds and the bees. She wouldn't have felt comfortable with this even under the most ordinary circumstances, but the *non evidens* thing raised the embarrassment factor exponentially. Take this exchange, for example: Janet's attempt to impress on her daughter the uncouth nature of masturbation after noticing that Harper locked herself away in her room for hours on end. "Don't do it," Janet warned, "it's not ladylike." Harper shrugged and agreed to comply. "I don't feel that much down there, anyway. Not with the skin on, at least."

How could Janet not find this conversation mortifying?

If she didn't have an interest in having grandchildren one day, she might have decided to ask the plastic surgeon to refer Harper to a gynecological surgeon to perform a hysterectomy. But Janet *did* want grandkids, and this meant that she'd have to find a way to convince Harper to lower her expectations in regard to sensation. Or, possibly, to engage in some conversation with the surgeon about how sensitivity might be increased.

Obviously, no mother wants to think of her daughter in *that way*. If she considered it at all, it was in a fleeting manner — associated with the birth of grandchildren. Hopefully, *visible* grandchildren. She reasoned that ordinary sexual functioning had to be *possible*. There was, after all, a special apparatus in the skin that facilitated other, unspeakable functions of the nether regions. The next time the plastic surgeon came for a house call, they'd sit down, like mature adults, and talk about it.

He came to the house as planned, but brought trouble along with him. "This is my son, Pax."

"Beg pardon," Janet said. "Did you say his name was, well, Pax?"

"It's Latin," the young buck said, "for peace." The lad had a strong jaw, a handsome brow, and piercing blue eyes.

"It's take-your-kid-to-work day, and Pax wanted to see what his old man's job was like. Please be assured that he'll keep all this completely confidential."

"I, well, I guess I'll have to trust that now, won't I, doctor."

The plastic surgeon grinned. "You don't have to worry about Pax. He won't blab to the *Enquirer*. He doesn't want anything to do with the limelight. I keep telling him he ought to go into movies. He's had a director or two interested already."

"I don't want to be in movies," Pax said. "The media gets all up in your business."

"Smart guy," Harper said. "A lot of times I don't want to be in movies, either."

Janet let out a clumsy laugh. "You'll have to indulge my daughter in her flights of fancy, doctor. Harper says the craziest things sometimes. I tell her that she can do that here, but outside of this house such statements might be misunderstood. Anyway, I suppose we should be getting down to business. She'll need her yearly adjustment and maturing work done. We also had, well, a sort of private question to ask you. Something that might best be handled without your son around."

"Fair enough. Can we meet in your den? Just the three of us?"

"Just the two of you," Harper said. "I don't want to talk about it. My mom can tell you everything. It's really her question more than mine."

"Not a problem," the plastic surgeon said. "Shall we then, Mrs. Pruitt?"

Janet looked at Pax and Harper smiling at each other. She didn't like it. Smiling led to holding hands. Holding hands led to, well, other things. It felt almost incestuous, the notion of Harper admiring her plastic surgeon's son. Images flashed through her brain. First dates. Second dates. Someday a wedding, and the specter of her daughter taking the boy's last name, going around Los Angeles with the name Harper Harper. She felt the need to nip this in the bud.

Janet glared at her daughter. "Harper, are you quite *sure* you don't want to *join us*?"

Harper rolled her eyes. "I. Am. Sure."

Janet fumed. The girl sassed her. For the first time. Right in front of company. Oh, how she'd pay when the doctor and his son left!

Footfalls pounded on the basement steps. Greg ascended them, coming up to the living room for the first time in many hours. "Oh, hey . . . I didn't think . . . you know . . . think there'd be anyone up here. *Wow* . . . it's a party! I mean, we usually don't hang out in the living room on this day—you know, Harper's house call day."

Janet snapped at him. "What are *you* doing up here?" She quickly realized she might make a scene in front of company. She couldn't let herself seem too strident. "What I mean is, I thought you'd be downstairs with your model trains all day."

"Parts," Greg said. "UPS was supposed to bring parts, you know. Have they . . . well, have they come yet?"

"No dear, I'll let you know when they do."

"All right then, I'll just go back to polishing the tracks

while I'm waiting." He clomped back down the stairs to his man cave.

"Well, Mrs. Pruitt?"

"Yes?"

"You did want to talk, right? I have another appointment back at the office in two hours and you know how traffic is. We need to get things moving."

"Yes," she said. "Of course." They went into the den. Janet explained everything to the plastic surgeon. She emphasized that this was a discussion that didn't have any practical bearing now, but something worth thinking about "down the road . . . a few years from now, after she gets married." The surgeon admitted to her that the sort of skin that had been engineered for Harper maximized realism at the cost of sensation. "There's a trade-off there, I'm afraid. We could have a new suit made, of course—one that enhanced her sense of touch; but it would be, by necessity, thinner—less convincing."

"I see," Janet said. She wouldn't allow Harper to wear anything that might endanger her career. "Well, it sounds like for now we'll just keep things as they are."

"As you wish. Now is that all you want to say to me in private?"

"Yes, of course."

"Okay, then let's bring Harper in."

Janet went to fetch her. The girl came into the room, grinning like the proverbial cat that ate the canary. "What are you so happy about?" Janet said, worried she already knew the answer.

"I have a date tonight."

That night, Janet went down to Greg's man cave. They needed to have a talk. "I'm worried about our little girl."

Greg's blue-and-white-striped conductor's hat wobbled around his head as he followed the course of his Lionel Super Chief. "Well, yeah, I think any parent would be worried on a first date. But he's, like—what?—the plastic surgeon's son? So, um, *yeah*. Wow, you don't have to worry about this being some guy who's just after her for her money, y'know?"

"She's going to want to *feel* something, honey. That

means she's going to want to take off her suit."

Greg flicked a switch, and the train switched tracks. "But the boy came here with his dad. I mean, well . . . I guess . . . he knows why his dad was here."

"It was a violation of our privacy rights. Doctor Harper should never have been able to bring the boy here. I could sue him for that."

"Well, in that case you'd be, I mean—sheesh, we'd all be—in the news, yanno? *Wow*, you'd really want that?"

"Well . . . I could *threaten* to sue and see if his lawyers capitulated, just to teach him a lesson."

"Wow, you'd really do that? I mean—seriously alienate the one doctor equipped to take care of her skin? Just—oh my God—*wow*."

Her husband, for the first time, had won an argument.

Harper started dating Pax when she was seventeen. Under the boy's influence, she became increasingly rebellious. Curfews came and went unheeded. Outfits that had left home perfectly draping Harper's increasingly curvy frame came back in the door with a rumpled, disheveled look suggestive of a roll in the hay.

Worst of all, she began to refuse to do movies.

Janet saw the writing on the wall. She was losing her hold on the girl, and the boy was gaining a hold on her. She went down to Greg's man cave one day to commiserate about it. Ordinarily, she couldn't stand the racket of dozens of trains chugging along a football-field-size collection of tracks, but she needed to vent.

Greg didn't hear her approach, and so she had to tap him on the shoulder. He was so severely startled that he almost lost his conductor's cap, then flicked a switch to turn off the trains so he could hear her.

Janet decided she'd better not pussyfoot when it came to this topic. She needed to start off the conversation with a hook to snag Greg's interest. "How," she asked, "are you going to pay for all this when your little girl leaves the house at eighteen?"

"Wow," Greg said. "You know, that is . . . we have savings, y'know? Put some money away."

"It's all hers at eighteen. She could cut us out completely and give it all to that boy."

"We'll just talk to her, I guess. I mean. Yeah. She's not eighteen yet. So, really, there's nothing she can *do*."

"But it's only months until then."

"Yeah . . . um . . . we'll talk to her. Yanno? Just ask if we can have some money." He turned the trains back on.

Janet gritted her teeth and tapped Greg's shoulder again. He flicked the switch to stop the trains. He trembled. "You really want to keep yammering about this, huh?"

Janet gasped. ("Yammering"?)

"Look, my goal is for the Super Chief to make five thousand laps today. It's only made four thousand and there's less than three hours left before midnight. So, yanno . . . just . . . well . . . get out and leave me alone." He flicked the switch to start the trains up again. Pulled the conductor's hat over his eyes.

Janet marched out of the basement. Even though the route was familiar, she almost lost her way, so clouded was her vision with tears.

Somehow, Janet's personal cell phone number had gotten leaked to the tabloids. Two weeks before Harper's eighteenth birthday, they called Janet asking for remarks on Harper's imminent early retirement from the motion picture industry. The little bitch must have released a statement to that effect without consulting her!

"No comment," Janet said, over and over again. It was the first time since she'd been in L.A. that she actually *dreaded* the specter of media attention. She felt like the world's worst mother. She had to confess to herself that, for the past several days, she didn't even know where Harper *was*. She tried calling the girl over and over, and always the call went to voicemail.

She had to tolerate news footage of man-on-the-street interviews with fellows old enough to be Harper's father, all of them confessing their attraction for the "healthy-looking" young lady. For two weeks, it was nothing but "Harper this," "Harper that." Harper on the cover of a tabloid. Harper on the cover of a slick entertainment magazine. The entire media seemed to be doing nothing at all except harping on Harper.

Then came the day itself. The eighteenth anniversary of

that day with all the heat-imaging devices and the sounds-but-not-sights and the asking them to take the baby away until it had fake skin on. The paparazzi had the mansion surrounded, anticipating there would be a blow-out birthday party.

But nothing happened. Not even a trace of Harper. Not until that night, when Janet got this email:

*Dear Mom,*

*I'm coming by tomorrow to get some of my things and say goodbye. Today would have been just too crazy, with all the media. But I hear that another coked-up celebrity just bit the dust, so they'll all be covering that now. I'm old news.*

*Sincerely,*
*H. I. Pruitt*

She was "H. I." now, eh? Harper Isabella Pruitt. H.I.P. Janet pondered for a moment why she hadn't thought of leveraging the initials into some sort of catchy marketing phrase. Such were the lost opportunities, the regrets of parenting.

There were no paparazzi in sight at ten A.M. the following day, when the doorbell rang. Janet opened it and found Harper and Pax on the other side. They'd brought a U-Haul. Janet shook her head. Really, they should have hired *assistants* to do this.

"Well," Harper said, "I guess this is goodbye."

Janet scowled. "Just remember, when the world gets brutal and nasty to you—and mark my words, you little hussy, it will—you can always come running home to Mom."

Harper ignored her. Pax brought in boxes. They went to Harper's room and began packing, closing the door behind them. For ten minutes, Janet heard the muffled sounds of coat hangers clanging, zippers unzipping, dull thuds against cardboard.

"The world doesn't like people like you," Janet said through the door. "It will be scary, it will be—"

The door opened. Pax stood on the other side, alongside Harper's skin-suit—which appeared to levitate in mid-air. "This isn't mine," Harper's disembodied voice said. Then, abruptly, something—no, some*one*: an *invisible* someone—shoved the skin-suit toward Janet. "It belongs to you. You purchased it. You wanted it. You never asked me what I thought. That goes for these, too." Invisible Harper piled two plastic cases on top of the skin that now hung limp and lifeless in Janet's arms: one case contained the latest pair of contacts, the other the dental edifice.

Janet snarled. "Why, you ungrateful little bitch!" She let the cosmetic equipment fall to the floor, took the flat of her hand and swatted in the air, trying to slap her daughter right in the face. She missed, and Harper giggled. Pax moved forward, out of the room. "C'mon, H. I., let's make tracks."

"And *you*," Janet said to Pax. "I can't believe that *you'd* allow yourself to be associated with—with this *freak*. What's *wrong* with you that you find an invisible girl attractive?"

"Maybe it's the way her hips feel in my hands when I'm dancing with her," Pax said. "Or maybe it's the soft smoothness of her legs. But honestly, I think it has something to do with the fact that I'm *non evidens*, too. The oscillating type. Why do you think my dad went into a specialty with such a limited clientele? He wanted to help kids like me blend in. But I like to think that if he knew how far some parents would take it, he never would have invented the suits."

"Yesterday we didn't want to come because it was Pax's *non evidens* day," the Harper-monster said. "Today he's *evidens*. It helps that he's visible fifty percent of the time; like, when we want to run errands and that kind of thing. Most people still haven't adjusted to the notion that there are some cars on the freeway that will look as if no one's behind the wheel. We try not to alarm people—especially on the highway. That could be dangerous."

"Yeah," Pax said. "We don't want to alarm people, but we don't want to apologize for our lives either. We just want to be ourselves, and H. I. can't do that here, Mrs. Pruitt. At least, not now. We hope someday you'll change."

And then the two of them started taking boxes out.

Janet began desperately scrolling through her options to rescue victory from the jaws of defeat. "Your father!" she said. "Your father will be *quite* disappointed that you're leaving without saying goodbye to him. You should go down to the basement and see him."

"I'll just catch him on Skype," the Harper-monster said. "That's how we've been keeping in touch the last few months."

Janet fumed. She went downstairs to give Greg a good

tongue-lashing. How *dare* he keep secrets from her! He was in the middle of talking to a couple of men in suits. "Oh, um, hey this is uh—my wife."

One of the men in suits, a bald man with a goatee, extended his hand. "Ah, so this is *Mrs.* Railroad Fanatic, eh?"

Janet didn't understand what was happening. "Beg pardon?"

"I made it, honey!" Greg said. "I, um, now have the world record for—you know, most, um, revolutions of a toy train around a track in a single day! I, um, *wow* . . . I mean, I thought I told you about this earlier."

"You won't mind if we get your husband out of your hair for a few months, will you, Mrs. Pruitt? We at Guinness World Records would like to take his toy trains on the road: we're making a tour of children's hospitals! Just think how many kids your husband will be making happy!"

"He's . . . leaving?"

Greg played with his cap nervously. Rubbed his three-day growth of beard-stubble. "Well, um . . . you know, with H. I. on her way out of the house and everything, I just thought . . . well, you know . . ."

*H. I.?* "Fine," she said. "Leave me. I'll be fine here all by myself."

"Oh, wow . . . just *wow*, that's good to hear. Okay, then, I just gotta go talk to these guys for a bit longer about the details, yanno?"

"But—"

The three men started talking again. Janet walked back upstairs.

In a few days, Greg and his trains were out the door, destined to entertain gaggles of waifs and guttersnipes. Janet guessed he was too good to entertain his wife anymore. Too good to entertain *anyone* anymore, unless there was a goddamned camera rolling.

After the toy train tour, Greg didn't come back home. *Must have finally found a way to gather shekels,* Janet mused. She let him go.

For many years, Janet lived alone in the mansion. Maids and assistants left, in a slow trickle. But the bills always got paid. It seems that the invisible-Harper-thing wasn't *completely* heartless. She made some provision for the woman who had sacrificed so much for her. She probably looked down her nose at her whenever she wrote the checks to the electric company and so forth, but at least she wrote them.

Years passed without any real contact between the two of them, and Janet began to grieve the loss less and less. This new entity, this so-called "H. I.," was just a phantom. Just a cruel ghost who decided she could no longer inhabit the precious skin Janet had scrimped and saved to purchase for her.

*The skin* was the important thing. One day, when she let her thoughts drift toward the subject, when she let herself feel some flicker of sadness, she reminded herself that she still had *that*. She'd wrapped the plastic skin in a plastic bag and kept it in the hope chest that still lingered in her daughter's old room. *"Yes,"* Janet repeated to herself, aloud, "I still have the *skin!"*

This notion energized her in a way she hadn't been energized for years. For the first time in what seemed like an eternity, she left the house to go somewhere other than the grocery store—Home Depot, to be exact. She purchased two large bags of sawdust there and had a nice man carry them out to her aging Cadillac. When he asked her, in the course of making small talk, what she planned to do with them, she told him she was planning to use them as a remedy, to make her sick daughter well. He gave her a strange look and walked away without saying another word.

Some months after the trip to the Home Depot, a journalist called and asked her if she had any comment about the tell-all book written by her daughter, H. I. Was she aware that the young lady had painted an unflattering portrait of her? Was she aware that H. I. Pruitt had become one of the first celebrities in the world to come out as *non evidens?* Was she aware that she was starting a foundation to help *non evidens* kids? That she was becoming an advocate for the cause?

"There must be some mistake," Janet said. "My daughter's name is *Harper* and she lives here with me. She's never felt the need to leave home. Each day we have a mother-daughter brunch in the sun room. Each night we have drinks out on the veranda. She's a beautiful girl, my daughter. Hasn't aged a bit since her eighteenth birthday. She's the loveliest girl I've ever seen."

# THE SQUATTERS

I have every right to get rid of the squatters.

I'm the sheriff of Conowingo County, Indiana. Just that, in and of itself, should be enough to grant me the authority to do the job. But if *that's* not enough, I'm also the man who owns the particular tract of land in question: the ugly, vine-smothered place called Orescular Island.

It's not an actual island. Just a mile-long stretch of land jutting out into the Ohio River, about forty-five minutes southwest of Cincinnati. A peninsula. But folks around these parts don't know a peninsula from penicillin, so they call it an island. It's a fucked-up place to find squatters. There's not even a house on Orescular Island to squat *in*. Just an old barn, left over from God-knows-when. And even that has a collapsed roof. Even that has succumbed to the vines.

I'm no horticulturalist. I can't tell you what the fuck that vine is. I know it's not kudzu because, A. I don't think kudzu has *quite* worked its way this far north yet, and B. I Googled "kudzu" and the picture doesn't match. But whatever it is, it's aggressive. Creepy, too. Green and gray and brown. Grows all over the ground and all over the trees and then all over *itself* in tufts and mounds. I always tell myself I'm going to make a clearing, but Mother Nature works at Orescular Island year round and I'm only there a few weekends during the summer. Whenever I try to cut some of it out, it grows back within a month. I'm no glutton for punishment, so I leave it as is.

Now I know why the land was so cheap. It wasn't that the seller was sucking up to me; it's that he knew it wasn't worth a damn. I think the moon's more hospitable. That's probably why my ex-wife let me keep it in the divorce, too.

It makes no fucking sense for someone to squat there.

But people—I swear to Jesus—people *on the other shore*, in Kentucky, spot a campfire on the land and call my cell phone at six in the morning. It's that old couple who spots it, the retirees from Michigan. The ones I drink with a lot in the summertime. The ones who take their boat over to my dock and bring over lots of gin in the summertime. The ones I never usually hear from this time of year.

"There are hippies on your land," the husband says. He has a warble in his voice that makes everything he says sound demented.

"*Homeless* hippies," his wife adds in the background. Her voice is a grating, three-pack-a-day smoker's croak that sounds distant but still distinct. "Pretty lookin' birds," she adds sarcastically. The slurred ess in "birds" tells me all I need to know.

"Probably just hunters," I tell them. "Deer season started a week ago."

"They ain't no hunters," the wife says. They're on speakerphone. "Me personally, I think they're devil worshipers. All prancin' around naked. And one of 'em's a man, covered in thick hair. He lets out loud grunts, like a wild boar. Maybe he's Satan himself. The great hairy goat-man! The other one is a young lady. Over by the campfire, I could see her dancin' and chantin' with the others. I think she worships Satan!"

"The third one, though, that one's the scariest, if you ask me," says the husband.

"That one, it's not man nor woman," says the wife. "It's somewheres in between 'em." She starts giggling. "Both . . . neither . . ."

I think the old couple is pulling a prank on me. Or maybe they're going through hallucinations—senility is bad enough without spiking it with gin. I'm not gonna call them full-blown alcoholics, but they've been known to get weird like this when they've been going for awhile. "How can you tell what these folks look like, from across the river?"

"Because," the husband says, "last night we got out my binoculars and took a gander at 'em. Once, on Jerry Springer, I saw one of 'em—what you call 'em?—Afro-dites? I think that's what the third one is."

"Hermaphrodites," I say, correcting him.

The wife interrupts again. "Jerry Springer said they like to be called 'intersexed' now." She giggles. "Don't want to take the wrong turn at *that* intersextion."

I force out a chuckle. I want to acknowledge their distress but also defuse it. "Look," I say, "let's suppose there *are* hippies out on my property. It doesn't sound like they're doing any harm. Hell, if they're making a campfire it might-could help make a clearing in all those vines."

"Not the sort of response I'd expect from a man in law enforcement," the husband says. That part gets on my nerves. He makes it sound like I'm not doing my job. Living across the river in Kentucky, they aren't, technically, even in my fucking *jurisdiction*, but they want to bitch at me.

"They're making a ruckus," the husband says. "Disturbing the peace. They're not as loud as they were a few hours ago, but they're still going. Kept us up all night. It sure would be nice if you saw to it to at least *investigate*, sheriff."

So, round about nine in the morning, I investigate.

It's November, and there's a ragged, smacking wind along the shore of the Ohio. The sky is the color of suffocation — gray here, blue there. The trees are naked and gaunt.

The vines are dying but not quite dead. Their green is gone. Now they're just gray and brown. Most have dried up and become more brittle than they appeared during the summer. That helps, because I have to tramp though an awful lot of them to get to the campfire. I follow the smoke and the smell of burning wood.

When I arrive, a passed-out, hairy ass greets me. Fella looks like a fucking caveman. He's on his stomach and holding the hand of the hermaphrodite, who's sleeping on his/her/its back. Damn, I've been in law enforcement almost fifteen years now, and I've never seen anything like that before. A tiny dick sittin' on top of labia. Small boobs. A girly face, except for the sunken brow. Mannish hands. Tiny shoulders. The hermaphrodite, in turn, holds hands with a damn sexy-looking young lady. She's on her stomach, showing me her tight little ass and the sides of her tits. Bitch is curvy as all get-out. In her mid-twenties. Brunette. (They're *all* in their mid-twenties and have brown hair, actually.)

I clear my throat.

The hermaphrodite stirs.

"Folks . . ." I say.

The others stir.

"Foe-olks . . ." I say, a little louder, like I'm trying to

call a cat. (In my head, I imagine saying: "Heeere, hippy-hippy-hippy-hippy!" But I don't, because I'm a professional.)

The hermaphrodite wakens. Gasps. Starts to crab walk away from me. Looks at me like I'm a grizzly bear, on its hind legs, about to attack.

"Look, I ain't gonna hurt you, I just need to—"

The man seems bothered when the hermaphrodite's hand slips out of his. He stirs awake. Grunts. The woman seems bothered when the hermaphrodite's hand slips out of *hers*. *She* stirs awake. Whimpers.

"Look, what I mean is . . ."

I see the man's front now. He has a long beard and long hair and his dick's just hanging there—as shamelessly as a bull's. He's grunting louder. Sounds like something's the matter with him. Like he's, well, as we say in this neck of the woods . . . *touched*, or something. The woman is now starting to cry. I mean, for no apparent reason, just starting to bawl. Her pale skin is turning pink and red around her cheeks and forehead.

"Folks, you gotta move . . . I can't let you stay here."

The man grunts louder. The woman cries louder. The hermaphrodite gasps and trembles. I point at him/her/it. "You . . ." I say, "you seem like the calmest one here. You're going to have to leave this land. This is private property. You can't stay here. And you can't just go around naked, either. I'm going to have to arrest you for trespassing and indecent exposure. Where are your clothes?"

Finally the hermaphrodite speaks. A deep voice, husky but a little whiny. "We cannot be banished from this land, officer. We will be here forever."

"Now look, I didn't want to do this, but this situation being what it is . . . What I mean is, if you aren't going to find your clothes and come peacefully I'll have to call for backup."

I get out my cell and call the office. Tell them there's troublemakers out here. I recite the charges and explain that, because of the nature of all that's going on, I'd like at least two deputies on the scene. I request that at least one of them be female, because I don't want the crying girl to say I touched her inappropriately while loading her into the back of my squad car. The deputies bitch and moan about going out this far, because Orescular Island is a hell of a long drive from the county seat. But they do as they're told, because I'm the sheriff.

Procedure says I need to obtain a statement from the suspects, but the man's grunting is getting worse—almost animalistic. And the woman's crying is getting damned near hysterical. So I point to the hermaphrodite and tell him/her/it that we need to have a chat, away from the other two.

"You can't expect me to leave them alone, officer," the hermaphrodite says. "I need to keep an eye on them at all times. There will be terrible consequences if I don't. Far worse than indecent exposure, I can assure you."

At this point I'm just about to lose my patience. I want to slap his/her/its face. I don't do that, though, because I'm a professional.

But I'm not perfect.

And by that I mean I'm human. This is a bit much for me to handle before I've had my third cup of coffee. I don't like the hermaphrodite's tone. Not at all respectful. So I go and grab him/her/it by the wrist. Pull him/her/it out away from the others so we can have a chat.

The man's now howling like a wolf and leering at the woman. The woman's freaking out, trembling.

I pull the hermaphrodite a good twenty feet away, behind a cluster of vine-covered trees, just so we can have a little privacy. There's a struggle all the way. But I need to take a statement, and there's no way I can do it in the middle of chaos. *Someone* has to speak for these weirdos, and the hermaphrodite is, relatively speaking, the only calm candidate.

"You imbecile!" he/she/it hisses.

Then there's a woman's shriek, followed by a long, loud male scream. There's a thud of something heavy landing in something wet. I jog away from the hermaphrodite, back around the trees and their vines, to see what's the matter.

The caveman is heaving a large stone into the woman's face, over and over.

I pull my pistol out of its holster. I scream as loud as I can. Aspire to scream even louder than the caveman. "Stop it now! Drop that rock and put your hands over your head!"

The hermaphrodite lets out a coarse laugh. "I told you so, officer. This is what happens if I'm separated from them. This is what happens. This is what happens. This is what—"

And on the third repetition, the hermaphrodite's voice gets deeper. And the legs grow longer, right before my eyes.

And the shoulders broaden. And the cock gets longer and the labia turn into scrotum and the breasts recede and he/she/it sprouts more body hair. And a beard. And it becomes clear the hermaphrodite is no longer a hermaphrodite.

The hermaphrodite is now a man. I stagger. Whimper. The carotid arteries in my neck are dancing to the pounding beat of my heart.

"When I'm not around to watch them," the gruff voice says, "he kills her. And then the female aspect of *me* dies with her. You're a man of justice, so you know what—regrettably—has to be done next." The once-hermaphrodite-now-man wrestles my pistol out of my grip. It's not hard to do. My palms are sweaty. The gun slips out.

The murderous caveman is still hunched over the dead woman's body. The head is bashed in. Skull bones jut out of the head at odd angles, but he doesn't find the sight unattractive. He's grinning and starting to fuck her. He's so absorbed in his pleasure that he doesn't notice the once-hermaphrodite-now-man's approach. A voice cries out: "This is justice!" And then there's a shot. And there's blood blowing in the wind. And the caveman slumps onto his victim.

The shot wakes me out of my astonishment. There have been two murders—both of which happened after I arrived on the scene. Luckily, no one else saw anything. (Unless the retired couple is watching at the window with their binoculars. *That* prospect doesn't help my nerves any.) I go over to apprehend the shooter, but just as I grab a hold of him, his flesh starts to feel like butter. Mushy. Insubstantial. Then a gust of wind kicks up and tears pieces off of him. They fly into the air, briefly circle around one another like a tornado of flesh, and then dissolve. This process starts at his hairy feet and proceeds upward. When it reaches his hands, the gun falls onto the ground. When it reaches his chest, he shrugs and says: "I was them and they were me. I can't exist without the two of them. But still, we cannot be banished. We will be here forever."

When my backup arrives, the bodies of all three of them are gone.

The hermaphrodite went away in the flesh tornado,

but the other two bodies just . . . faded. It was the damnedest thing. Faded as soon as I heard the squad cars approaching in the distance. There's still a thin wisp of smoke trailing up into the sky from their campfire, though. That assures me I haven't gone mad.

What can I say under these circumstances? I think on my feet. Tell the deputies the suspects have escaped to somewhere else on the island. The retired couple get out on their dock, take their boat over to *my* dock, and insist on giving my deputies their statement. They look badly hung over. "We got woke up by a gunshot," the wife says. There's a cigarette dangling from her mouth. She doesn't bother removing it when she talks. "Figured 'em hippies murdered the sheriff. Hid in the basement until we heard police sirens. Then we figured we'd better come over and testify."

The deputies look at me weird. Ask if I'm all right. Say it looks like I need to sit down. Say I look like I just ran a mile through the desert. I feel my uniform clinging to my back, it's so sweaty.

The deputies search the island, but can't find anyone. I go back to my office and file a report, but it's vague and brief. Part of that stems from necessity. (Clearly, I can't document everything I saw.)

But it's more than that. I have trouble concentrating. The words can't seem to find their way on to paper. I can't seem to pull my mind away from the scene.

Ragged, smacking wind along the shore of the Ohio.

A sky the color of suffocation—gray here, blue there.

Trees—naked and gaunt.

The vines.

Blood blowing in the wind. Dancing through my veins.

The vines.

The caveman smashing open the woman's head, then fucking her.

The hermaphrodite stealing my gun for the execution.

The flesh tornado, the fading.

The vines.

The vines.

The vines. Green and gray and brown. It's November outside but it's May in my brain and the vines are growing and they're twisting around each cauliflower-curve of gray matter and they squeeze all resistance out.

*Go there*, they insist. *Go back.*

So, around one in the afternoon, I go back.

There's been a crazy increase in temperature over the last few hours. A good twenty degrees at least. The thermometer on my dash says it's now sixty-three outside.

When I arrive at Orescular Island, I see that the retired couple's boat is still on my side of the Ohio. Two figures sit on the dock. One is shaggy, the other curvy. I run toward them. I need answers.

The shaggy man raises a glass. "We were hopin' you'd come back out," he says with his warbling voice. He is the old man, but hairier. Heftier. More robust. Moment by moment, his gray turns brown. He smiles and takes a sip of gin.

Even more alarming is the curvy young-old woman. Each moment she grows less frail and more luscious. Time works backwards on her body. Once desiccated, she's now delicious—morphing into a clone of the tight-assed vixen I saw earlier.

She pours some gin in a glass for me. "Care for a drink?"

More than anything, I need a drink. I need many drinks.

And together we drink and we laugh and we talk about how much we enjoy one another's company. Afternoon stretches into evening. As the sun goes down we get on our bellies, on the dock, and look out at the Ohio. And as the sun slips over the horizon we look *down into* the Ohio. And we see one another in the water's reflection, as we really are, for the first time. Caveman. Vixen. Intersexed. And, exceedingly curious about our bodies, we remove our clothes. (They already seem like foreign things—unwelcome chains tethering us to some outrageous time and space.)

And I run my hand over my breasts and down to my tiny penis and labia. And the caveman rubs my rump, and I kiss the curvy maiden. And we roll against each other, on the dock. And the caveman howls. And the maiden lets out yippy little squeals of delight.

Our bodies writhe around one another like vines until we are one. We must be one. A hideous imbalance strikes if we are separated from one another.

We make solemn vows to always stay together. To always stay on this land. To never again let ourselves be separated, under any circumstances. We have every right to dwell in this zone of existence forever. We belong here. We cannot be banished.

# The Mirrors

he day the mirrors took over, you could still see a reflection—it just wasn't yours. It made no difference whether you looked in the bedroom mirror, medicine cabinet mirror, rearview mirror, or sideview mirror. Always, someone else who *wasn't you* stared back (a *different* someone else in each mirror). In many cases, the image in the glass held not even the slightest hint of a resemblance to you. Hair, eyes, nose, weight, skin color—all different. Occasionally, it wasn't even the right gender.

This tormented you, but you said nothing about it to anyone else. You didn't want to sound crazy. Besides, everyone looked so frazzled, you felt certain you'd not find an understanding ear. That day, you almost wet yourself because your coworkers constantly occupied the office's single-stall bathroom.

The second day, you woke up, rubbed the sleep out of your eyes, and lurched toward your bureau to take a glance. You wanted to think the worst was over. You sought to confirm a hunch that reality had just taken a personal day, and had now returned.

But the second day proved even more distressing than the first. At least then, your reflections had all been more or less ordinary human beings. The second day, you looked in the mirror and saw a dummy made out of clay, with hair made out of yarn. Dull, asymmetrical eyes glanced back at you. A drooping mouth drooled. Stubby appendages hung from the torso, more like fins than arms. Worse, the whole thing began to melt. The mirror had concocted a clumsy effigy, not even real enough to scare away crows. You whimpered and put a sheet over it. That made things better until you went to take a shower.

This day, everyone called in sick. The folks on TV called it a flu epidemic, since so many people feigned illness.

It was also the first day the Prophet appeared. The initial reports placed him smack dab in the middle of downtown. The five o'clock news teased you, promising an upcoming feature about him and his robe of tiny mirrors woven together like chain mail. Reporters at the scene tossed around phrases like "mentally ill" and "traffic nuisance" and "coming up next," but the station never broadcast actual photos of the man creating the disturbance. The promised story never materialized. You waited a long time for it, too. Later in the program, the anchors pretended they'd never mentioned it. They weren't quite themselves that day. The male anchor's hair looked too tousled. The female's eyeliner looked as if it had been applied by a fourth grader.

The third day, mirrors stopped working altogether: they reflected everything else *but* you. *So this*, you thought, *is how a vampire must feel*. This posed a problem, of course, as far as preparing for the workday (you only had so much sick time left, you had to make a go of it). But you realized that seeing *nothing* felt better than seeing what you had seen in the mirror the previous two days. You prepared yourself to make the best of it.

It wasn't to be. The governor declared a state of emergency. You couldn't leave your house. You had to stay tuned to the television for further instructions. The governor would read a statement and answer questions at a press conference scheduled for noon. Twelve came and went. Three came and went. It wasn't until after dark that new information became available, but it wasn't the governor who delivered it.

## A PRIVILEGE, NOT A RIGHT

Something wrote those words in a simple, savage script—carved (as if by claws) out of the newly molten surface of your mirror. You turned off the light and hoped the glass would become glass again, that the message-wound would heal overnight.

The fourth day, the news reported that many people now had their normal reflections restored, while some still suffered "outages." That day, all the anchorwomen wore a gratuitous excess of perfectly applied makeup, sending a message to the audience about what side of the divide they were on. Not a single anchorman suffered a cowlicky coif. Reports trickled in, and before long the new normal began to establish itself. High school principals fared well, as did realtors and many civil servants. Most teachers found themselves Reflected, but a substantial minority didn't. All doctors and the vast majority of lawyers made the cut, as did their secretaries. The unemployed didn't. Farmers didn't. Skilled tradesmen split fifty-fifty.

During man-on-the-street interviews, some expressed a belief that one's reflection-status had more to do with geography than occupation. These theorists pointed to the dearth of Reflected persons in the dingy heart of the city and among the dilapidated trailers in the countryside, beyond the reach of the Interstate.

Debates raged about the so-called Reflection-gap—on TV, Facebook, Twitter, and even good old-fashioned street corners. Some of the latter ended in brawls. Some of the brawls ended in riots. Some of the riots ended in curfews. You obeyed them.

The fifth day, your bureau mirror still rippled with molten silver, but a new message had been scrawled into it:

## UNDESERVING

You felt punished and didn't know why. That one scornful word managed to scourge your every nerve. You went back to bed for several hours, but fidgeted—unable to sleep. You both sought answers and feared them. You decided to turn on the TV.

One local network affiliate grabbed an exclusive interview with the Prophet. What transpired wasn't so much an interview as a monologue (or, as some might say, a sermon). By now, his garish outfit had become familiar. In the eyes of the reporters, he'd undergone an elevation in status—from maniac to messiah. He offered an "exegesis" of the mirror messages, but this was little more than an unpleasant rant.

"They've separated us," the Prophet said, "the wheat from the chaff, the Reflected from the Undeserving, and the Undeserving from the Condemned. When you look into the mirror, it *tells* you what you are. *They* tell us what *we* are. Gone now are the days of denying what you see there. Gone are the days of hiding the truth." He contorted his mouth and let out a loud, raspy cry. "Accept your judgment, accept it with humility, ye Undeserving ones, and in time even you might find yourself Reflected! There is still time before you find yourself

# THE MIRRORS

Condemned!"

That's when the phone rang. The caller ID said it was work. You picked it up and listened to a recording. "We're hoping to return to normal business operations tomorrow. As always, we expect all staff to maintain superb standards of personal grooming."

You needed a Reflection.

You tried using windows, but they invariably fogged, despite the moderate temperatures. You tried using your cell phone to take pictures or movies of yourself, but a ghostly white haze lingered over your face in each and every image.

You left in search of a fountain. You tried the wishing well at the mall. A phalanx of well-groomed policemen surrounded it, standing between you and Reflection. They began staring at you, perhaps noting your inordinate interest in the wishing well, perhaps noting some irregularity about your appearance—a crumb stuck to the side of your mouth or a few too many hairs out of place. A policeman gestured toward a mall security guard, who then waddled over to him with alacrity. The cop whispered in his ear and pointed in your direction. Then the security guard huffed his way toward you. You turned around. You walked into a crowd of happy faces, hoping to get lost in them so you could escape to your waiting car. It worked.

To clear your mind, you drove to the outskirts of the city. It still wasn't clear, so you kept driving into the country. By then it was sunset. Orange light flickered off a farmer's pond. Lots of land, and not another soul in sight. You pulled over, got out, and wriggled through the rusty barbed wire and into high, rustling rows of corn. The country air reeked, and you chalked it up to all the fertilizer. Undeterred by the stench, you kept walking in the direction of the water. You heard buzzing. When you arrived, you discovered the pond's surface was covered with dead fish and flies.

"Been like that since the first day."

You turned around and saw a scrawny farmer resting against a dead tree. From a distance, you must have mistaken him for just another gnarled root. "Reckon 'em mirrors don't like the competition. Jealous gods, don't you think?"

You nodded, clenched your fists, bit your lip, returned to your car, and kicked the driver's side mirror off. You worried afterward that such blasphemy might only make things worse. You drove farther away from the city. You stopped along the road to sleep. For the first time, you began to notice you smelled bad. A heavy rain rattled the car's roof.

The sixth day, you drove until you saw the sign (handmade and stenciled on wood—as many were this far out in the boonies).

## SALVATION FOR THE UNREFLECTED

A spray-painted arrow pointed down a dirt road. You'd never before put stock in words like "salvation," but felt heartened by the word "unreflected." You felt this a more respectful term than "undeserving" or "condemned."

The uneven road made the trip feel as though it were being made on sea rather than land. Your car wasn't made for this terrain, and your muffler was one of the casualties. It dragged and scraped against the soggy clay, but you persisted.

After too long a drive, you arrived at a clearing occupied by several large tents of the types used for outdoor festivities. A weather-beaten wooden cross—at least twice your own height—stood in the midst of them. Perhaps this had been the staging area for a wedding reception, a particularly low-rent circus, or, more likely, the site of an annual summer revival meeting hosted by the local Baptists. Last night's storm had by then exhausted itself. The barest hint of drizzle beaded your windshield. Disheveled men shambled toward your car. They all wore bloodied bandages around their eyes. The youngest (in his early twenties) spoke up.

"Welcome to the land of blessed blackness."

You kept your mouth shut, locked the doors, and shifted gears into reverse.

"Have your eyes caused you to sin? Gouge them out and throw them away. Better to enter eternal life without eyes than to worship the demon, Reflection."

You made a quick sweeping turn, kicking up mud and forcing the loose muffler free. Your engine roared.

A naked figure ran out of a tent. "Don't go!" the woman hollered. A wisp of a woman—tiny, thin, and milky-pale, her blonde hair shorn to stubble. You shifted gears into park. She jogged toward you and paused to catch her breath. "Let me greet the newcomer, Jacob. I think this is just someone who's a little lost." In the distance, the blind men grunted and shrugged. They took stumbling steps backward, then continued milling around the field.

"Are they hurting you? Do you need to get away from here?"

"No," she said. "I work for them."

Your stomach churned. "Of your own consent?"

She sighed. "It's not what it looks like. The minister blinded all the members of his flock, but then they needed someone from outside the congregation to come in and *blind the minister*. The idea revolted me, but with, well, all the recent *changes*, I don't have many options as far as making a living. Besides, if I didn't perform the operation he'd find someone else who would. So I did it. Now I just cook and clean for them. They tolerate nonbelievers who are willing to help." She lowered her voice to a whisper. "I'm lonely. They're not much in the way of good company, as you can imagine. But they're a wealthy congregation. In exchange for my duties I'm well compensated."

"I'm sorry I made assumptions. It's just, well, with you being . . ."

She lowered her voice into an even quieter whisper. "Naked? Please don't say anything about it. They wouldn't like it if they found out. It's just that the weather has been warm, and I always have my tent to duck into if it rains, so why not? Same thing with the hair. They'd freak if they knew I cut it all off. But it's just so much easier this way. It feels right."

"They don't know?"

"When I blinded them, I wore clothes and had hair down to my butt. That was a few days ago."

"But those bandages, still bloody. That can't be sanit—"

"They refuse to let me change the dressings. They believe that only *blood* will serve as sufficient testimony to their sacrifice. At first I debated it with them. I mean, I'm no doctor, but everyone knows they need to keep those things clean to avoid infection. They said infections only happened to those with lapsed faith. Then I realized it's crazy to expect self-mutilators to give a damn about hygiene."

You felt yourself smile for the first time in days.

She smiled back. "You're not from around here, are

you?"

"I live—well, used to live—in the city. How did you know?"

"You followed the sign. Nobody from around here would have followed it. Everyone discounted them as lunatics, even before the changes."

"And you *are* from around here?"

"Not originally. I moved here to teach science at the county high school. I haven't been here all that long, but long enough to know that even the hardcore fundamentalists thought these folks were a little nutty. But you never know ... I suppose this little cult's theories about what the mirrors are up to make as much sense as anyone else's."

"They think they have it figured out?"

"Like everyone else, they filter the events of the last week through their pre-existing worldview. They say the Prophet is the *False* Prophet from the Book of Revelation, and that the force controlling the mirrors is a satanic one, of course. All the usual bells and whistles of end times fear-mongering. There is one part of their dogma that actually makes sense, though. They think that it was all brought on by vanity. They say that as the human population has grown, and the number of mirrors has multiplied, and the time spent *in front of* mirrors has risen exponentially, we've given them power over us. Oh, they drape it in the language of their own fanaticism—say that by 'worshipping false idols' we've 'displeased God,' allowing 'Satan an opening'—but even in their madness, there seems to be a kernel of truth."

You asked about food and fuel. She said the congregation had long ago stockpiled both for the end times. You offered to pay. She took the money, but said that if you stayed on to help her take care of the others, room and board would be free. The tents were heated, she added. They had a generator.

You felt exhausted from running and assumed you didn't have a job still waiting for you back home. You decided to trust her, at least for the night. You told her you'd sleep on it.

You didn't want to do another night in your car, but the blind men banned you from spending the night in any of their residence-tents. They explained these were reserved only for dwellers of the blessed blackness. They said that, as a nonbeliever, you were likely still contaminated with vanity.

# THE MIRRORS

They offered you other places—perhaps you could reside, just for the night, in the surgery tent? You tried it, but couldn't get to sleep. It was too close to the generator's growl. Besides, you thought you smelled the coppery scent of blood still linger in the place.

You found only one tiny tent left available to you. Light glowed inside of it, and one of its flaps remained open—perhaps offering invitation, or else indicating a sort of carelessness that you found oddly charming. The woman lived there. It looked as though she'd fallen asleep reading.

You didn't want to wake her. You put out her lamp and took a seat on the grass, just under her cot. You weren't the kind of person to invade someone's privacy. You weren't the kind of person to feel this close to a total stranger either. But times change, and maybe the kind of person you were was changing with them.

That night, you heard her let out a soft moan in the warm dark. You heard the bones in her back crackle and her cot squeak.

The seventh day, you woke to find that she'd gotten on the grass with you, that she'd put a hand on yours. When she saw that you'd wakened, she whispered. "Please don't leave me. I need a friend, someone who isn't insane."

A trail of sunlight filtered into the tent, giving the grass its green back. You gazed at her. Her eyes gleamed. You looked into them, past the pale blue irises, into the depths of the pupils themselves. You saw ghostly hints of yourself inside them. Colorless, spectral reflections—distorted by the curve of cornea. Neither clear enough to groom by nor crisp enough to provoke the jealousy of mirrors. They could only provide assurance that you were, indeed, there—face to face with her.

You decided that was good enough.

# STORY NOTES

# Broken Mirrors

"The Truth, as Told by a Bottle of Liquid Morphine"

There is, perhaps, no more desperate place than the intersection of poverty and terminal illness. While this story isn't inspired by any one particular instance, I'd say that it's deeply influenced by the *overall flavor* of hospice work with the marginalized. The events of this story are entirely fictional, obviously. Yet, the shady-goings-on at the funeral home don't seem (to my jaded sensibilities, at least) completely outside the realm of possibility. I have to believe that, *somewhere* in the world, there's a crooked mortician up to such nefarious hijinx.

This was one of those rare stories that essentially wrote itself. The entire plot (beginning, middle, and end) came together in my brain one night as I was resting in bed. The next morning I sat down and wrote the first two-thirds of the tale. The rest was finished shortly thereafter.

At the end of the story, the morphine bottle sounds pretty gung-ho about suicide. This is probably a good place to state what should be obvious (simply from the fact that I'm here to write this sentence): any opinions expressed by the morphine bottle are the morphine bottle's, exclusively, and do not reflect those of the author.

"The Cat in the Cage"

This story was inspired, in part, by Jack Ketchum's Stoker-winning tale "Gone". At the time I wrote the story, I wanted to write an ending that stated certain horrors and left other (even worse?) horrors implied. (Just like Ketchum had).

I find that some folks who read this story grasp all of the horrors on the first read, but others need to read it twice before they understand the full magnitude of the tragedy (that two lives, not just one, will end with great suffering).

"The Orchard of Hanging Trees"

If I recall correctly, this story made the rounds to eleven or twelve different markets before finding its original home on *Pseudopod* (the weekly horror fiction podcast). Once it debuted there, though, some listeners shared that they thought it was one of the better stories *Pseudopod* had featured that year. It also received a fair bit of positive attention when it was reprinted by *DarkFuse Magazine*.

Why was it rejected so many times? I have to think it's because it's an odd duck. It has elements of extreme horror, elements of philosophical horror, elements of surrealism, and elements of good old-fashioned morality-driven EC Comics-style horror. Not a cocktail to everyone's taste, to be sure.

This version of "The Orchard of Hanging Trees" has a slightly different ending from the version on *Pseudopod*. I made this change because I wanted more readers to feel a kinship with the protagonist. I didn't want him to be *so* evil that the reader couldn't identify with him. I also wanted the story to have more of a mythic, universal feel (less pinned down to a specific nation's politics).

"The Fourteenth"

This tale was born out of grief and despair. In reviewing my records, I see I sent this one in to editor D. F. Lewis just a little over two months after my friend Sara J. Larson died from inflammatory breast cancer. At around the same time, my father barely survived a pulmonary embolism. My mother told me that he'd fallen with such force that he knocked a hole in the wall. I became obsessed with my mental image of the hole he'd made in the wall. The hole worked its way into the story.

There are two other ingredients that were essential

to the writing of this story: Dmitri Shostakovich and his Symphony No. 14. After watching the Shostakovich biopic *Testimony*, I found myself wanting to know everything I could about the man. After my friend Sara died, I played the Fourteenth over and over and over. It is, to this day, my hymn of grief–a fine secular substitute for a requiem mass.

The text for the Fourteenth comes from the work of various poets in the public domain (Rilke, Apollinaire, et al). The transliterated Russian text can be found in several places online, along with English translations (I found it on an international classical music site; here is the full attribution: "Authorship [transliteration] by T. Silman, based on a text in German by Rainer Maria Rilke (1875-1926), "Der Tod des Dichters," from *Neue Gedichte*, published 1907. Authorship [music] by Dmitri Dmitriyevich Shostakovich (1906-1975), "Smert' po`eta," op. 135 no. 10, from Symphony no. 14, no. 10.").

Shostakovich's brief dialogue in this story is paraphrased from a quote attributed to him in Solomon Volkov's book *Testimony*, specifically in reference to the ending of the Fourteenth: "They wanted the finale to be comforting, to say that death is only the beginning. But it's not a beginning, it's the real end, there will be nothing afterwards, nothing." Note that the alleged authenticity of this quote (and, indeed, many others in the biography) has been disputed.

"A Catechism for Aspiring Amnesiacs"

On one level, this story is my temper tantrum against southern Indiana. On another level, this story is my temper tantrum against life. Obviously, I think it's a relatively well-written temper tantrum. But yeah, at its core, that's what this is. A scream. A flailing about on the floor.

Oh, and one other thing: there really is a place

in southern Indiana called Rose Island and it really was a former Depression-era resort that got wiped out by a flood. Up until recently, it really was pretty fucking creepy, too. But then, do-gooders had to go and clean it up, thus ruining a perfectly good wasteland. (Note: I'm pretty sure "a perfectly good wasteland" is a phrase Thomas Ligotti used in one of his interviews. Just giving credit where credit's due.)

## "White Flag"

I've never been homeless, but I've had reasonably close acquaintances in my personal life who've been homeless. This story was born, in part, from my conversations with one of them—a rough-around-the-edges gal who was blatantly honest about what her life in a shelter was like.

Despite periodic surges of interest in ending homelessness, it's a problem that doesn't seem to be going away. It seems perfectly reasonable to assume that, a hundred years from now, there will be homeless shelters. And yet, I don't know of any writer who has addressed this possibility in speculative fiction. (Maybe other authors have, but I'm not aware of them.)

Anyway, science fiction films are rife with flying cars. But I think I'm the first person to imagine homeless people throwing themselves off of flying *buses*.

## "The Company Town"

This story first appeared in the Thomas Ligotti tribute anthology *The Grimscribe's Puppets*. And, in some ways, this makes all the sense in the world. It has so many qualities that dovetail with Ligotti's frame of reference. Suicidal ideation? Check! Bizarre corporations? Check! A town that has long ago "gone to seed"? Check!

But in other ways, it's really not that much like Ligotti's work. After all, in this tale, grief and loss are the portals to the Liggotiesque state of mind. Ligotti's characters need no such portal to arrive at their unholy city. But this is another example of how we're quite different from one another: as much as I might seem to feel uncomfortable with the other members of the human race, I'm interested in them enough to find loss a worthy topic to explore. (And, the truth is, grief and loss reverberate through this book like the tolling of a bell.)

### "The Choir of Beasts"

Here's the secret history of "The Choir of Beasts": it, too, was originally written for *The Grimscribe's Puppets* (but was rejected in favor of "The Company Town"). And so, it made its way to publication as one tale in a three-story chapbook published by Dunhams Manor Press (likewise called *The Choir of Beasts*).

Here's how the story came about: I had a daydream of the Plain of Drau Meghena and the singing Beasts while my husband and I drove through the rural Indiana countryside. For some time, these were visions that just knocked around in my head (with no story to contain them). The morning I found out my friend Sara Larson died, I took a walk in my favorite stretch of woods and the story began to assemble itself in my brain. As I recall, I started work on it immediately upon returning home.

### "All I Really Need to Know I Learned in Piggy Class"

This is one of the earliest stories in this collection. When I got the email from John Skipp telling me he was buying the story for his anthology *Werewolves and Shape Shifters: Encounters with the Beast Within*, I engaged in no small amount of celebration. I'd sold short stories before, but never to a publication with that level of distribution.

The story was inspired, in part, by a scene in Ligotti's *My Work is Not Yet Done* , in which a man is transformed into a pig. What if, I thought, an entire society *depended* on the transformation of people into livestock. What are some of the ways that society *already* treats people like livestock? These are the questions that motivated the story.

## "The Last Kid Scared by Lugosi"

A few years ago, I went to see a showing of the original '31 *Dracula* at Louisville's Palace Theater. I was appalled at how many people were laughing at the film. So this story is my love letter to the classic monster movies of Universal Studios. It's also a reflection of my concern that–in my lifetime–they may begin to fade into obscurity.

Of course, given enough time, we *all* fade into obscurity. No matter how large a mark we make on the world while we're alive, the sands of time will eventually erase it.

## "I Am Moonflower"

Originally this was a parable told by a character in a much longer work. That much longer work didn't hold together very well, and was sent off to the virtual scrap heap. But I was able to salvage this little piece of it. Sometimes I'll do that. I'll salvage a worthwhile nugget from a story that doesn't otherwise work, and use it for a new project.

## "The Meaning"

In a collection brimming with bizarre stories, this one may just be the *most* bizarre. I blame the folks at the

UK-based literary magazine *Polluto* for that. They were running an issue with the theme "Witchfinders Vs. The Evil Red," and so I had to come up with a story that fit into that framework.

I dig that this story references both Schopenhauer and Rocky Balboa.


## "The Suffering Clown"

The central fantasy elements in this story (the clown and his influence over the stars) came to me in a nightmare. If my memory serves me correctly, I woke up around four in the morning and went downstairs to my office to immediately start working on the story.

Obviously, a nightmare–in and of itself–lacks the narrative structure required for a successful story. But I've found that nightmares can provide visceral images *around which to build* stories.

# Funhouse Mirrors

"Eulogy to be Given by Whoever's Still Sober"

The publishing world tends to romanticize the lives of writers who just didn't take very good care of themselves (Poe, Hemingway, Phillip K. Dick, etc.) Noticing this trend, I felt compelled to vent with a little dark satire.

"Youth to be Proud Of"

Parents in southern Indiana sometimes struggle to accept their kids as they are. Noticing this trend, I felt compelled to vent with a little dark satire.

"Subcontractors"

I had a dream about an unknown man's corpse hanging out, on funereal display, in my living room. So, I spent some time trying to work out just how a corpse could end up on funereal display in someone's living room. This story is the result.

I suppose another influence behind this story is my observation that people often survive life by minimizing its bad news (or even denying it). Noticing this trend (you know what's coming next),I felt compelled to vent with a little dark satire.

## Boudoir Mirrors

"The Peculiar Salesgirl"

This is yet another story inspired by a nightmare (specifically, a nightmare about being offered a variety of skins to wear–some of which were hideously misshapen). Let me ask you, dear readers, could *you* get back to sleep after suffering through such mental anguish? I couldn't. So I went down to my office at about four a.m. and tried to capture the experience in a story. As I've implied in some of the other story notes, there's a sort of reverse-engineering that goes on in such situations. I had to work backwards to determine how such a scenario could come about. "The Peculiar Salesgirl" was my answer.

*"Non Evidens"*

Written shortly before a visit to my parents, this piece gushed out of me quite easily. I've never felt that my mother has seen me for who I really am. I've felt that–from birth–she never really understood me. *"Non Evidens"* simply takes that idea and renders it literally.

"The Squatters"

The central fantasy element of "The Squatters" came to me as I drifted in and out of a nap. It originated as an experience of thought, imagery, and feeling somewhere between dream and daydream. On awakening, I found that the story's three interdependent characters demanded my immediate attention. I hadn't planned on writing a short story after my nap, but that's what I did. The story wouldn't go away until I addressed it. It was every bit as persistent as Orescular Island's vines and the squatters themselves. The whole thing was finished in a matter of days.

# Coda

### "The Mirrors"

Yet another story that first came to me as a nightmare. (In the nightmare, I was looking into the mirror and saw only a melting mannequin as my reflection.) How I went from that nightmarish start to a relatively happy ending, I'll never know. I do like the fact that the story ends on a high note (embracing the idea that a connection with at least one other sane person helps us survive even the most identity-dissolving nightmares).

There's a reason why it's the last story in this collection. There's a reason why it's the title story. It underscores why I keep on living.

## About the Author

Nicole Cushing was born in June, 1973–the youngest of four children. She was raised in rural Maryland, where she attended public school. Her hometown was within driving distance to various historical sites related to Edgar Allan Poe. She counts her childhood visits to these sites as formative experiences that threw fuel on her already-morbid imagination.

She attended St. Mary's College of Maryland (the state's public honors college), graduating *magna cum laude* with a degree in psychology. It was there that she undertook her first studies of psychopathology (a subject that frequently appears in her writing).

Following college, she worked at a public mental health facility while simultaneously going to the University of Maryland–Baltimore to earn her Master of Social Work degree. This extended education (and later personal and family crises) delayed the start of her writing career. In 2003, she relocated to Louisville, Kentucky. Shortly thereafter, she moved to nearby southern Indiana. She is married and presently childless.

Although in her twenties she had occasionally sold short stories, it was not until the fall of 2008 that she pursued a writing career in earnest. Since that time, she has gone on to sell dozens of short stories, two stand-alone novellas, and a novel (*Mr. Suicide*, Word Horde). She received a nomination for the 2013 Shirley Jackson Award for her debut novella, *Children of No One*. She is currently working on her second novel and building her career as a nonfiction contributor to *Nameless* digest and the UK-based horror film magazine *Scream*.

Made in the USA
Charleston, SC
24 October 2015